INHABITATION

INHABITATION

A NOVEL

Translated from the Japanese
by Roger K. Thomas

TERU MIYAMOTO

Counterpoint
Berkeley, California

INHABITATION

春の夢

Library of Congress Cataloging-in-Publication Data
Names: Miyamoto, Teru, author. | Thomas, Roger K., translator.
Title: Inhabitation : a novel / Teru Miyamoto ; translated from
the Japanese by Roger K. Thomas.
Other titles: Haru no yume. English
Description: Berkeley, California : Counterpoint, [2019] | "First published
in Japan in 1984 by Bungei Shunju"— Title page verso.
Identifiers: LCCN 2018050853 | ISBN 9781640092174
Subjects: LCSH: Osaka (Japan)—Fiction.
Classification: LCC PL856.I8735 H3713 2019 | DDC 895.63/5—dc23
LC record available at https://lccn.loc.gov/2018050853

Cover design by Sarah Brody
Book design by Wah-Ming Chang
Calligraphy by Shih-Ming Chang

COUNTERPOINT
2560 Ninth Street, Suite 318
Berkeley, CA 94710
www.counterpointpress.com

Printed in the United States of America
Distributed by Publishers Group West

1 3 5 7 9 10 8 6 4 2

INHABITATION

1

Cherry blossom petals were falling on the twilit path. It was at the end of a shopping arcade with no cherry trees in sight. Feeling as if someone were scattering bits of garbage toward him as some kind of joke, Iryō Tetsuyuki cast his eyes about with vague misgivings.

The single road from the shopping arcade led to a railroad crossing, beyond which it began to twist and turn until it was soon following a small stream. A little farther, the stream turned to the right and the road extended straight ahead toward Mount Ikoma. There was a liquor store and a vacant lot thick with weeds. The signboard of a coffee shop that appeared to have closed several months before was shaking noisily in the unseasonably cold wind. After turning right by a general store and a barbershop, he took another twenty minutes before arriving at the apartment he was renting in a crowded, cheaply built residential area. He had only a short while ago moved from Fukushima Ward in Osaka to this apartment on the outskirts of Daitō, his belongings loaded in a friend's small truck. In exchange for the deposit and advance payment of rent, his land-lady had handed him the key. Aside from minimal necessary eat-ing utensils and kitchenware, his meager belongings consisted of a decrepit low desk, a small television set, a refrigerator, a chest of drawers that had been part of his mother's trousseau, and a futon. Within fifteen minutes, he and his friend had fin-ished unloading and carrying everything to his new room on the second floor. His friend left immediately to return to work, and only when Tetsuyuki set about putting things away by him-self did he realize that there was not a single light bulb in the apartment. He went to the landlady's house to inquire.

"Sorry, I guess the former tenant took them when he moved out."

The landlady, a fortyish woman who ran a tiny beauty salon in this squalid residential area, continued to brush a customer's hair and paid no more attention to Tetsuyuki, as if to say "Go buy light bulbs yourself." *Light bulbs should be her responsibility*, he thought, but the expression on her face conveyed what a tightwad she was and he reluctantly walked to the station, where he bought two 60-watt bulbs and a fluorescent light for the small apartment.

The sun had almost disappeared and a faintly bluish tint of dusk was spreading in the room. From a cardboard box he pulled out the tennis cap Yōko had given him for his birth-day, wanting before anything else to find a place to hang it. He screwed in a light bulb and flipped the switch, but it did not turn on. He inserted a new fluorescent light and turned the switch, but it did not come on either. Checking the me-ter located just outside the door, he found that a tag had been attached to it by the power company. He again went to the landlady's beauty parlor.

"The lights won't come on."

The landlady glanced at Tetsuyuki. "Oh no! I forgot to contact the power company. It must be turned off at the meter."

"Does that mean I'll have to spend the night in the dark?" Tetsuyuki suppressed his anger with a calm voice.

"I'll bring some candles by later. I'll just have to ask you to put up with it for one night."

Tetsuyuki returned to his dark room and sat down on the tatami. *Oh well, what can I expect for 7,500 yen in rent?* The landlady hadn't been going to budge from her demand for 10,000, but when he pleaded that he was a student after all and couldn't she knock it down a bit, she reluctantly reduced it to 7,500. The musty-smelling six-mat room looked as though it hadn't been renovated in more than ten years.

He cast his eyes about the darkening apartment. *Well, at least it has its own toilet, not a communal one.* He placed the low writing table in a corner and set the chest of drawers next to it. He put the futon away in the cramped closet, set the box of eating utensils in the kitchen, and then took out his toolbox with its cutting pliers, nails, and hammer. He looked for a short nail, but in the now pitch darkness of the room was not able to find one shorter than two inches. He moved the chest of drawers slightly, creating a space between it and the low table, and groping about, drove the nail into a four-inch pillar where the two walls intersected. Roughly estimating the location, he pounded the nail with all his might. The room shook at the

5

reverberation of the pounding. Tetsuyuki hung his tennis cap on the nail, and then smoked a cigarette in the darkness. Then the landlady stopped by.

"Please don't go pounding nails in the walls." She handed him five slender candles. "I turned the gas on, but it's propane here, so don't use a stove that requires anything else." Then she left without further ado.

The stove Tetsuyuki had brought with him was not made for propane. Would he have to buy that new as well? Having lit a candle, he emptied the money out of his pockets and counted it. Since he had purchased light bulbs and eaten dinner at a Chinese restaurant in front of the station, the money his mother had given him was down to 47,000 yen. He snuffed out the candle and left the apartment to look for a public telephone, but with no success. He expected to find one at the entrance to the general store, but it was already closed even though it was not yet seven o'clock. Following instructions given by a woman he asked, it took him more than fifteen minutes at a quick pace before he finally saw the phone booth, and during that time he did not encounter a single other person, nor was a single streetlight on. His hands in his pockets and hunched over, he muttered to himself, "Is this really part of Osaka?"

When Yōko answered the phone, he said, "This place is a ghost town!"

"Are you coming to school tomorrow?" she asked in a worried tone.

"No, I'm going to crash here tomorrow, 'cause I'll have to start work the day after." Then he told her how to get to his apartment. After a pause she said in a barely audible voice, "I'll be there tomorrow."

"Okay."

"Is there anything you'd like me to pick up and bring with me?"

"I need a gas stove that uses propane. A small, cheap one will do."

After hanging up, he next dialed the number of the café in Kita Shinchi where his mother worked. It was the busiest time, and he worried that they might not call her to the phone, but the young waitress who answered affably summoned his mother from the kitchen. She seemed to have been expecting Tetsuyuki's call, asking whether he had eaten dinner, whether there was anything he needed, and telling him to be sure to make every effort to go to every class. Then she added, "Be sure to call every day. I'll be waiting in front of the phone at twelve noon."

"There'll be times when I won't be able to call right at twelve."

"It doesn't have to be exactly at twelve. But make sure to call me around noon. All right?"

"Yeah."

As he returned along the cold, unlit path, Tetsuyuki thought about his need to graduate from college soon. This year he had failed in four classes and was not able to graduate. Any more extension of his time in school would not be permitted. He needed to secure employment that summer, and then graduate next year. And after being employed, he would need to fulfill his promise to pay 15,000 yen monthly for a period of three years to the Naniwa Commerce Bank. There were five promissory notes his father had drawn shortly before his death, and three of the five had been canceled by the other party out of pity for the impoverished circumstances of the bereaved. Some recalled how they had been obliged to his father when he was alive, and others finally gave up after showering Tetsuyuki and his mother mercilessly with cutting remarks and seeing them hang their heads. But the collectors for the remaining two were tenacious. One had found its way to the Naniwa Commerce Bank, and another had ended up with a broker of promissory notes. The person in charge who came from the Naniwa Commerce Bank, a mild-mannered man well past sixty, asked, "Since it's not a very large sum, why don't you pay it off in monthly installments?"

This "not very large sum" was 540,000 yen, a huge amount for Tetsuyuki and his mother in their present straits. Without consulting his mother, Tetsuyuki went to the Naniwa Commerce Bank and petitioned the elderly man, saying that he was currently a college student who planned to find a permanent job the following year, and asking if he might not be allowed to begin paying it off over several years following that. An agreement was reached: no interest would be assessed in the intervening period. Tetsuyuki affixed his seal to the memorandum.

The remaining six-month promissory note for 323,000 yen that had gone to a broker was a problem. Its holders had no interest in negotiation or anyone's circumstances. Over a period of three months someone would come to the house where Tetsuyuki and his mother were living, sometimes showing up in the middle of the night and making threatening statements

8

until nearly daybreak, other times pleading gently. Eventually his mother became neurotic and would start trembling all over when night came, hiding in the closet and not coming out until morning. Tetsuyuki would hide elsewhere, spending nights at his friends' places. Then one night a week ago, the man who had always come by himself showed up with three gangsters. They kicked down the front door and rushed into the house, dragged his trembling mother out of the closet and threatened her, saying that if she did not come up with the money, they would take one of her son's arms as payment. The next morning, Tetsuyuki and his mother assembled all of their household belongings, explained the situation to their landlord, and for the time being sequestered themselves at an aunt's place in Amagasaki. The widowed aunt made ends meet with the pittance she received from a pension and from part-time work with a nearby auto-parts maker. She lived alone in a small rented home, and was worried that the loan shark would track down their location and come barging into her place. After discussing the matter, Tetsuyuki and his mother decided to live separately in an attempt to evade the gangsters. Through the introduction of an acquaintance, his mother decided to work as a live-in employee at the Yūki restaurant in Kita Shinchi, while Tetsuyuki rented a single-room apartment he had found with the help of a college friend living in Daitō. Tetsuyuki thought that it would be just like gangsters to spend entire days lying in wait by the school gates, and so he had not attended a single lecture of the new semester that had begun five days ago. Did they think they'd get any money if they came to this place? No, he resolved that he would just keep dodging them.

When he got back to his apartment, he struck a match, lit a candle, and fixed his gaze on the tennis cap hanging on the nail he had driven into the pillar. He had been active in the tennis club, but realizing he would no longer have time for such things, he had quit the sport shortly before his father died. When he announced his decision to the other club members, they said they would retain his membership, and that anytime he wanted to play he need only come to the courts. Under the flickering light of the candle, Tetsuyuki lay down in the narrow room and stared intently at the French-made tennis cap, a gift from Yōko. With no heat in the room, he soon spread out his futon and dived under the covers. He heard coughing in the room next door, and then later a telephone rang. "Ah, so my neighbor has a phone." He thought about taking some cake or saké next door the following day to say hello, ask for the phone number, and see if his neighbor would be willing to take calls for him. The only calls would be from his mother or Yōko, at most only one or two a week, so his neighbor might be accommodating. He blew out the candle and turned his thoughts to Yōko's visit tomorrow. For the first time in a long time, they would be alone.

Tetsuyuki recalled the first time he saw her on campus three years ago. She was a new freshman, he a sophomore. On that warm day she was wearing a white blouse and a light blue crepe georgette skirt. She was not an outstanding beauty, but her facial expression had a soft roundness about it that he had never seen in other girls. An overflowing feeling of purity and a reserved lightheartedness about her drew his unending attention.

"That girl's cute," Tetsuyuki remarked to the tennis club member next to him.

"Then you'd better act fast. Yamashita in the rugby club has his eyes on her, and about three others in the karate club are taken with her."

"I think I'm in love with her."

"Make your move now. Show me what you're made of."

Tetsuyuki set aside his unfinished ramen noodles, went up to Yōko, who had just entered the student cafeteria, and tapped on her shoulder. She turned around and gave him a suspicious look.

"Would you like to join the tennis club?"

Yōko blushed and said apologetically that she had no interest.

"That was just a pretext. Actually, I wonder if you'd lend me your notes for French. I'm a sophomore, but I flunked French last year and have to take it over again. But I haven't gone to class even once. Is it okay if I copy your French notes from now on?"

Even as he was talking, Tetsuyuki felt disgusted with himself: *What a clumsy approach!* And yet, Yōko cheerfully lent him the notes. Two weeks later they met at a coffee shop in Umeda and then went to see a movie. Some days after that, he visited Yōko at her house, where he was treated to dinner. That evening as she saw him off to the station, he kissed her and could feel her breasts under her thin blouse.

Tetsuyuki had a feeling that tomorrow they would surely spend the night together under his quilt. He had never been with a woman before, and Yōko had not let him do more than touch her breasts. He imagined her carrying the groceries, the cake, and the gas stove on the long path through the unfamiliar town, and determined that he must never do anything to hurt her. There was not a shred of mean-spiritedness about her, and she was totally without worldly guile. He desired to see her unclothed body, and the way she had said "I'll be there tomorrow" seemed to hint at something. In his mind he embraced the naked Yōko, and fell asleep.

After waking up the next morning, Tetsuyuki unlocked the door and then went back to bed. When he awoke again, Yōko was sitting next to his futon looking down into his face. He had been aching to see her, and there she was. *She didn't wake me up, but just watched me sleep.* The thought was accompanied by an incomparable euphoria as the two looked at each other. He raised his hand from under the quilt and caressed her cheek, eliciting a smile from her.

"Here I am," she whispered, as if humoring a child.

"When did you get here?"

"About twenty minutes ago."

"You should've woken me."

"Why? I was just thinking how much I like you, even though you're not all that handsome, you wear dirty shoes, and you never give me any presents."

"But I *am* handsome!"

"Well, depending on how one looks at you. Your face looks strange." Yōko had a light complexion, with just a few freckles under her eyes.

"How is it strange?"

"It's so strange I couldn't begin to say how."

"I guess it must be a disgusting face."

Yōko giggled and squeezed Tetsuyuki's hand on her cheek. "I like your face." She embraced him. Her cheek was cold.

"I left home at eight o'clock, and it took me two hours to get here," Yōko whispered as she lightly bit Tetsuyuki's lip. Then she added reproachfully, "It's cold. You don't even have a heater."

Tetsuyuki pulled her into the futon and for a long time briskly rubbed her cheeks, back, and shoulders. He slipped out from under the bedding to wash his face and brush his teeth. Having finished, he turned around and was stunned to see Yōko clad only in scant underwear, sitting on top of the futon with her back turned to him. Hiding her breasts with her hands, she turned her head and looked at him. With a slight smile on her face, she was brimming with shyness. Of all her facial expressions, this was his favorite: that faint smile projecting both innocence and reserved allure. As he sat down, she lay back, whispering that she was cold and asking him to put the quilt over her. Tetsuyuki sat staring silently into her face; although she had already willingly taken off her clothing, she was overcome with shame. Coming to his senses, he took off his pajamas and underwear and stood there naked. Bright morning sunlight was streaming through the still-curtainless window. She asked him to darken the room. In place of a curtain, he took off the quilt cover, securing it over the window with thumbtacks. Then, in the darkened shabby old room he glanced at Yōko, who was waiting for him under the musky-smelling quilt with an expression that combined fear and a broader than usual smile.

Since it was the first time for both, they were clumsy and things did not go smoothly. He sensed that she was feeling warm, and before they knew it the covers were down around their feet.

"Just relax," Tetsuyuki kept telling her, but Yōko remained rigid. Then in an instant, she clung to him tightly and began to cry. The cloth that had been serving as a curtain fell down, filling the room with spring sunlight. The two of them lay still, their bodies intertwined. There was no heat in the room, but his back was covered with sweat, and her skin was flushed and burning. Bathed in the spring light, her tense body relaxed and, exhausted, she let herself go. For his part, Tetsuyuki was carried away by an illusion of embracing her on a warm, deserted field of flowers in full bloom.

For nearly three hours, they cuddled under the covers.

"My mother said she likes you."

"What about your father?"

"He doesn't seem to think too highly of our relationship."

"I wonder if he'd let me marry you."

"That's hard to say."

Tetsuyuki again uncovered her. Gazing on her body illumined by the spring sunlight, he thought how beautiful she was. She responded by clinging to him even more firmly than the first time, again crying.

"Are you going to cry every time?"

"I just can't help crying."

Tetsuyuki had never had more tender feelings toward anyone before. Yōko lightly brushed away his insistently groping
hand. She glanced at the tennis cap hanging on the pillar and
asked, "What happened to your rackets?"

"I sold them to friends. All three of them."

"So, you've given up on tennis?"

"Tomorrow I start working as a bellboy at a hotel. My
mom's working now, and I won't have time for anything like
tennis."

"Take good care of that cap."

"Sure. I'll wear it every day this summer."

Yōko asked Tetsuyuki to turn his face away, and then got
dressed. She prepared a meal using the meat and canned soup
she had bought. When he tried to pay for the gas range, she
smiled.

"My mother bought it. She said it was a housewarming
gift."

"It wasn't a matter of moving. It was more fly-by-night. Or,
rather, fly-by-morning."

They ate and then they left the apartment, walking the long
path to the station, where they took the ancient Katamachi Line
to Kyōbashi, and from there rode the Kanjō Line to Osaka. They
went into a hotel coffee shop to the side of Osaka Station. Yōko
was taciturn, occasionally stealing glances at Tetsuyuki as she
sipped her coffee. He mentioned that after securing full-time

employment next year, he would have to spend the next three years making monthly payments on his father's debts.

"I won't be able to get married until I've paid off the debts." Yōko was about to say something in response, but then held her tongue.

"What were you about to say?"

Her palms pressed against her round cheeks, Yōko muttered, her eyes cast down, "I'd like to marry you right now." She had allowed him to enter her for the first time that day, and seemed somehow dejected, but her skin was more radiant than usual and her moist eyes glistened. She had grown up as the only child of an executive in a large company. Superficially she gave the impression of being easygoing and willing to agree to anything, and yet she possessed a stubborn streak that Tetsuyuki admired, and found challenging. Once she said something, she would not budge from it, and whenever the two got together they would argue about trivial things. But as Tetsuyuki came to understand her personality, even that hard core that coexisted with her mild manners and her adaptability became something precious to him, something that gave him a certain feeling of security.

"I'll start working too after I graduate. We can both work, can't we?"

They left the coffee shop and got on the escalator to the ticket gate of the Hankyū station, where a train bound for Sannomiya was about to depart. Yōko said she would take the next train but, goaded by Tetsuyuki to run for it, she dashed up the stairs to the platform, waving at him repeatedly.

Tetsuyuki looked at his watch—9:00 p.m.—and realized that he had forgotten his promise to his mother. She had told him to be sure to call every day around noon, but it had completely slipped his mind. At noon that day, he had in his arms Yōko's white, naked body, which had soon become warm inside the futon and was as sleek as if it had been brushed with oil.

He thought of phoning the Yūki restaurant, but it occurred to him that if he called too often while his mother was busy at work, it might reflect badly on her. He set off toward Osaka Station and took the Kanjō Line to Kyōbashi, where he descended the dark stairs to the platform of the Katamachi Line and looked at the schedule. A train had left just two minutes ago, and he would have to wait a full thirty minutes for the next one. He sat down on a bench and lit a cigarette. On the deserted platform, he thought of his sickly mother.

Through spaces between billboards on the other side of the tracks, the entertainment district in front of Kyōbashi Station was visible. A red lantern with the words STAND-UP BAR was swaying. There appeared in his mind the image of Yōko as she ascended the stairs to the platform, reluctant to part. Every time after saying goodbye, he would soon recall her face and manners at their parting moment and would feel lonely and dejected.

He rose from the bench. Hurrying up the stairs and out the ticket gate, he walked toward the red stand-up-bar lantern where working-class men were drinking saké and munching on peanuts and shredded dried squid. Oldies could be heard playing somewhere in the distance. An odor was wafting from the gutter.

"House saké, please."

"What would you like to go with it?" asked the owner, who was wearing a hachimaki around his head.

"Nothing, just saké."

Nervously keeping track of the time, he guzzled the warmed saké. He sensed that if he drank this fast he would feel queasy by the time he got to the station, but if he missed the next train he would have to wait another forty minutes after that.

He drained the saké from his cup, paid for it, bought another ticket, and again descended the stairs to the Katamachi Line. Five minutes later the train arrived. It would stop at Shigino, Hanaten, Tokuan, Kōnoike Shinden, and his own destination of Suminodō before going on to the limits of Osaka and then Nara. Though he was born and had grown up in Osaka, he had never realized that there were stations with such odd names on the line extending beyond Kyōbashi. Sitting in a corner of the empty car with its metallic smell, he glanced at a sports newspaper lying at his feet. As he read its headlines he gave himself over to the fantasy that he was headed for some distant, foreign land. It was nearly half an hour to Suminodō Station.

Most of the stores in the shopping street along the railway were already shuttered. Groups of what looked like country ruffians were hanging out here and there, casting their vacant stares at people who were hurrying home. It took another half hour to get to his apartment. The saké he had gulped down was taking its effect, and the damp, chilly wind was unpleasant.

Tetsuyuki could taste the strong smell of alcohol on his own breath. As he approached his apartment his sense of loneliness grew. It began to rain.

He ascended the steps and as he was about to unlock the door, the next-door tenant came out: a lean, fiftyish woman. Tetsuyuki introduced himself, and said that he had just moved in the day before. He thought of bringing up the matter of the telephone, but decided that it would be awkward to make such a request while he was reeking of alcohol, and left it with only a simple greeting. She soon disappeared into her room without looking at his face. She seemed somehow somber, a sad expression on her mouth.

The fluorescent light came on when he flipped the switch; the landlady had contacted the power company.

"That's only as it should be. After all, I paid my deposit, and forked over a month's rent in advance." Standing alone in the room, Tetsuyuki spoke to himself. The quilt that had enveloped Yōko's naked body was still spread out, and leftovers from the food she had prepared were on top of the refrigerator. He plugged in the refrigerator, and sat down at the low table to eat the leftovers.

He lay prone on the futon, taking in its scent. Yōko's fragrance had dissipated, but there was a slight trace of her lipstick on the pillowcase. He pressed his lips against it and for some time lay motionless. He pricked up his ears at the sound of someone climbing the stairs, and a powerful anxiety made him grow tense at the thought that perhaps the loan shark had already sniffed out his location. The sound of the footsteps stopped in front of the next-door apartment, followed by the sound of a conversation, immediately after which the footsteps descended the stairs. The feeling of relief revived in his mind the feel of Yōko's body. The first time he was a bit frightened and not at ease, but the second time the pleasure was really wonderful. It was so incredibly warm and soft inside her. He pressed his erection against the futon and turned his head to glance at the tennis cap hanging on the pillar. He got up and, using a marker, wrote FROM YOKO on the inside. As he was about to return the cap to its nail, he jumped back with a start. A small lizard was stuck on the pillar.

For a while Tetsuyuki was glued to the spot, but then cautiously drew close and stared intently at the creature, finally emitting a gasp that was almost a scream and falling back to the opposite wall. The nail that Tetsuyuki had driven into the pillar as he groped in the darkness the previous night had pierced the lizard right in the middle. When he approached it again, it squirmed, moving its legs and tail. Tetsuyuki sat down and for a long time gazed at the creature he had nailed, alive, to the pillar.

2

The glare of the fluorescent light made the lizard's body appear dark, and yet Tetsuyuki was able to tell that it was unmistakably a lizard, not a gecko or a newt. The small striped reptilian pattern was the same as he had seen in the crevices of stone walls, clumps of grass, and on ridges between rice fields when he was a child.

When Tetsuyuki remained motionless, the lizard likewise stopped its writhing and kept still, but as soon as he moved his face even slightly toward the creature, its head, legs, and tail would thrash about in a desperate attempt to escape. In order not to frighten it, he slowly sidled his way over to the closet, noiselessly opened its sliding panel, and took out a hammer that had a claw. With that in hand, he again stood in front of the lizard and puzzled over how best to pull out the nail.

The creature had been fastened to the very middle of the pillar at a slightly crooked angle but with its head up. He was certain that the nail was about two inches long, and more than half of it was driven into the pillar. Tetsuyuki thought about the optimal angle of the claw to pull the nail out of the poor thing.

It seemed strange that it had not died; it occurred to him that if he pulled the nail out, it would leave in the lizard's abdomen a hole out of which its innards might protrude. He could not help imagining how that might only plunge this reptile that had barely escaped death into its final agony.

His hand holding the hammer gradually relaxed. Seating himself on top of the low desk, he mused that if he just left it alone, it would die anyway. The nail was nearly an eighth of an inch thick, so in terms of a human body it would be like being pierced by a utility pole. Whether it would die of internal injuries or of starvation, it could not last long. Tetsuyuki decided just to wait until it died, and put the hammer back in the toolbox. He could not very well hang the French-made cap on the nail to cover the lizard, but neither could he just neglect that valuable gift from Yōko.

He tried hanging a white towel on the nail, but then only the reptile's head protruded, making him feel like a little girl at play putting her doll to bed under a blanket. An idea came to him: he took down the towel and pulled a small, flat wooden dish out of a cardboard box left unopened in the corner of the kitchen. Then, fumbling about in the toolbox, he produced an awl and bored a hole right in the middle of the dish. The hole was smaller than the head of the nail, and he spent considerable time enlarging it with a knife. Then he gently placed the dish over the lizard. The head of the nail passed through the hole in the dish, which he pressed firmly against the pillar, neatly covering the lizard.

Tetsuyuki left a small space between the dish and the pillar in order not to smother the creature. Then he reconsidered, and thought that he ought in fact to smother it. Using cellophane tape, he carefully sealed off the space between the pillar and the perimeter of the dish, and for good measure put several layers of tape over the hole as well. With that, he was sure the lizard would be dead by the following evening.

He addressed the reptile that was now completely airtight under the small brown dish: "What a dumb thing you are! What were you doing there anyway, not paying attention? The room was pitch-dark, and I had no idea you were there. When a human approaches, you're supposed to run the hell away."

Considering a lizard's agile movements, Tetsuyuki wondered how he could possibly not have noticed its presence. He tried to recall driving the nail, but was only able to remember the resistance of the hard wood and could not recollect feeling the slightest hint of hitting anything living. Feeling sorry for the lizard, his mood darkened, and he looked at the small dish taped up with such determination. "When I think of things I can't stand, reptiles top the list."

He glanced at the alarm clock: 1:00 a.m. He washed his face and hands, brushed his teeth, and changed into his pajamas. Overcome by an irresistible fatigue, he turned off the light, dived into the quilts left spread out from the night before, and closed his eyes. He had long since sobered up from the half-pint of saké and was feeling a chill. Hugging his knees he kept repeating in his mind, *Go to sleep! Go to sleep!* At length he did doze off, but soon awoke and realized that his sleep had been very brief.

He had not looked at the clock to determine this; the ache in the middle of his head and the heavy feeling of his body informed him of the brevity of his slumber. He got up, turned on the miniature lamp, and looked at the clock: only a little over an hour had passed.

Wrapped in the quilts, Tetsuyuki stared at the small wooden bowl covering the lizard and thought, *A small creature under there has been robbed of its freedom, and I'm the robber.* Though it had not been intentional, he nevertheless felt a deep contrition for the suffering he had caused. Wouldn't it be better just to kill it once and for all? An image began to flit across his mind of the lizard left alive in the small, sealed-off space between the dish and the pillar, desperately trying to breathe in the last of the oxygen that was certain to run out. With a sweater over his pajamas, Tetsuyuki went to the kitchen and lit a burner on the gas stove since he had no space heater.

Soon the room grew warm. Tetsuyuki thrust his head inside the closet and took a hammer out of the toolbox. He tore off the several layers of cellophane tape he had affixed around the small dish, and removed with his fingernail the many strips he had placed over the hole in the center. Since it had spent more than an hour in the narrow, sealed-off space, perhaps it would already have died of suffocation. Hoping that would be the case, Tetsuyuki removed the dish from the pillar.

The lizard was motionless. Relieved, Tetsuyuki tossed the hammer onto the quilt. Had it still been alive, he had intended

24

to kill it with a blow to the head. Sitting on the low desk, he hunched over and rested his head in both hands with his elbows on his knees. He wondered how Yōko was doing. She was no doubt mumbling to herself in deep sleep, all warm and curled up in quilts.

Counting on his fingers, he realized that exactly three years had passed since they had first met. Three years ago she was eighteen, he nineteen. During those three years he had desired her every time they'd seen each other, but he had never once expressed what he was feeling. There were several couples among his friends at the university who, it seemed, readily formed physical relationships, later very casually parting ways; after they parted, they would soon be walking about holding hands with someone else. If he had pressed her insistently—or perhaps even not so insistently—Yōko would have yielded to him long ago. Even though both of them had this on their minds when they were together, they had not said it aloud during these three years. And yet today . . .

Then he saw that the hands on the clock were already pointing to three, and he realized, *Ah, that's right. That was yesterday!* He recalled her face as she removed her clothes and got under the quilts. There could be no doubt that she had resolved long before to do that. She had mustered all her courage and gotten naked in this shabby, dirty apartment.

That dreamlike act of supreme bliss, accompanied by Yōko's plump-cheeked smile, appeared like a mirage beneath the light of the miniature lamp. Tetsuyuki vowed that after graduation he would work as hard as he could to make Yōko happy. The thought made his heart sink to even greater darkness: why, after an event of such happiness, did he feel so depressed? It seemed so strange to him. He had a sort of premonition that a great unhappiness lay far ahead. That premonition had been with him for three months: a vague and unreasoned feeling stubbornly occupying a corner of his mind.

At one time he had mentioned to his mother that, after graduating, he was going to marry a young woman named Ōsugi Yōko. And then he introduced Yōko to her at an arranged meeting in front of a department store in Umeda. That was about a month after his father had died. Using most of her carefully saved nest egg, his cash-strapped mother had treated them to sushi at a restaurant well known for being expensive, but made no mention of her sacrifice.

"She's a nice young lady, isn't she? She isn't exactly a knockout, but she shows a certain refinement, and is really adorable," she said.

Tetsuyuki kept mentioning marriage; intending to caution him against despair should that prove impossible, she whispered, "Would Yōko's parents allow their daughter to join a family like ours?" Recalling his mother's smile, Tetsuyuki puffed on a cigarette. Perhaps because the heat from the gas stove had warmed the upper air, the smoke from his cigarette neither rose nor sank, but drifted in a thick, silent fog in the middle of the room.

Tetsuyuki again took the claw out of the toolbox and stood before the pillar, ready to pull out the nail and dispose of the dead lizard. The moment he inserted the head of the nail into the cleft of the claw, ready to apply all his strength to pry it out, the lizard's entire body began to writhe. Quickly removing the claw from the nail, he stared at the still-living creature with a weary feeling, yet at the same time amazed at its vitality. Retrieving the hammer he had tossed onto the futon, he raised his arm and took aim at the reptile's head. But somehow, a feeling of dread prevented him from going through with it. For the first time, he fixed his eyes on the lizard's body and studied it in detail.

Its back was dark brown with a greenish cast, rendered gray by the darkness of the room. Its tail was blue. Along both sides of its body, beginning from its nose, ran a wide black band that was bordered with a narrow stripe of dubious color, neither yellow nor blue. On its back were five yellowish-white bands reaching from one side of its body to the other, three of them extending down toward the middle of its tail. The part of its body around where the nail had penetrated was slightly concave, suggesting that its flesh had already begun to heal up around the metal.

"Enough! Why don't you just die?" Tetsuyuki addressed the creature. "Sure, it'd be easy to kill you, but even the thought of it gives me the creeps. I'm the kind who turns and runs when he sees a lizard thirty feet away, and now I've got one alive here with me in this tiny room. It gives me goose bumps!" And in fact, as he spoke he got gooseflesh.

"But it was all my fault. Sorry . . ." With that, he again placed the dish over the reptile, but he no longer felt like sealing it with tape. In any case it was sure to die in two or three days. He turned off the gas range and opened the window to let some fresh air in.

It was at the appointed time of 5:00 p.m. on the dot that Tetsuyuki arrived at the business office of the large hotel in Umeda. He had intended to go a bit early, but missed the train on the Katamachi Line and again he had to wait a whole half hour until the next one, and almost ended up being late. The head of the Personnel Section, Shimazaki, called a young man whose name badge identified its wearer as BELLBOY CAPTAIN and introduced Tetsuyuki to him.

"This is Iryō. Starting today, he'll be working a shift from five until ten."

The bellboy captain, Isogai Kōichi, objected, "Unless he stays until twelve, it'll create a lot of problems."

Shimazaki turned his angular face toward Tetsuyuki and asked, "You live far away, don't you? Let's see . . . What time did you say the last train leaves?"

"At three minutes after eleven."

Shimazaki nodded several times. "If you finish work at ten, by the time you change your clothes and take the Kanjō Line to Kyōbashi, it'll be about eleven. This is only a part-time position, so we've taken that into account."

Isogai—clad in a beige uniform with double gold braid on the shoulders, sleeves, and both sides of the trousers—darted an upward glance at the newcomer and wordlessly motioned with his chin for Tetsuyuki to follow him. An oppressive odor of food filled the narrow, dim passageway, which was strangely sweltering though not near any furnace.

"Why is it so hot here?" Tetsuyuki asked. Isogai, who was thin and looked a bit older than Tetsuyuki, thumped the walls on both sides. "The grill's kitchen is on this side, and over here is the laundry room. The air-conditioning doesn't extend this far, so it gets hot as hell during the summer."

At the end of the passageway a heavy steel door opened to the employees' locker room. Isogai took a uniform out of a large box in the far end of the room and tossed it at Tetsuyuki. "Here!"

After Tetsuyuki had put on the uniform, Isogai looked him over with deliberation, mumbling curtly that it was a bit small but a part-timer ought to be able to put up with it.

Isogai opened an empty locker. "You can use this one. Be sure to lock it. There are thieves around here too, you know."

The hotel had several branches. Two years previously they had torn down the old building and erected this magnificent twenty-four-story structure, but it seemed somehow dreary and dirty behind its façade. No doubt Tetsuyuki could expect to encounter maliciousness at every turn. He glanced at Isogai, noting his poor complexion and the lack of redness in his lips. But his hair was properly groomed, and he appeared gallant in his uniform with its gold braid. Tetsuyuki stowed his own clothes in the locker and turned the key.

"I'll show you around the whole place. Altogether, there are eighty boys."

"Huh? That many?" At Tetsuyuki's surprise, Isogai cracked a smile for the first time.

"They're all 'boys,' but they have various responsibilities. You and I are page boys. We do things like show guests to their rooms, carry luggage, and arrange for cabs. Ten of us are full-time employees, and three, including you, are part-time. Another thirty take care of banquets. Some are the hotel's regular servers, and when we're busy we also have part-timers come. Fifteen people work at the grill, and another fifteen at the coffee shop, where there are also five part-timers. Finally, there are four in the basement bar. The ones I've mentioned so far are all men. In addition, there are thirty women, including maids, waitresses in the grill and coffee shop, and servers for banquets."

"So then, with men and women combined, it comes to a hundred and twelve. Are you captain over all those employees?"

Isogai shook his head. "Just over the page boys." Then he glared at Tetsuyuki intensely. "Part-timers have no sense of responsibility. They go about their tasks with the attitude of 'It's just part-time anyway.' But my expectations are exactly the same for everyone, so keep that in mind."

Isogai continued down the dim winding passageway to a door that opened into the office behind the front desk. He led Tetsuyuki to a man whose name badge identified him as FRONT DESK MANAGER. Not even glancing up in response to Tetsuyuki's greeting, the man said indifferently, "Pleased to meet you," as he continued to check reservation cards. Tetsuyuki looked at his badge: NAKAOKA MINEO in both Japanese characters and Romanization.

Next, Isogai showed Tetsuyuki the time clock located in a

room to the side of the lobby. Bellboys in the same beige uni-
forms were lying on the table, leaning back in chairs smoking,
or playing cards.

"This is Iryō Tetsuyuki, who'll be working part-time starting today. Everyone get acquainted with him."

Everyone turned toward Tetsuyuki in unison without saying anything. They struck him as a potentially spiteful bunch,
but he resolved not to get into arguments with anyone and just
do as he was told.

Isogai and Tetsuyuki took the elevator to the banquet room
on the second floor. It would have been faster to use the emergency stairs, but Isogai took the elevator from floor to floor.
The third floor was also a banquet hall, and the fourth consisted
of several large conference rooms. All floors from the fifth to
the twenty-third were guest rooms, and on the twenty-fourth
were a grill and a Chinese restaurant. It was already past six by
the time they completed their brief tour, since they had to wait
for the elevator each time.

"Your name badge will be ready in two or three days."
Isogai stood somewhat removed from the front desk. "You
should always stand at attention, and never let your posture
become sloppy." Isogai told Tetsuyuki to watch him closely
for a while. A guest was filling out a form at the front desk.
The clerk took out the room key and called for a bellboy. With
snappy motions Isogai took the key, picked up the guest's luggage, and said, "Room 2500 on the sixth floor!"

Isogai beckoned, and Tetsuyuki followed him and the
guest, whom Isogai allowed to enter the elevator first, then

pressed a button and said again in a firm voice, "Allow me to show you to the sixth floor." When the elevator stopped, he allowed the guest to exit first and then nimbly took the lead down the long maroon-carpeted hall.

Opening the door to room 2500, he switched the light on and, again allowing the guest to enter first, placed the luggage on a stand next to the desk. Then, opening the bathroom door and turning on the light, he explained, "This is the bath and commode. For room service, please dial six. For other matters, you may dial one to reach the front desk."

As he handed the key to the guest, Isogai said with a bow, "We hope you have a pleasant stay with us." Then he exited the room.

"This is how you show guests to their rooms."

"How do you know which floor and which room?"

"You can tell by looking at the key. If it says 6-2500, then that means 'sixth floor, room 2500.'"

"So then, if it's room 1324 on the twenty-second floor, 22-1324 will appear on the key, right?"

"Right. But there aren't any room numbers that end below five hundred."

Isogai told him to do the next one by himself. As they were waiting for the elevator, he whispered to Tetsuyuki, "Some guests will tip you. As a rule, we're not supposed to accept tips, but if you're offered one, just say 'Thank you' and take it." He gave Tetsuyuki a sideways glance and smiled.

"Some people really tip?"

"They sure do. It might be three hundred-yen coins, or a

five-hundred-yen note . . . You'll get all kinds. On a good day, your tips might even be more than your wages."

That's great, Tetsuyuki thought. The front desk was at its busiest when they returned to the lobby.

A voice called out, "Bellboy! Show this guest to his room." Isogai gave Tetsuyuki a shove on the back. Just as Isogai had done, he strode swiftly to the desk, took the key, and picked up the guest's Boston bag. The numbers 11-2562 were engraved in the plastic rod attached to the key. He announced in a loud voice, "Room 2562 on the eleventh floor." He had the guest board the elevator first and as he pressed the button, declared in a voice that sounded strangely loud even to himself, "Allow me to show you to the eleventh floor."

The middle-aged man looked at him with some surprise. "You're in good spirits, aren't you?" Tetsuyuki maintained a nervous silence. Upon exiting the elevator, he glanced at the directional arrows: rooms 2500–2549 to the right, rooms 2550–2599 to the left. Tetsuyuki turned left and proceeded town the hall, taking care not to overlook any numbers of the rooms on either side.

After unlocking the room, turning on the light, allowing the guest to enter, and setting the luggage down, he opened the bathroom door and repeated the lines he had hear Isogai use. Then, as he was handing over the key, he said, "For room service . . ." and stopped; he had forgotten which number Isogai had said to dial.

"Uh, let's see . . . room service is . . ."

"It's six, isn't it? And the front desk is one. I've stayed here several times, so I know that much."

"I'm terribly sorry. Today is my first day on the job," Tetsuyuki said, bowing.

"Oh, a greenie, huh? So then I know more about this hotel than you do." The guest pulled several hundred-yen coins out of his pocket and put them in Tetsuyuki's hand. Tetsuyuki thanked him politely and again bowed.

"But you're very good at accepting a tip," the guest said, laughing. Wishing him a pleasant stay, Tetsuyuki left. Making sure that no one was around, he counted the coins in his hand: 400 yen. That pleased him. He had no idea how many guests he would show to their rooms between five and ten o'clock, but if at least five of those tipped him, that could come to nearly 2,000 yen. In his impecunious state, that was a matchless bounty.

By ten o'clock he had shown twenty parties of guests to their rooms. Those who had tipped him included the first guest and a young woman accompanied by a man who looked like a gangster. The man was rather drunk, and no sooner had he entered the room than he collapsed on the bed. As Tetsuyuki was explaining to the woman how to dial for room service and the front desk, the man shouted, "We know that without having you tell us. It's written right next to the phone, isn't it? That's enough. Now get out!" He kicked Tetsuyuki in the knee with the tip of his shoe.

Tetsuyuki left and was walking down the hall when the woman trotted up behind him. "Sorry. That guy can be a real jerk. Take this." She pressed a 1,000-yen note into his hand. She appeared to be a hostess at some bar, but there was something little-girlish about her facial expression and figure.

Most of his work that evening was between six and ten o'clock, during which he was allowed to take only one break. Returning to the locker room, his feet ached, his whole body was heavy with exhaustion, and even speaking had become a bother. He had not imagined that having to work so long without sitting would be this hard. After changing his clothes, he remained for a while in a chair in the corner.

Behind its closed heavy steel door the room was deathly quiet, and Tetsuyuki was overcome by a feeling that he was locked in a jail cell. The pattern of colors on the lizard flitted across his mind. *Was it already dead?* He stood up, switched off the light, and trudged down the narrow, stiflingly hot passageway.

He had no desire to return to that room where the lizard was nailed to the pillar. A thought flashed in his mind: perhaps the creature was still alive, pondering how it might free itself. *Maybe it's waiting for me to come home.* "Pull this nail out! Please, pull it out!" It seemed as if he could hear the lizard screaming.

He climbed the concrete stairs, and exited through the employee entrance, next to which a vent spewed out all of the fumes from the grill and the laundry room. Tetsuyuki held his breath. The foul essence of human beings who deck themselves out so gorgeously, the hidden unhappiness of people who pretend to be happy . . . the stench that poured forth with such violence and noise from a gigantic hotel brought such phrases into his mind.

Jostled by the crowds, he trudged toward Osaka Station. *Die, and be quick about it*, he mentally shouted to the lizard. *I won't pull the nail out until you've died, and I'm not going to kill you either. I'm just going to wait until you die, so just give up and kick the bucket!*

Tetsuyuki dialed a number at a public phone. Having anxiously awaited his call, Yōko answered in her animated voice.

"Does it look like a job you're up to doing?"

"A bellboy's work is a piece of cake."

"You must be tired since it's your first day."

"The first day on any job is tiring."

"Take a bath and get a good sleep. Then you'll feel better."

"I think I'll stay at Nakazawa's tonight. I don't have what it takes to ride the Katamachi Line and then walk another half hour along a dark street."

Yōko paused for a moment, and then said, "When you get to Nakazawa's place, call me again, okay?"

Nakazawa Masami lived right in the middle of the business district of Honmachi. He was a friend of Tetsuyuki's since high school, whose father managed a real estate rental agency, and who owned the eight-story Nakazawa Second Building. There was also the Nakazawa First Building in Matsuyamachi, where his parents and siblings lived, but Masami occupied a small room on the eighth floor of the Nakazawa Second Building. He was the same age as Tetsuyuki and was attending the same university, but since he had spent two years in cram school, he was only a junior. When Tetsuyuki phoned him, he only got the usual terse response of "I'll open the back door for you in fifteen minutes."

As Tetsuyuki stood waiting on the subway platform, he again heard the lizard's voice. It was crying, *Pull out this nail! Pull out this nail!*

3

Having passed through the ticket gate in the subway, with drooping shoulders Iryō Tetsuyuki trudged up the deserted stairs furiously swept by air from aboveground. He then walked south down the late-night Midōsuji Avenue, turning east at the corner of an enormous building housing a foreign investment company, and then proceeding straight ahead. A ramen stall had been set up by a cluster of buildings whose lights had already been extinguished.

Next to the Nakazawa Second Building was an old three-story concrete structure, the narrow space between the two edifices barely wide enough for one person to pass through. Going through this urine-reeking passageway and turning to the right, one arrived at the back of the Nakazawa Second Building. Since the large shutter was pulled down over the front entrance at nine o'clock, when Tetsuyuki went to see Nakazawa Masami he had to call in advance and have Masami unlock the small private door in the rear.

Closing the small metal door and relocking it, Tetsuyuki

went over to the elevator, whose power had been shut off. He always took the stairs, but that night his legs lacked the strength to climb to the eighth floor. The power switch for the elevator was located in the custodian's closet next to Nakazawa's room. Using the house phone on the first floor, Tetsuyuki again phoned Nakazawa.

"I'm downstairs now. Turn on the elevator."

"Use the stairs. You need the exercise."

"I don't have the energy this time."

"Are you drunk?"

"Never mind about that. Just turn on the damned elevator!"

Tetsuyuki had become irritable, and was shouting into the phone. Shortly, the lamps on the elevator lit up. Tetsuyuki got off on the eighth floor. Standing there pajama-clad was Nakazawa, who went to the custodian's closet, switched off the elevator, and then turned his sleepy, listless gaze toward Tetsuyuki.

"You're in a pissy mood, aren't you?"

"You got something to eat?"

"Just saké and beer."

As soon as Nakazawa opened the door to his room, a modern jazz melody assaulted Tetsuyuki, just like the wind that had come blowing down on him as he climbed the stairs from the subway. A stereo set, several hundred LPs, an antique pendulum clock, hundreds of magazines on recordings and stereo equipment, a large globe, a small television set, a refrigerator, and a bed, next to whose pillow was a copy of the thirteenth-century Buddhist treatise *Lamenting the Deviations*.

The familiar clutter in Nakazawa's room abruptly brought a feeling of sadness over Tetsuyuki. He opened the refrigerator, took out a bowl containing two eggs and butter, and handed them to Nakazawa, saying, "Make some of the fried rice you're so good at. I haven't eaten any dinner." He'd had no appetite at all when Isogai gave him an employee meal pass, and left it in the pocket of his uniform.

Shaking his head and pulling behind his ears the long locks that had fallen in front of his eyes, Nakazawa peered inside the rice cooker and said, "If I let you eat this, there won't be anything for breakfast tomorrow."

"You can just cook more for tomorrow, can't you?"

Lying on Nakazawa's bed, Tetsuyuki smoked a cigarette. Nakazawa poured saké into a cup and mutely thrust it toward Tetsuyuki's face. Listening to the popping of the melting butter, he slowly drank down all the chilled saké.

"Is that old guy, the custodian, still in the hospital?"

"He died," Nakazawa answered as he deftly handled the frying pan. Tetsuyuki sat up and stared at Nakazawa's back.

"When?"

"Three days ago. Now I won't have to play chess with him in the evenings anymore."

"That's a heartless way of putting it. Did you get some sort of strange enlightenment from reading *Lamenting the Deviations*?"

Nakazawa glanced at Tetsuyuki. "There's nothing you can do about it, is there? We humans are subject to death." With that, he heaped the readied fried rice on a plate and handed it to Tetsuyuki along with a spoon.

The elderly custodian had often handed money to Tetsuyuki, asking him to buy betting tickets for horse races. Since it was right on Tetsuyuki's way from Hankyū-Umeda Station to the university, the custodian would stuff small amounts of money along with numbers written on memo paper into his pocket, asking him to stop by and purchase tickets. There was an off-site-betting office behind Osaka Station, but Tetsuyuki had never once bought the requested tickets.

The old man's predictions for betting had never once been right, and the small sums had always just turned into Tetsuyuki's drinking money. He never gave thought to what he would do if the predictions ever proved correct, thinking it unlikely that the custodian, who would spend only a small portion of his sparse pocket change on safe tickets, possessed sufficient sense about the competition that he would ever end up with a winning bet, and that even if by chance he did, Tetsuyuki calculated that with the kinds of stakes the old guy put out, he would be able somehow or other to come up with the dividend.

"Until they hire a new custodian, I have to take care of things. I'll get up at seven in the morning to open the shutter." Nakazawa turned down the volume on the stereo, and started to drink some saké himself. "Your work is pretty tough, huh?"

"No, out of all the jobs I've had so far, this one's on the easier side."

"But for all that, you look pretty worn out," Nakazawa said as he studied Tetsuyuki's face, his cheeks stuffed with fried rice.

Tetsuyuki thought of telling Nakazawa about the lizard,

but decided against it. He sensed that Nakazawa would not be interested, but more than anything else he was simply too tired. All Nakazawa was interested in talking about was modern jazz. Sometimes he would hole up in this eighth-floor room and for three or four days do nothing but listen to records. His stereo system was one that he had spent several months assembling by himself, using amplifiers, a turntable, and speakers all of different brands, selecting the best of each.

"Is there something you want to listen to?"

"Put on 'Lady Jane.'" Tetsuyuki did not particularly want to listen to anything, but answered anyway.

"'Lady Jane,' huh? That used to be a popular tune . . . I haven't listened to it for a long time either."

Nakazawa quickly picked out the record from among his collection of more than eight hundred LPs and placed it on the turntable. Just as Tetsuyuki finished eating the fried rice and started drinking the saké remaining in his cup, the saxophone began playing the low, soft melody he had heard so many times.

Listening intently to the tune, he sat down in a corner of the room leaning against the wall and staring at Nakazawa, who was looking vacantly into space. It occurred to him that this woman "Jane" must have been a prostitute, and he pictured in his mind how, after finishing her work, she put on her clothes, leaving the room and the man in it and going back out into the empty late-night street. This image coincided with the glance he had stolen of Yōko as, half reclining, half sitting, she asked him to look the other way when she began to put on her underwear. At that moment, she had appeared lovely and at the same time a bit degenerate, and this image of her conflated in his mind with that of Lady Jane. Again the thought of the lizard nailed to the pillar crossed his mind.

"Jazz is decadent . . ." Tetsuyuki muttered. When the piece ended, Nakazawa got up and, switching off the amplifier, said: "That's because humans are decadent. I have no faith in music that isn't decadent."

Tetsuyuki asked if he could use Nakazawa's telephone. "Is it time for your phone call?" Nakazawa asked in a deadpan voice as he went to the kitchen to fill his empty saké cup.

Yōko chided Tetsuyuki for the tardiness of his call, but immediately returned to her usual easygoing tone, and volunteered to attend the next day's English lecture in his place. She had asked Yamashita to answer the roll call for him in the lecture for Introduction to Philosophy. In the English lecture, the professor passed out attendance slips at the end of class, and Yōko would fill in Tetsuyuki's name and student number.

"You must pay Yamashita two hundred yen. That's cheap compared to you repeating the grade for another year." Yōko's voice suggested she was smiling.

"I'll start attending classes next week."

Following a long pause, Yōko asked anxiously: "What will you do if you're caught?" She was worried that a debt collector might lie in wait at the gates of the university.

"If those guys find me, there's nothing I can do. I'll just have to resign myself to it."

"Resign yourself . . . ?"

While working at the hotel that day, it had occurred to Tetsuyuki that he would not likely be able to evade them longer than two or three months, and so he resolved to settle things sooner than that. They were not such fools that they would kill someone over 320,000 yen. Even if he ended up getting beaten within an inch of his life, that would be better than constantly running about in fear. He had resigned himself to that.

Yōko said she was sad that they wouldn't be able to get together because of his work, and Tetsuyuki wasn't able to whisper reassuring sweet nothings because Nakazawa was right next to him. So he remained silent.

"I'll take a day off next Sunday . . ."

Now it was Yōko who remained silent. Tetsuyuki sensed that she didn't feel she could offer to come to his apartment, so he said: "There's something I'd like you to bring, so come on over. It's a bit far, but . . ."

Yōko understood immediately what it was he wanted her to bring. "Sure. It is a bit far, though."

After Tetsuyuki hung up, Nakazawa put on another record, a quiet piece.

"Just like a diligent, loyal housewife!" Nakazawa commented as if to himself, then crawled into bed. Beneath the bookshelves there was a long sofa where Tetsuyuki always slept. Blankets and quilts were constantly stacked up on it. He borrowed and changed into some pajamas, then made up a bed and lay down. Lying there, he drank some more saké from his cup.

For the following three days, after work Tetsuyuki stayed in Nakazawa's room. On the fourth day, a Saturday, as soon as his shift ended he hurriedly changed into his own clothing, then jogged to the platform on the Kanjō Line. He thought that with some luck he might be able to catch the 10:46 train bound for Suminodō rather than the last train of the evening, which was bound for Nagao.

He had not bathed in several days. There was no bath in his apartment, and he wanted to go to the public bath near the station to wash his hair, clean the oil from his body, and change his underwear. It would be too late if he returned to his apartment first, so during his lunch break he purchased underwear and requested a guest towel and soap from the young woman in charge of room amenities. He got off at Kyōbashi Station and looked at the clock on the platform: 10:45. He raced down the stairs at full speed. The train for Sumidō had already stopped at the platform. As soon as he jumped into the car, the doors closed.

The train lumbered along slowly. Quite a few passengers got off at Hanaten, and by the time it reached Kōnoike Shinden, the car was almost empty. When he looked out the window, in the distance he could see lights apparently from a new residential district.

Arriving at the station, several men—probably office workers—who had been on the same train went through the shopping arcade and disappeared down various narrow lanes, leaving Tetsuyuki by himself on the dark street. After he turned left at a shuttered liquor store and then left again at a corner by a row of apartment buildings, the shop curtain of the public bath came into view. After washing himself thoroughly, he soaked so long in the hot water he became a bit dizzy. Putting on his new underwear, he felt fully relaxed and stared at his own face in an enormous mirror. It seemed to him that his cheeks were a bit more wan, and the look in his eyes had become tense. He mounted the scales and found that he had lost nearly five pounds.

Teased by the spring breezes, Tetsuyuki felt as if he were bracing himself for something as he made his way along the dark path to his apartment. No matter what, the lizard would have to be dead already. Yet he had a premonition somewhere in his mind that it was still alive.

The cramped room of his apartment, which he had vacated for four days, felt chillier than outside in the spring breeze. Tetsuyuki turned on the light and glanced at the pillar. He could see the head of the nail and the gleam of the brown saucer placed over it. He cautiously approached and peered into the hole in the bottom of the saucer, but it was pitch-black inside. In a moment of resolve he tore the saucer off the pillar, and with a heavy sigh pressed both palms against his head as he saw the lizard, still pierced by the nail, slowly squirm.

Staring at it, his forehead broke out in sweat. The lizard stuck out its long, slender red tongue, which remained stuck to the pillar. Tetsuyuki wondered how lizards take in liquids. Do they lap, like dogs or cats?

He went to the kitchen, poured some water into a small spoon, and stood as far as possible from the lizard, stretching his arm out to full length until the spoon reached the creature's tongue, which did not retract. It remained motionless, only blinking now and then.

Just as Tetsuyuki was about to abandon this approach, the lizard began to lap at the water, like a dog or cat. When his right arm grew tired, Tetsuyuki changed it to the left, continuing to offer water until the creature's thirst was slaked. At length, it drew its tongue into its mouth and no longer moved.

Tetsuyuki spread out his futon and lay down on it, staring at the nail-pierced body of the lizard, which he had forgotten to cover with the small saucer. He finally drifted off to sleep. Once during the night he awoke, turned off the light, and again fell into a deep slumber.

It was a little past ten when Tetsuyuki opened his eyes, his face illumined by the glare of the morning sun. The light filled the entire room, bringing the lizard into sharp focus as well. Lighting a cigarette as he lay prone on his quilts, he pressed his ear against his pillow and waited for Yōko to arrive. Still in bed, he took off his pajamas and removed his underwear, imagining his stark nakedness responding to the buoyancy of her unclothed body. When she came into the room, without saying a word he would pull her under the covers and would be rough in achieving his aim, all the while maintaining silence. How would she respond to him if he were like that? The spring sunlight filling the room seemed like a reflection of his own carnal craving.

He jumped up in his nude state, letting out a small cry: he realized that it would not do to leave the lizard in full view.

46

Yōko would no doubt be shocked to see the creature nailed to the wall like that, and would demand an explanation. Why hadn't he pulled out the nail and let it go? If that were put to him, he would have no idea how to answer. Perhaps the best answer would be that, since the whole thing gave him the creeps, he was just waiting for the creature to die, but he sensed that such an explanation by itself would leave something unresolved.

He put the hole in the bottom of the saucer through the head of the nail, upon which he hung his tennis cap. He then unlocked the door and, still in a state of undress, washed his face and brushed his teeth. Hearing footsteps ascending the stairs, he hurriedly wiped his face with a towel, dived back under the quilts, and waited. He could hear the door being opened, then locked. After placing something in the kitchen, Yōko sat down by the quilts.

"It's almost eleven."

Tetsuyuki didn't respond. When Yōko gently pulled the quilts back, he grabbed her arm and pulled her toward him, using all his strength to draw her inside the covers.

"So, you were just pretending to be asleep after all!"

Taking Yōko in a firm embrace, he guided her hand down below his waist to let her know that he was completely naked. She was wearing a yellow skirt and an orange cardigan over a white blouse, and it took rather a long time to remove everything. When that was completed, he embraced her tenderly. They spent nearly two hours under the covers.

"I'm starved." Those were the first words to issue from Tetsuyuki's mouth. Wrapping her arms around his neck, Yōko smiled. "I got up early this morning and fixed some sandwiches. I lied to my mom, saying that I was going on a picnic with some friends." Then, pressing her lips against his, she mumbled almost inaudibly: "You held your tongue on purpose, didn't you?"

"Uh-huh."

"Why?"

"I wanted to test you to see whether or not that'd tick you off."

"Liar! You knew very well that it wouldn't."

It was indeed a lie. He had just wanted to try treating her once as if he were despoiling her. "Well then, why do you think I did it?"

Tracing the tip of his nose with her unmade-up lips, she blushed. "Whatever. I enjoyed it."

"Can you come to my apartment like this once a week?"

Yōko nodded, and whispered to him to turn the other way. Lying with his back turned to her, Tetsuyuki glanced at the tennis cap hanging on the pillar, and every now and then would stealthily steal a peek at Yōko as she put on her underwear. The drooping line described by her neck and shoulders as she went about this task had a note of sadness and ruin about it.

"Why are you so embarrassed about putting on your clothes even though no one's watching?"

"I'm embarrassing to myself." Then she hit him with a pillow. "You were watching after all, weren't you?"

"Just a little."

"For me, the most embarrassing thing is to be seen putting on my underwear."

48

As he was eating the sandwiches Yōko had made, Tetsuyuki related some of the goings-on at work. The matter of the lizard was on the tip of his tongue, but he refrained from mentioning it.

As before, he went with her to Osaka Station. She had told him that he did not need to see her farther than Suminodō Station, but he felt loath to part. Entering a coffee shop in a subterranean mall near the platforms for the Hankyū trains, the two of them kept up their conversation for nearly two hours. When a lull finally occurred in their exchange, they both gazed at each other mutely, waiting with smiles for the other to break the silence.

"There's no end to it, is there?" Yōko remarked.

Having seen her off as she passed through the ticket gate and ascended the escalator to the Kobe Line, Tetsuyuki went into a nearby bookstore. Standing in front of the shelves marked NATURAL SCIENCES, he looked for books on lizards and flipped through the pages of *Reptiles of Japan Illustrated*, which featured many pictures but did not contain the information he sought. He glanced through several volumes before finally finding what he was looking for. Near the end of a book titled *Reptiles of Japan* was the section "How to Care for Lizards." The book was rather expensive, but he purchased it.

It was a Sunday evening, but more people were out and about than on a weekday and both the station concourse and the platforms were overflowing with the crowd. Arriving at Kyōbashi Station, he glanced at his watch and dashed down the stairs, but the train did not come: the timetable for the weekend was not the same as for weekdays. He waited on a bench for more than half an hour, his thoughts focused solely on Yōko. Such a sweet, beautiful young woman, and she loved him! That thought brought a fervent swelling within his lean chest. For Yōko's sake, for his mother's sake, and even for his own sake he simply had to secure permanent employment and graduate.

Taking a seat in the sluggish, antiquated car of the Katama-chi Line, Tetsuyuki took out the book and read "How to Care for Lizards."

> A lizard may be kept in a small wooden box (about one foot in size), but ideally it should be in a tank used for fish. The lid should be of metal. Spread some moist soil in the box, and place some wood chips over that. Take care not to let the soil become compacted, because lizards like to burrow in it. For water, a low, shallow dish is best. When the lizard finds this, it will place its front legs on the lip of the dish and lap the water like a dog. It is necessary to keep the dish filled up to the edge.

> The best food is such things as maggots or chestnut weevil larvae, which can be obtained at fishing tackle shops. Additionally, they will eat spiders, crickets, flies, and small ants. Some will also eat earthworms, depending on their species. Where feeding occurs in a single session, once every two days is sufficient

in the summer, and once every seven days in the winter. Since lizards require some sunlight, the box should be placed where it will be in partial sunlight in the morning or near sundown. If a glass tank is placed in direct sustained sunlight, the interior will become extremely hot and the lizard will die. Even when placing the box or tank in some sunlight in the morning or late in the day, part of it should be shaded. That way, the lizard can control its body temperature by either basking in the sun or hiding in the shade. An owner who takes such precautions will receive great satisfaction from keeping a healthy and active lizard.

The conclusion of that section included a precaution about keeping lizards indoors: an infrared lamp should be used when no sunlight reaches the room.

So, what should be done with a lizard that's nailed to a pillar in a room? Tetsuyuki thought to himself. At that point, he realized that he was seriously intending to keep the creature as a pet. He flipped through the book, stopping to stare fixedly at the photographs of several of the reptiles. His eyes fell on a line: "Young lizards have three gold-colored lines on their backs." He closed the book and concluded that he should just kill the thing after all. One blow on its head with a hammer, and it would be finished. Wouldn't that be simplest?

But having gotten off the train and hurrying down the mid-night street, the thought came to him: though he had not done it intentionally, it was he who had put the poor thing in such a plight. It had amazingly survived these several days pierced by a thick nail, without eating or drinking. It must possess a very tenacious vitality. Tetsuyuki came to a sudden standstill: the thought of entering his apartment felt frightening. Not just the lizard, but even the nail seemed like a mysterious living entity.

4

That day was hectic. A group of 160 foreign tourists arrived from the airport in sightseeing buses, and the full-time bellboys were marshaled to the task of escorting the mostly middle-aged and older group to their rooms. Tetsuyuki and two other student part-timers were assigned to unload the luggage from the three enormous buses.

Room assignments and preparations had been made in advance, but upon seeing 160 foreign tourists along with other guests standing at the counter waiting to be escorted, Isogai Kōichi, the bellboy captain, impatiently glanced at Tetsuyuki as he loaded the heavy luggage onto a cart.

"It's amazing that each one of them could carry two or three heavy trunks like this," one of the student workers remarked, out of breath. And indeed, each of the large trunks was so heavy as to make one wonder what could possibly be in them. Tetsuyuki answered, "Americans must have more muscles than we do."

He was simply unable to lift them with one hand, and as he was using both hands to heft one, Isogai came by, remarking sharply: "You'll get nowhere at that leisurely pace. The first thing guests want to do as soon as they get to their rooms is to relax, and you're keeping them waiting for the change of clothing in their trunks. At the rate you guys are going, it'll be hours."

At that, one of the part-timers, Tanaka, who had the habit of always arguing with the full-time bellboys at every opportunity, retorted with a flushed face: "Including everything besides the trunks there are over three hundred pieces of luggage, and only three of us to get them off the buses, check the names on each one, assemble them in the lobby, and then carry them to the rooms. And you're telling us to do all of that in thirty minutes? That's impossible."

Fixing his upturned eyes in an angry glare and taking a few steps toward Tanaka, Isogai said: "If you work efficiently, you can move at twice the speed. You guys just look as if you're trying to have fun or something."

"Then you try lifting them with one hand, and I'll show you that I can work efficiently with both. Come on! Let's see you lift them with one hand."

Tetsuyuki tried patting Tanaka on the shoulder to calm him down but he, prone to irascibility, shook off the appeasing hand and grabbed Isogai by the lapels. "There are only three of us part-timers, and you saddle us with backbreaking work like this. How about getting one or two of your henchmen to come help?"

"The front desk is shorthanded and in turmoil. The first

54

order of business is to take care of the guests." Isogai tried to remove Tanaka's hands from his lapels.

"In that case, all the bellboys should work at getting the guests settled in, and then all work at carrying luggage, shouldn't they? Wouldn't that be more efficient?"

Isogai answered in a quavering voice. "The guests will make fun of us if they see hotel employees scuffling with each other at the entrance. Let go of me!" After Tanaka released his grasp, Isogai explained: "Since the flight arrived late, the chartered tour buses were also an hour late getting to the hotel. The drivers are eager to get back to the garage as soon as possible, and are pressing us to unload the luggage."

"Then at the very least you, as bellboy captain, ought to pitch in and help. The staff at the front desk can manage the bellboys seeing guests to their rooms. Try carrying a couple of these trunks to the lobby!" With that, Tanaka unleashed on Isogai the grievances that had been building inside him for some time. "Today's not the first time you've pushed this kind of thing off onto us part-timers. Should I knock two or three front teeth out of your smart mouth?" Tanaka was on the karate team of a private university in Kyoto. With a slight smile, he cracked his knuckles. Isogai looked at Tetsuyuki as if pleading for help, but immediately returned his gaze to Tanaka.

"Tanaka, you're fired. Ever since you came here you've done nothing but cause trouble with the bellboys. I can't very well keep someone like you on."

A threatening gleam flashed in Tanaka's eyes, and Tetsuyuki hurriedly interposed himself between the two. His attempt to say something was halted by Tanaka's spiteful laugh directed at the two other part-timers. "Well then, I quit. Sorry, but you two will have to haul all the luggage." With that parting shot, he headed toward the lobby, but soon wheeled about and returned. "Let Yamaguchi and Takakura know that I'll be stopping by in a few days to say hello. I have lots to settle with those two." Yamaguchi and Takakura were full-time bellboys who were always bullying the part-time student workers about one thing or another.

One of the bus drivers hollered from his seat. "Hey, what're you doing? Hurry up and unload the luggage!"

After Tanaka's departure, Tetsuyuki had no choice but to board the bus and set about the task of unloading the baggage, more than half of which remained. Isogai disappeared into the lobby, but soon returned and began setting onto a cart the bags the two part-timers had unloaded.

"Only five more. Thank you for waiting." No sooner had he said this to the cigarette-smoking driver than Tetsuyuki saw Isogai fall over onto the luggage cart. He rushed down off the bus to Isogai's side.

"What's wrong?" Isogai's forehead was perspiring, he was clutching his chest with both hands, his breathing was labored, and his lips had a bluish cast. The other part-timer dashed off to the lobby.

"I'm okay. Is all the luggage off?" he asked in a broken, pained voice. Shimazaki, the head of personnel, came running up, reprimanding Tetsuyuki: "You shouldn't be making Isogai haul heavy luggage!"

"Yes, sir . . ." Unsure of what it all meant, Tetsuyuki remained standing there until the driver lost his temper and
shouted, "Hey, haven't you finished yet?" At that, Tetsuyuki
again boarded the bus and began hauling the trunks one at a
time. The last one was especially heavy and, unable to lift it
even with both hands, he dragged it down the aisle and finally
finished the task of unloading. Even after the tour buses had
pulled away from the hotel entrance, Isogai remained sitting on
the luggage cart, pressing his hands against his chest. Shimazaki
ordered Tetsuyuki to take him to the employees' nap room.

"You mustn't make him climb stairs. Use the elevator."

The nap room, known as the Peacock Room, was off to the
side of the hotel's largest banquet hall on the third floor, at the
end of a passageway for employees. In it, triple-decker beds
were lined up like shelves in a silkworm nursery to allow as
many as thirty employees to nap at any one time. Light snoring
could be heard coming from the farthest bed, where someone
was apparently asleep. Isogai lay down on a bed and closed his
eyes. A bit of redness had returned to his lips, and his breathing
no longer seemed so labored.

"Shouldn't we call a doctor?" Tetsuyuki asked in a hushed
voice. Isogai shook his head. "It's always like this. It's passed
now. If I just rest for a while I'll be okay." At length, after some
deliberation, he said hesitantly: "I trust that you won't mention
to Nakaoka that I had another bout of chest pains today."

"Nakaoka?"

"Nakaoka Mineo, the front-desk manager."

"Oh yes . . . that guy." Tetsuyuki called to mind the

somewhat aloof features of the young manager to whom he had only paid brief respects on his first day on the job, and with whom he had never again exchanged words. Feeling uneasy about Isogai's use of the word "another," he asked: "Is this a chronic condition?"

Isogai evaded an answer by changing the topic of conversation. "Is your family in some kind of business?"

"My dad was, but he died about the same time his company went broke. So now my mom works at an eatery in the Kita Shinchi district . . . ."

Isogai seemed to have regained strength, so Tetsuyuki started to rise from the edge of the bed where he was seated in order to return to work. Isogai reminded him: "Whatever you do, don't let Nakaoka know about this." Tetsuyuki again sat down on the bed and asked: "Why mustn't he know?"

"He and I are the same age, and were hired here at the same time. But he has a college degree, and I only graduated from high school. At first, both of us were put to work as bellboys, but it wasn't long before a gap arose in status. Since he can speak English, he was assigned to the front desk and almost immediately made manager. But oddly enough, he has it in for me. At first I thought he was just feeling smug and superior, but that doesn't seem to be it."

"Then what leads you to think he feels that way?"

"He makes a big deal of my slightest mistakes, as if he were trying to create an even bigger gap between us."

The person who had been snoring in the farthest bed, a newly hired cook trainee, suddenly got up and hurried out of the nap room in a panic. The cooks did not have a night shift, so Tetsuyuki concluded that he had probably slipped away from his post and ended up falling asleep. Though it was none of his business to pry into things Isogai didn't want to talk about, he ended up asking: "You have a bad heart, don't you?"

As he lay there, Isogai set a finger aside the well-defined ridge of his nose, his eyes darting about. "It's been bad ever since I was kid. The doctor says I need an operation."

When introducing him to the job, Isogai had guided him all the way to the twenty-fourth floor. Tetsuyuki had thought it strange that they didn't just take the emergency stairs when the elevator was slow in coming. So that was it: he was avoiding the stairs. And it became clear why Section Chief Shimazaki insisted that he should not be allowed to lift heavy luggage.

"They told me that since it's a valve disorder, surgery could fix it . . ."

"Well then, you should just resign yourself to having surgery."

Isogai turned to Tetsuyuki, smiling, and muttered: "That's easy for you to say, since it's not your problem." It seemed to Tetsuyuki that he was seeing Isogai smile for the first time.

Returning to the lobby, he went to Section Chief Shimazaki in the front office.

"It seems to have subsided."

Shimazaki raised his angular face from the documents he had been inspecting. "Oh? That's good." Then he halted Tetsuyuki, who had turned toward the lobby to return to work.

"There's something I want to talk to you about." Having

filed away the documents on his desk, Shimazaki headed for the employees' cafeteria with his restless, somewhat bow-legged gait. Purchasing two cans of cola from the vending machines, he sat down at a table and motioned to Tetsuyuki to take a seat.

"Let's see, you'll graduate next year, won't you?"

"Yes, I plan to."

"What kind of company are you thinking of applying to for work?"

"I haven't thought about that yet. I might fail an employment examination . . ."

Though there was no one else in the cafeteria, Shimazaki suddenly lowered his voice and leaned over the table.

"How about full-time work at our hotel?"

"At this hotel . . . ?"

"Being a hotelier doesn't appeal to you?"

At a loss for an answer, Tetsuyuki sipped the cola that was offered to him.

"These past two months, I've been observing your work habits, and have thought that I'd really like to have you work for us after you graduate. These days, so many student part-timers aren't serious, but you're well-mannered and a hard worker. Some of our guests have also had praise for you."

"Oh?" Tetsuyuki could not recall having done anything that would merit praise.

"Next year, we're planning to hire ten college graduates and twenty high school graduates. How about it? Why not go ahead and make an early decision about employment?"

"Can that be decided before I even take the employment examination?"

A somewhat smug smile arose in the candid features of Shimazaki's face. "If I recommend you, it'll be settled in one shot." Then, as was apparently his habit, he lit his cigarette after resting the filter on his tongue and licking it around once.

"I also saw to it that Isogai was hired here." Shimazaki explained that he and Isogai were from the same town. "His father was a doctor, an otorhinologist, whose practice was in the Marutamachi area of Kyoto. Our house was in the lane behind that. I knew Isogai when he was just a kid." Then lowering his voice, Shimazaki added, "Nobody's had it rougher than that guy."

"The Isogai Otorhinolaryngology Clinic was flourishing, and everyone assumed that the oldest son, Isogai Kōichi, would one day take his father's place. However, an unexpected disaster struck the family: leaving for a trip to the northwestern coast with a fellow doctor, his father for some reason fell from the station platform into the path of a special express train that was passing through at full speed.

"But that wasn't all," Shimazaki continued in a small voice. Less than a year after his father's accidental death, his mother also died after being hit by a train. Returning from taking care of some matter with relatives in Katsura, she was waiting at an unmanned railway crossing on the Hankyū Line for an Umeda-bound train from Kawaramachi to pass by. She must have been in a hurry, because after the train had passed she ducked under the crossing gate, which was still down, and started to cross the tracks, unaware of the train rushing in the opposite direction.

"It's as if they were under some kind of curse, isn't it?" With that, Shimazaki broke off speaking and took out another cigarette, again licking the filter. "At that time, Isogai was still in his first year of high school, and his sister was in sixth grade at elementary school. He went to live with an uncle, while she was taken in by a different relative. For a long time they continued to live separately, but in February of this year they finally rented an apartment in Toyonaka and are again together. If that accident had not happened, by now Isogai would be a doctor, filling his father's shoes."

Glancing at his watch, Shimazaki stood up and, urging Tetsuyuki to give his offer serious thought, hurried back to his office. The smell of food hung heavily in the air of the employees' cafeteria. Three vending machines stood side by side, and on each table there was a plastic cylinder packed tightly with light brown chopsticks. On a large sign was written: PLEASE RETURN UTENSILS TO THE PROPER PLACE AFTER WASHING THEM THOROUGHLY. Tetsuyuki stared vacantly at the sign, his chin propped on one hand.

He was, to be sure, diligent in his work, but Tetsuyuki was not particularly fond of Isogai and the constantly probing look in his eyes that was a part of his standoffish expression. As he recalled Section Chief Shimazaki's narrative, he reflected, *Strange things do happen in this world.* He also thought of Isogai's need of an operation for his chronic heart condition. But concluding that none of that had anything to do with himself, he left the cafeteria and headed for the lobby.

The foreign guests' luggage had been placed in a corner of the lobby, to the side of the main entrance. The bellboys had apparently already taken most of the roughly fifty remaining pieces to the rooms of their respective owners. There were five trunks tagged with the name "E. H. Thomas." Having loaded them onto a cart, Tetsuyuki inquired at the front desk about their owner's room number.

"Number 2588, on the twelfth floor." As Tetsuyuki began to walk toward the elevators with the luggage, Nakaoka, his back turned as he checked the cards, called out to him in a sharp tone: "Iryō! You're supposed to say 'Yes, sir, I understand.'"

"I'm sorry, that was careless of me."

Then, finally facing Tetsuyuki, Nakaoka summoned him with an exasperated gesture.

"Yes, what is it?"

"You were goldbricking for a whole hour. Were you in the nap room? Or in the cafeteria?"

"I wasn't goldbricking. Section Chief Shimazaki had something he wanted to discuss with me, and the two of us went to the cafeteria."

"What did you discuss?" The shirt on Nakaoka, who was tall and thin, had at least an inch-wide opening between the collar and his slender neck. Tetsuyuki had once heard him complain to coworkers that, if he bought shirts adequately long in the sleeves, they would fit poorly around his neck. Feeling no obligation to respond, Tetsuyuki remained silent. Nakaoka's long, slender neck oddly appeared to magnify his twitching

63

Adam's apple. Arranging his disheveled bangs, he asked with a sly smirk: "Isogai had another one of his attacks, didn't he? And Shimazaki told you to keep it from me, huh?"

"What do you mean by 'attack'?"

Nakakoa glanced at Tetsuyuki, then turned away with an insouciant air and said, "Get back to work. You're paid by the hour here, after all."

Tetsuyuki vaguely remembered hearing rumors about a struggle over succession in the hotel, and he sensed that Naka-oka's rudeness had something to do with it.

It was a little before midnight when Tetsuyuki returned to his apartment. Turning on the light, he called out the name he had given the lizard: Kin-chan. As usual, Tetsuyuki filled a spoon with water and held it toward Kin, who lapped at it with his narrow tongue. After giving his pet water, he took the lid from a square wooden box on top of the refrigerator and, using tweezers to extract chestnut weevil larvae out of the sawdust, held them in front of Kin's nose. He released the tension on the tweezers as soon as Kin's long, agile tongue wrapped itself around the larvae. At first, he could not coordinate the timing of the release, and ended up dropping several on the floor. All of two weeks passed before Kin began eating them directly from him.

"Hey, we're getting good at this," Tetsuyuki said after Kin had consumed four larvae. Then, tapping the lizard's nose with the tweezers, he added: "It'll be summer before long, and this room will turn into a sauna. But I can't very well leave the windows open when I'm away."

Kin curled his tail back and forth and blinked several times. Having cleaned the droppings off the pillar, Tetsuyuki was finally able to stretch out on the tatami and fixed his gaze on the nail piercing the lizard's back. "You know, it might get so hot in here that you could die by the time I come home, Kin-chan." He wondered how long he intended to keep this reptile, and thought to himself that if it died, then it died, and that couldn't be helped.

"Kin-chan, when summer comes, I'm going to pull the nail out." Even as he spoke the words, he realized that the lizard's internal organs had probably already knit with the nail, which had thus become part of its body. By pulling the nail out, he would be opening a large wound that had finally healed. Tetsuyuki agonized over what to do.

"Today I did nothing but haul luggage, and only got fifteen hundred yen in tips. Foreign guests have been told that tipping isn't necessary in Japan, so even after hauling all those heavy trunks, I got nothing but 'thank you.' But three newlywed couples did give me five hundred yen each." Tetsuyuki kept up his monologue directed to the small creature that, deprived of its freedom, remained silent in the phosphorescent glow. "But I have it a lot better than Isogai. I never imagined he had it so bad, poor guy. I just thought he was obnoxious."

At that moment, there was a knock at the door. Tetsuyuki sat up with a start, his body tense. A feeling of panic gripped him. The knock was repeated, followed by a man's voice.

"Iryō." It was a peculiarly gravelly voice, one he could never forget. "It's Kobori. Open up!"

Kobori entered as soon as the door opened. He was extremely nearsighted, and the long narrow slits of his eyes blinked behind thick, brown-tinted lenses. "I found you! I never thought it'd take this long, but I had no idea where you'd gone. I finally tracked you down." Kobori sat cross-legged and barked at Tetsuyuki: "Sit!" Kobori kept his red-and-white-striped blazer on until Tetsuyuki took a seat. "Where's your old lady?"

"She's living where she works, at a restaurant."

"Well then, she must have a bit of dough by now. I'm not saying that it all has to be paid back at once. I'll wait three months. After that, be prepared to fork over 350,000 yen."

"It's 323,000 yen, isn't it?"

"You've put me to a lot of unpaid expense and trouble tracking you down."

"There's no way I could come up with money like that. Besides, it has nothing to do with me. My dad didn't leave me a thing, and I am under no obligation to repay his debts."

"You'll end up in a condition where you'll never be able to spout that argument again."

"I'll report your threat to the police."

Instantly, a tremendous blow filled Tetsuyuki's mind with sparks. Standing up, Kobori again punched Tetsuyuki in the face and kicked him in his side repeatedly after he had fallen over.

"I'll come again tomorrow. Be prepared to give me a more sensible answer."

Slinging his blazer over his shoulder, Kobori left. Blood was dripping on the tatami from Tetsuyuki's nose and from a deep gash inside his upper lip. He staggered upright, but was not able to walk in a straight line. He washed his face in the kitchen sink and, stuffing tissue paper up his bleeding nostrils, used a towel to wipe the blood off the floor and then lay down. His nosebleed appeared to be stanched quickly, but blood from his lip continued to flow endlessly. *What if I killed that jerk?* That thought crossed his mind as he looked at Kin, nailed to the pillar. *When he shows up tomorrow, he'll get a carving knife stuck in him.* Tetsuyuki was shaking with fear and mortification. No matter how hard he tried to calm himself, his trembling only grew stronger.

Sleeping fitfully, Tetsuyuki awoke several times during the night. His nose and upper lip throbbed and he was repeatedly attacked by an anxiety that constricted his chest. Each time he awoke he smoked a cigarette. Once when he dozed off, he dreamed that he had become a lizard, scurrying about through clumps of grass and stone fences. Dying and being reborn, he continually passed through the cycle of life and death as a lizard. Through decades—even through centuries—he continued as a lizard and clearly sensed the long passage of time in his dream. Hiding in the shadow of grass on footpaths between paddies, he would look up to see Yōko, Isogai, and many other people he knew as they passed by, and wondered when his time would finally end.

Then he awoke and glanced at his alarm clock: 3:30. He had not been dozing for longer than forty minutes. Pondering the several centuries he had clearly just spent as a lizard, he lay facedown and lit a cigarette. He was enveloped in a feeling

of glowing intoxication. He had no idea why he was so enrap-
tured, but it seemed as if something akin to hope had grown
in one corner of his body, which was otherwise bound by tremendous anxiety.

During forty minutes, he had spent centuries going through
countless lives as a lizard. What a frightening dream that had
been. And still, that strange and frightening dream had put his
mind at ease. Savoring the flavor of the smoke, he reflected
deeply. The bitterness of the tobacco penetrated the wound behind his upper lip. The dream had been vividly engraved in his
mind and had not faded.

He could recall everything: whether the sensation of the
blazing sun on his back, or rapturously stretching his limbs out
to imbibe from dew-drenched grasses, or the feeling of terror at soaring high into the sky in the beak of a shrike. Dying
from hunger and thirst, or being devoured by some unidenti-
fied creature, or being clubbed to death by human children, he
had died countless times and had been reborn as many times.
He had unmistakably passed through a dreadfully long time.
And yet all that had happened in only forty minutes. The idea
that the lizard that had passed through centuries of recurring
life and death, and the person who had awoken and was here
smoking a cigarette were the same "self" produced a point of
clarity in his hollowed-out spirit.

Tetsuyuki got up and switched on the miniature light. He
approached Kin and, leaning against the wall, gazed at the nail.
Kin opened his eyes, blinked, moved his face to look at the human, and flicked his long, slender tongue.

"Are you thirsty?" Tetsuyuki spoke to the reptile in a lowered voice. "You didn't die even after being nailed to a pillar . . . Why didn't you die, Kin-chan? Why are you alive?"

He stroked Kin's head gently with his fingertip. The lizard's skin was rough, lacking any moisture. Filling a cup with water in the kitchen, Tetsuyuki returned and dipped his fingers into the cup, then let the drops from them fall onto Kin's back.

"Why were you born as a lizard? And why was I born human? There must be some reason for that. What do you think the reason is?"

Tetsuyuki's tongue licked the wound inside his upper lip. It had stopped bleeding, but a wide, deep gash remained. "There's no way I'm going to pay anything to a gangster like that, Kin-chan. Even though I ended up in a mess like this, I didn't die. And I won't give in. Whether they break my nose, or even kill me, I'll be damned if I do as that jerk says. I'll kill him before he kills me!"

Then a slight smile appeared on Tetsuyuki's face as he corrected himself: "Yeah, but if I did that, my life would be over. No matter that he is only a louse as far as gangsters go, if I killed him everything would be at an end." Then he told Kin about his dream.

"This was the first time I've ever had such a strange dream. For centuries, I had actually become a lizard, just like you, going through life and death over and over." The moment he spoke these words, it occurred to Tetsuyuki that during those forty minutes of dozing, perhaps he really had gone through all those cycles of birth and death as a lizard. But then he quickly banished the absurd notion from his mind. Such things could not be. It was a dream, after all, and here he was awake and human, talking to Kin, wasn't he?

Tetsuyuki continued to lean against the wall, staring fixedly at the bluish light reflected on Kin's skin. As he did so, it became unclear which was dream, which was reality: his self as a human being, or his self as a lizard. It seemed as if both were dreams. Then again, it seemed as if both were real.

"I'll have to tell Yōko not to come here anymore." He had no idea when Kobori might show up again, and he couldn't let her be anywhere nearby.

"Yōko, why do you care for someone like me and even say you want to marry me? I might never be anything more than a grunt salaryman."

The darkness outside the window was just beginning to yield to the faintest blue. Tetsuyuki left Kin's side and tumbled into bed, curling up tightly. He slept soundly until nearly noon.

Tetsuyuki remained in bed for a while, reflecting. Then he got up and looked at his face in the mirror. Both his nose and lip were swollen; he could not very well go out among people looking like that. He fixed himself a meal, making some toast and warming some milk. The wound smarted when he ate, and it took him three times longer than usual to get down one slice of toast and a glass of milk.

Then, his face cast downward and his eyes on the ground, he walked the long path to the police box in front of the station. He peered inside and saw a middle-aged policeman sitting at a desk, scribbling notes on a document. Tetsuyuki returned to the shopping arcade, mustered his resolve, and then again went to the police box.

"Excuse me . . ." At Tetsuyuki's voice, the policeman looked up. "There's a matter on which I'd be grateful for your advice."

The policeman's gaze was fixed for a moment on Tetsuyuki's swollen nose and lip. He asked, motioning for him to take a seat, "What is it?"

Tetsuyuki summarized the matter from the beginning up to the incident the night before.

"Apart from the issue of the debt, this is a clear case of extortion, and a charge of assault would also apply," the policeman said as he removed his hat and smoothed his thinning hair with the palms of both hands. "It's not unusual for collectors to make threats, but they rarely resort to violence. But since he actually assaulted you, you could have this petty gangster Kobori arrested."

"I'm worried about what would come after that."

"You mean, you're afraid of reprisals?"

"That's right. He's not working alone."

"They all capitulate without a fight. As for the debt, that could be solved legally as a civil suit. But since you've come to discuss the matter with the police—and especially now that there is the fact of your having been threatened and beaten—we are obliged to take action. Press charges against that gangster."

Looking at this officer, who somehow had the air of a middle school principal about him, Tetsuyuki hesitantly responded, "I'll press charges." He felt the blood drain from his face. The policeman poured some tea for him, but it was hot and made the wound smart, so he took only two or three sips and then vacantly stared at the steam rising from the cup.

Leaving the police box, Tetsuyuki quickly went into a phone booth and dialed the hotel. He told Shimazaki that he had caught a cold and was running a fever, and asked to be excused from work. Then he hung up and returned to his apartment.

Night fell. Around eight o'clock, Tetsuyuki's heart began to pound violently. He had to keep wiping his sweaty palms on his trousers. He could hear footsteps climbing the metal stairs, and assumed a formal sitting posture in the middle of the room, with both fists clenched. There was a knock on the door, but before he could respond, Kobori had already entered.

"So, have you thought of a good answer?" Kobori's words hardly entered Tetsuyuki's ears, which were listening intently for any hint of the arrival of the policeman who was supposed to be keeping watch.

"What's this? You're trembling, aren't you?" As soon as Kobori spoke, the door opened to reveal the familiar middle-aged policeman and a young officer. His mouth partly agape, Kobori glanced back and forth between Tetsuyuki and the policemen. The middle-aged policeman stepped into the room and, patting Kobori on the shoulder, said calmly, "You're under arrest for extortion and assault." Then he took out a pair of handcuffs.

"Do you have a warrant?" Kobori was staring at Tetsuyuki, and his face was drained of blood."

"We do. I can show it to you if you want." Then, handcuffing

Kobori, the policeman smiled at Tetsuyuki. "If something else comes up, please come see us anytime." The policeman's voice echoed as they descended the stairs. "You'll have plenty of other charges against you anyway, and we'll have you fess up to all of them. It'll be five or six years before you'll be back on the streets."

Tetsuyuki quietly went to the kitchen and opened the window to peer out. Sometime or other, a police car had parked there. He hurriedly closed the window and, leaning against the wall, sank down, pressing his forehead against his knees, and remained motionless for a long time. He wondered how his mother was doing.

They had been in contact by telephone two or three times a week, but over the two months since moving into this apartment, he had not met with her even once. He wanted desperately to see her. Feeling like a child lost in a crowd, he hurriedly put on his shoes and left the apartment. As he walked briskly down the dark path toward the station, he realized that he had not given Kin anything to eat or drink, and ran back.

He opened the box containing the chestnut weevil larvae to find only four of the creatures left among the sawdust. After feeding those to Kin, Tetsuyuki got down on all fours in the kitchen and began looking about. Two young cockroaches ran out from underneath the refrigerator, and so he trapped them with a cup, then, holding the insects with tweezers, thrust them in front of Kin's nose. Up to now he had only alternated between larvae and grubs, and had never tried feeding him cockroaches. Kin just fixed his beady black eyes on the baby

73

cockroaches squirming in the grasp of the tweezers, but made no move to consume them.

"What's the matter, Kin-chan? You don't like roaches?" As if at that urging, Kin's tongue adroitly wrapped itself around a cockroach. One of the insect's legs dangled out of Kin's mouth. It finally disappeared, but it took a very long time for the lump to move from Kin's throat down to his stomach. Tetsuyuki waited impatiently. Then he administered some water with a spoon.

"Drink up. Who knows? Maybe I won't be coming back today." He dampened Kin's body all over with the water remaining in the spoon, and then left.

There were few people at Suminodō Station, where he waited a good half hour for a train to Katamachi. As soon as he sat down in the nearly empty car, he realized that he had eaten no dinner, and apart from his lunch of milk and a slice of toast he had consumed nothing at all. He had spent all that time so anxiously wondering where the policeman was keeping watch and when Kobori might show up that he had not felt hunger.

From the central entrance of Osaka Station, he went down to an underground arcade and glanced at a clock—11:30. Five or six vagrants had fashioned enclosures out of cardboard and had made beds in them for the night. Hurriedly turning right in the arcade, Tetsuyuki headed toward Sakura Bridge.

No sooner had he started down the main avenue of Kita Shinchi than the restaurant curtain of Yūki came into view. Yūki was a two-story wooden structure sandwiched between large office buildings on either side. It was an unpretentious shop, marked only by an indigo-dyed curtain hanging in front

74

of its latticed door, but it was numbered among the distinguished old establishments of Kita Shinchi, and it had a reputation both for its refined patronage and for its steep prices. It had a regular chef, and at first his mother was put in charge of cleaning up, but it was soon recognized that she was better at flavoring the appetizers and two weeks previously had been put in charge of that.

Tetsuyuki stood in front of a florist's shop not far from Yūki, waiting for the restaurant's closing time. A man accompanied by a woman who looked like a bar hostess was purchasing armloads of orchids. Tetsuyuki watched through the window as the man paid, pulling money from a leather wallet bulging with 10,000-yen bills.

As its last group of customers left, the lights inside Yūki went out and a young woman attired in a splash-patterned kimono came out to put away the shop curtain. Tetsuyuki approached her.

"I'm Iryō Kinuko's son. I'd like to see her for a moment." The woman affably urged him to enter, loudly calling inside, "Mrs. Iryō, your son is here."

The light that was on in the kitchen soon spread to the interior of the darkened shop. His mother emerged, her slim body wrapped in an apron, wiping her wet hands with a towel. Tetsuyuki was still standing hesitantly outside.

"The customers have all left. Don't just stand there. Come on in." When Tetsuyuki entered, she introduced him to the elderly chef who had poked his face out of the kitchen.

"This is my son. And this is Mr. Ishii, the very best chef in

75

Kita Shinchi." At her words, a smile came to his lips and he said gruffly, "You're the only one who calls me the best, auntie."

"Have you had dinner?" His mother's face darkened as she looked at him. Then she pulled him by the arm into the brightly lit kitchen. "What happened to you? Your face . . ." She stared at his swollen nose and lip.

"I stumbled and fell down on the apartment stairs." Tetsuyuki had never before deceived his mother. As soon as she tried to say something, he cut her off. "I haven't eaten dinner. And I only had a slice of bread for lunch."

Apparently having overheard him, Chef Ishii chimed in. "We have a bit of sliced squid left, along with some stewed pork and red miso." With that, he opened a pot, heaped the food on a plate, and set it on the counter. His mother thanked Mr. Ishii as she filled a bowl with rice.

"This is really good, so thank Mr. Ishii and eat up." Tetsuyuki thanked Mr. Ishii, as well as the young woman who had come into the kitchen, for all they had done for his mother. The latticed door opened and a heavily made-up woman in Japanese attire staggered in, reeking of perfume. "That's the proprietress," Tetsuyuki's mother whispered to him.

"This is my son. He stopped by to discuss something with me, and hadn't had any dinner, so the chef picked out a few leftovers for him," she explained in a flustered tone.

"Well, well, you have such a grown-up son." The proprietress cast a sidelong glance at Tetsuyuki, who said, "Thank you for treating me." He began to add an expression of thanks for all she had done for his mother, but the proprietress paid no

attention to him, and asked the young woman who was putting things away in the kitchen to call a cab for her. Tetsuyuki
judged her age to be forty-two or -three.

"Yokota's gotten so that he drinks too much, and I can't
keep up with him. Maybe that's what happens when you're
down and out." As the proprietress talked, Ishii changed out
of his apron and responded briefly. "Aside from what you drink
with him here, it's not necessary to accompany him to other
clubs, is it?"

"Yes, but he and I go way back together, and he's trying to
hide the fact that his business isn't going well, and I can't all of a
sudden give him the cold treatment. I had to down three glasses
of brandy, and now I'm drunk."

"That's because before that you'd already had five rounds
of saké."

Both her cosmetics and her kimono made her look youth-
ful, and her profile still had traces that suggested remarkable
beauty in her younger years, but from the front, under strong
light, her heavy makeup made her look older. In the middle of
her face, which expressed both craftiness and innocence, was
a pair of inorganic eyes that seemed like those of an exquisitely
crafted doll.

"Eat it up quickly, or it'll get cold." Urged by the proprietress, Tetsuyuki slurped the miso and stuffed his mouth with
rice. There was no warmth in her words, and it seemed to him
that she did not want him eating her shop's leftovers for free.
"How much do I owe you?" His intention was to show consideration, but the proprietress threw him a sharp look and said,

"What do you mean? You want to pay? I'm sure our chef didn't serve it with the intention of being paid." With that, she got into the cab parked in front of the shop. Ishii and the young woman also went home, leaving only Tetsuyuki and his mother.

"The proprietress seems a bit touchy."

"Well, she used to be a geisha." Wiping the countertop, his mother named a major railroad company. "The president of that company set her up in this shop." She held a pinkie erect as she spoke. "She's lived in the world of nightclubs and bars since she was a kid. And then she went from being a first-class geisha to being the mistress of a millionaire and got this shop here in Shin-chi. She's getting on in years, but is like a naïve little girl when it comes to how the world works. It was after her patron died that she really got serious about the business. Up till then, all of her customers came here because of connections with her patron."

"How old is she?"

"The same age as I am."

"Huh?! Then she's fifty?" Tetsuyuki found it amusing, thinking that in that case her heavy makeup really did a splendid job of exposing her age.

"She has her endearing qualities, but she's pretty capricious. But by now I've gotten used to dealing with her."

His mother appeared in better spirits than he had expected. "You've grown thin," she said. "Has something happened?" After finishing her work, she sat down next to him and began questioning.

"No. Just hanging around in my apartment, I suddenly wanted to see you, that's all."

"Does Yōko sometimes come to your apartment?"

"Yeah . . . Sometimes she brings groceries." Under his mother's gaze, he sensed in her words that she had caught on to everything about them.

"I really like that girl. She's cheerful and sweet, not a single blemish on her character. I wonder if she'd be willing to marry you." From a teapot she filled to the brim large teacups, the kind used at sushi restaurants. Cradling her cup in both hands, she looked down, focused on the tea stem floating in the brew. "About two months before your father died, I told him about you and Yōko, and said it seemed as if you had decided to tie the knot."

"What did Dad say?"

"He laughed, and said that people never get to marry their first love."

Tetsuyuki beamed at his mother. For the first time in a very long time he felt peace in his heart.

"My first love was cruelly shattered when I was in middle school." As a teenager, he had fallen for the girl who managed the equipment of the baseball club. He didn't like baseball, but joined with her as his aim.

"I was put out in right field and made to practice catching fly balls. I got so nervous with her watching me that I caught a ball with my forehead instead of my mitt, and that made her double over laughing. She had become the manager because she had a crush on the pitcher, a guy named Takakura. As soon as I realized that, I quit the club after just three days, and a senior teammate slapped me across the face three times.

Whenever I think about it, it seems so idiotic that I end up laughing."

On the street outside there was the insistent honking of a horn and a sudden surge of people. The noise of the bustle broke the silence of the closed restaurant.

"It's time for the hostesses to head home." With that lone comment, his mother fell back into pensive silence, not even sipping the tea she had poured. At length, she said, "What really happened? Tell me, and don't hide anything."

"There's nothing to tell. I really fell down on the apartment stairs and hit my face."

"You never heard again from that collector?"

"Never. There's no way he could trace me so far outside Osaka. By the time he finds either of us, I'll have saved three or four hundred thousand yen."

"It's not money that we particularly need to repay, but . . . there's no doubt that it's your father's debt." She told Tetsuyuki to stay the night in her room on the second floor. After making sure that the door was locked and the gas turned off, she extinguished the light. After climbing a steep staircase next to the enormous refrigerator in the kitchen, they came to a cramped room with a wooden floor, crowded with stacks of cardboard boxes, beside which was a sliding door. Opening the door, she turned on a fluorescent light. It was a six-mat room properly furnished with a tokonoma alcove and filled with her familiar scent.

"It won't matter if I stay without permission?" Tetsuyuki glanced around the room.

"No, it won't matter. The proprietress won't come to the shop until after seven p.m. Mr. Ishii will stop by at about six a.m. with a load of goods from the market, and will leave right after that."

"Then you have to get up at six?"

"He has a key, so I can stay in bed. If I'm awake, I get up and make him a cup of tea, but he returns home after that and goes to bed. He gets up at four a.m. and goes to the central market by himself to pick out produce for our pantry. Then he comes to work at four p.m., and the restaurant opens at six." She opened the closet and pulled out futons and quilts, arranging beds for two. Tetsuyuki sat down by a latticed window facing the street.

"This is a nice room."

"Until two years ago it was used for guests. It even has an alcove for decorations."

"Why isn't it used that way now?"

"They said it's because they were so understaffed that they decided to limit the business to downstairs, but it's probably because their customer base has dwindled. It's rare that customers here request a separate room, and so they decided not to use the second floor."

"Where do you bathe?"

"I take the bus to Jōshō Bridge. There's an old public bath there." She sat in front of a small dressing mirror, applying lotion to her face.

"You take the bus, to go to a public bath?"

"It's only five minutes to Jōshō Bridge." She changed into a nightgown and got into bed, and so he also undressed, switched off the light, and got into bed in his underwear.

"I hope we can all live together someday soon, you and Yōko, the three of us . . ." she muttered, and yawned. It was not long until her regular breathing evinced slumber. Noting how exhausted she must have been, Tetsuyuki, too, closed his eyes.

There were signs of a steady stream of traffic on the main avenue through Shinchi, and he could hear laughter and voices calling for others among the human noises that had increased. He listened intently to the clamor, his eyes closed tight. He wondered about the meaning of the dream in which he had gone through centuries of cycles of birth and death as a lizard. In a mere forty minutes, he had gone through several hundred years. Though he dismissed it as only a dream, he felt that he had stood on the brink of a chasm opening onto a deep and distant world, and that he had peered down into something very strange. The self that was dreaming and the self of his waking consciousness—how were they different?

He thought of Kin, nailed to a pillar in a small dark apartment way beyond that distant station. Sometime, he would have to pull the nail out and set him free. He wanted to do this in a careful manner that would not kill him or aggravate the wound. Imagining Kin in the back of his mind, Tetsuyuki wanted to repeat the dream of the night before.

5

It was summer break at the university, and among Tetsuyuki's classmates, there were several whose employment following graduation had already been secured. If nothing else, he could always do as Section Chief Shimazaki recommended and take full-time employment at the hotel. This offer had dampened his ambition to take the examinations for more desirable jobs.

When he arrived at the employees' entrance to the hotel a little before five o'clock, as usual, he found Yōko standing on the adjoining sidewalk, trying to avoid the foul-smelling effusion of the exhaust. Bathed in the setting sun of summer, half of her body was tinted red, giving her features a melancholy cast. She trotted across the street, breaking into a smile only after reaching the other side. Tetsuyuki had also dashed out into the street, dodging traffic to meet her.

"What's wrong?" Yōko returned his gaze in silence. They turned down an alley and entered a coffee shop. During the month that had passed since they last met they had only talked on the telephone.

Until summer break arrived, Yōko had been attending lectures every day, and after that various errands seemed to come up for her, leaving them no opportunity to get together. Ever since the incident with the collector, Kobori, Tetsuyuki had told Yōko not to come to the apartment. On his days off he had always tried to arrange for them to meet in Umeda, but each time she either had errands to run for her mother, or she had to go help clean and do laundry for a cousin who had just given birth, and they were not able to meet.

Sitting at the very back of the coffee shop with bossa nova music in the background, Tetsuyuki studied the expression on Yōko's face.

"Did you cut your hair?"

"Yeah, it was getting hot, so I ended up cutting it."

"This is the first time I've seen you with short hair."

"This is the shortest it's been since I was in middle school. You don't like it?"

"It looks good on you." Then he asked again, "What's wrong?"

"When you've had a day off, I've had errands, and when I have time, you always have to work . . ."

It was his least favorite time of the day, and yet he felt happy. He glanced at his watch: the same 4:40 as when he arrived at Osaka Station. He took the watch off and held it to his ear, shook it and tapped it lightly, but it didn't move.

"Ah, it's stopped. It was cheap, so it was just a matter of time till it broke." He threw it down on the table. Yōko took a watch out of her purse, an old Rolex that had belonged to her father and that she had begged him for. She always kept it in her purse.

"I'll lend this to you."

"It would look odd for a hotel bellboy to wear an elegant timepiece like this."

"Yes, but you have to have a watch, don't you?" Then, quickly pulling the watch back from his hand as he tried to take it, she added it a jesting tone, "Now, you mustn't take it to a pawnshop."

Laughing, he put the Rolex on his wrist. "I've had my eye on this. I thought if I married you, it'd be mine."

"No matter how much I begged, 'Dad, pretty please,' he wouldn't give in. He'd say, 'What would a woman do with a man's watch?' or 'It has too many fond memories for me,' and wouldn't part with it."

"I'm surprised he gave it to you, then."

"He got a new Rolex at discount, and finally let me have this one."

"Why were you so set on having a man's watch like this?"

"You can't find vintage Rolexes like this anymore. And besides, I really liked it for some reason."

"These are the toughest ones in the world."

"Take good care of it, okay?"

It was 5:30. Finishing her iced coffee, Yōko stood up. At the sight of her breasts through the thin material of her blouse, Tetsuyuki felt a sudden surge of desire, darkening his expression and rendering him mute. Her words as they left the coffee shop were answered only with silence. He just ran his eyes from her lips to her breasts to her crotch, and then back down to the sidewalk.

"What's wrong? Are you angry about something?" Yōko cocked her head slightly, but Tetsuyuki only stared silently at the sidewalk. "Again! It's always like this . . . you suddenly fall into a foul mood . . ." She seemed now to be in a bad humor herself. They crossed the street and parted, and he watched her as she mixed into the crowd. Abruptly, she turned and made a derisive gesture toward him, pulling against one eye and sticking out her tongue. Several passersby looked at her in surprise.

Tetsuyuki changed into his uniform and hurried to the office.

"You're forty minutes late." Tsuruta, one of the bellboys, was sitting at the desk.

"I'm sorry." In spite of Tetsuyuki's apology, Tsuruta punched the time card himself and then wrote in some numbers with a red pencil.

"You're paid by the hour, so I'm docking forty minutes from your pay." Such determinations were supposed to be made by the bellboy captain, Isogai, but Tetsuyuki just meekly voiced his acknowledgment and headed toward the lobby. Tsuruta walked up behind him and whispered, "For the time being, I'm substituting as bellboy captain."

After escorting guests to their rooms, Tsuruta was in the habit of killing time by shooting the breeze with female employees in the bellboy stations on each floor. Scrutinizing his acne-studded face, Tetsuyuki asked, "Has something happened to Isogai?"

"He collapsed again, before noon. He's resting in the nap room now. The section chief asked me to fill in for him."

After escorting a foreign couple to a room on the four-teenth floor, Tetsuyuki headed for the nap room. Preparation was under way for what appeared to be a major event, with waiters and waitresses busily carrying plates and cups. One of them almost bumped into Tetsuyuki, nearly dropping his plates. Coming to a standstill, he said with a sigh, "Hey, if you've got that much time on your hands down in the lobby, help us out here. We have to prepare a buffet for eight hundred people by seven o'clock."

"What kind of event is it?"

The waiter named a well-known politician from a conser-vative party. "It's to celebrate his seventy-seventh birthday, but that's only the outward reason. It's really a membership event to raise campaign funds."

Promising that he would inquire at the front desk and come back to help out if permission were given, Tetsuyuki proceeded through the narrow passage to the nap room. Upon gently opening the door and looking inside, his eyes met those of Section Chief Shimazaki, who was sitting on the bed. Tet-suyuki tiptoed up beside him and sat down. Isogai appeared to be asleep.

"It's been rather hectic today." Shimazaki spoke softly. "He collapsed in the lobby. I was about to call an ambulance, but it so happened that there was a cardiologist right there who attended to him. He was here for some university class reunion, and there were about twenty doctors altogether. One of them had some medicine with him that saved Isogai's life."

"What did the doctor say?"

"He said to make sure Isogai received a thorough examination at a specialized hospital. He mentioned, too, that operations for valve disorders now have a fairly high success rate compared with other kinds of heart surgeries."

The door opened and a clerk from the front desk called for Shimazaki, who came back to the bedside after exchanging words with her. "Something's come up and I have to return to the office. Iryō, you stay with him for a while." As he was about to leave, Tetsuyuki hurriedly interjected. "Please tell Nakaoka at the front desk and the bellboy Tsuruta that you have asked me to remain here, or I'll be accused of goldbricking."

Shimazaki nodded and walked off with his usual brisk gait. When the metal door was closed, the bustle and noise of preparation in the banquet room ceased and the dimly lit nap room returned to silence.

Isogai's face, shadowed by the bunk beds, looked like a bronze bust. Staring at his closed eyes, Tetsuyuki wondered how Yōko would be spending the summer break. Every year she had spent the entire month of August working in the basement grocery section of a department store, using her earnings to travel and returning the day before classes resumed. That one week of travel spent with some close female friends from school had been her only time away from Tetsuyuki; all other times, both on and off campus, she was in close company with him. Even though they did not live together, her friends often teased her, saying that they were just like a married couple.

The question popped into Tetsuyuki's mind: *Why has Yōko not mentioned her summer plans to me?* Usually she began talking well beforehand about her plans for work and travel, but this year she had not touched on it at all. Last year and the year before, by the third day of summer break she would already be standing at a register in the basement of some department store. What plans did she have for this year? They were already ten days into summer break. Tetsuyuki recalled the downcast look on her sunbathed face as she stood on the sidewalk waiting for him.

"You don't have to stay here with me all the time."

At these words Tetsuyuki looked up with a start: Isogai wasn't asleep after all.

"I heard you had a bad time of it today." Isogai's eyes remained closed even when Tetsuyuki addressed him. "Did you lift something heavy?" Isogai shook his head. "Or were you running up a flight of stairs?"

Isogai finally opened his eyes. "I wouldn't do something that stupid."

There are things people dislike mentioning to others, or even hearing mentioned. Acknowledging that, Tetsuyuki added, "The other day, I heard from Section Chief Shimazaki . . . about your mother and father."

Isogai cast a glance at Tetsuyuki and muttered, "That guy blabs too much." Then he closed his eyes again.

"I think you ought to bite the bullet and have the operation . . ."

"What's that got to do with my mom and dad?"

After hesitating for some time, Tetsuyuki said, "If these attacks keep happening, I'm afraid you'll end up dying."

"You think I'd let myself die from something like this? People make a big deal of it, but I'm used to it. It always passes if I can just rest a bit."

"I have this feeling that you're going to be run over by a train . . ." Tetsuyuki was taken aback by his own words, as if they had come out independently of his will. Realizing how insensitive a remark it was, he lowered his gaze to the green carpet. "That just slipped out . . . What I meant was . . ."

Isogai cut him off. "I've had the same feeling." Tetsuyuki looked up. "Today I was a bit late getting out of the apartment, and I thought if I had to wait for another train I wouldn't make it to work on time. When I got to the station, the gate was already lowered, but if I wanted to catch the train for Umeda, I had to get past that to make it to the ticket gate. After the train had gone by I thought the gate had started to rise and was about to hurry across when someone next to me shouted, 'There's another one coming the other way!' I was in such a hurry I'd completely spaced out, and didn't even notice it."

Isogai's face, which had been immobile, turned toward Tetsuyuki but with his eyes focused on an indefinite point, as if recalling something. At length he resumed his story. For the first time Tetsuyuki was seeing emotions manifest in Isogai's countenance.

"As I was waiting for the train my heart began to pound, and I was gripped by a fear that someday I'd end up going the same way as my mom and dad. And not just me, but my kid sister, too. Then, when I was on the train I kept thinking, 'I can't go on like this.' When I arrived at Umeda and was walking to the hotel, everything in front of me started to blank out. I rested a bit in the locker room, but the moment I got to the lobby, I collapsed . . ." Then he fell silent.

Tetsuyuki's thoughts raced wildly through his mind in search of the right words that might put Isogai Kōichi at ease and give him some hope.

Was this the first time he had empathized with someone else so much? It seemed strange to him: a human unable to face another's suffering as his own. The face Yōko had pulled at him came to mind, and then the image of Kin. And the thought he'd had, if only momentarily, of wanting to kill Kobori. As he mused about these things, he began to talk.

"My father died and his business fell apart. My mother and I had no idea that the guy he'd depended on as his right-hand man had appropriated the company funds. What's more, the way he'd managed to put everything in his own name was both clever and legal, and by the time we realized what was going on, it was too late. All we were left with were my father's debts. Thugs came crashing in, pressing us for payment, so I'm hiding in an apartment outside Daitō while my mother is living where she works, in a restaurant in Kita Shinchi. But one of the thugs sniffed me out. He beat me and kicked me, leaving my face so mangled I couldn't go out for a week. I was afraid of reprisals, but I reported it to the police anyway. The guy was arrested, but I have no idea when his pals will come to retaliate. I thought of moving to a place even farther away, but a certain situation prevents me from leaving that apartment."

Having said all that, Tetsuyuki wondered what it could possibly mean to Isogai. What was he trying to get across? It also occurred to him that Isogai must know far greater unhappiness. By comparison, Tetsuyuki was the rather fortunate one: he was in good health, and his mother was alive. And what's more, he had a girlfriend: Yōko, whose charm was matchless. Yes, he was certainly blessed. Intending to raise Isogai's spirits with his life story, he had instead given himself a boost. Yet at the same time part of him fell into deeper dejection than before.

"Why can't you leave that apartment?" Isogai listened to the story of Kin, and then slowly straightened himself up with eyes wide. "Is that lizard alive, even now?"

"Yeah, it's alive. Before I left today, I gave it water and fed it."

"Why don't you just pull the nail out?"

"If I did that it might die. I don't know how many times I've thought of just killing it, but I can't bring myself to do it. After all, I was the one who got it into that situation, even if it was dark and I wasn't aware of what I was doing."

"Can a lizard stay alive if it's nailed to a pillar?"

"Well, it *is* alive."

"Is what you're saying really true?"

"If you think I'm lying, come take a look."

Isogai leaned forward and was about to say something when the door opened and Tsuruta poked his head in. Seeing that Isogai appeared to be feeling better he asked, "Are you all right?" The tone of his inquiry betrayed an indifference to Isogai's actual condition.

"Yes, I'm better now. Sorry to have caused so much trouble."

"There's some work I want Iryō to do."

"Sure, right away." Tetsuyuki stood up and, without saying more, brushed past Tsuruta and dashed through the passageway. The party in the banquet room had apparently begun. While he was waiting for the elevator there came a roar from behind the closed door: "*Banzai!*" shouted three times by hundreds of people. Two men were standing guard in front of the door, casting wary glances all about. Before he knew it, Tsuruta was standing beside him. He threw out a cutting remark. "You're good at slacking off, huh?"

"Section Chief Shimazaki told me not to leave Isogai's side until he had fully recovered."

"How noble of you! Maybe Isogai's just faking to get out of work himself."

Tetsuyuki ignored that comment and remained silent inside the elevator. Tsuruta perversely kept up his haranguing until they reached the lobby, at which point the expression on his face immediately tensed. He rushed to overtake Tetsuyuki in response to the professional tone of voice of a front-desk employee as he obsequiously handed over a room key: "Please see these guests to their room." The guests were the sort of couple—a seemingly well-off middle-aged man and a woman in a kimono who looked as if she might be in the nightclub business—that usually slipped a 500- or 1,000-yen tip to a bellboy. But when contrary to expectation no tip was forth-coming, Tsuruta would invariably return to the lobby and take out his irritation on one of the part-timers.

As Tetsuyuki was standing in the lobby looking forward to the end of his shift in another ten minutes, Isogai tapped him on the shoulder and whispered, "Let me see that lizard."

"Sure. When can you come by?"

"Today."

"Today?"

"Let me stay in your apartment tonight. You don't mind, do you?"

"I don't mind, but do you feel up to it?"

"I'll call my sister and let her know. Let's take a cab back. I'll pay the fare."

Isogai had changed his clothes and was waiting by the employee exit. Tetsuyuki went out to the street and quickly hailed a cab.

"Please take us to Suminodō."

The driver turned his head and looked at them. "Sumi-nodō . . . Where's that?"

"You don't know?"

The driver made an apologetic gesture with his hand, and explained that he had not been long on the job. Tetsuyuki had never taken a cab home and was at a loss to describe the route.

"At any rate, go straight on the Hanna Freeway until just be-fore you get to Mount Ikoma. From there I'll have a general idea."

When they set out, Isogai laughed aloud. "Even a taxi

driver has never heard of the place, but a collector was able to sniff it out."

"Those guys are good at it." The mood of gaiety affected Tetsuyuki and he joined in the laughter. As they approached the foothills of Mount Ikoma, a sign on the left with an arrow appeared: Suminodō Station. As they turned onto that road and continued some distance, Tetsuyuki guessed that a lane off to the right was the correct way, and told the driver to turn there. It was a dark street, barren except for a telephone booth, the one from which he always placed calls. Never once getting lost, the cab stopped in front of Tetsuyuki's apartment.

A rush of hot, humid air issued from inside when Tetsuyuki unlocked and opened the door. He hurriedly turned on the light and fan and opened the window. He wanted to open the screen to improve air circulation, but recalled that the area was infested with mosquitoes. An open screen could result in sleeplessness from bites. He pointed at Kin. "See, I was telling the truth."

Tetsuyuki gazed vacantly at Isogai, who was standing rigidly just inside the door, staring at Kin with a startled look. His mouth agape, Isogai's expression seemed at first glance to be absentminded, but his eyes gleamed with an eerily powerful light. His expression was of the same kind one might see on a person in the throes of madness, an aspect Tetsuyuki had never once seen during the several months of their association.

Sensing that it was rude of him to stare at Isogai like that, he began his routine. First, he opened the refrigerator, put some ice in a cup, and filled it with water. Then he poured the ice water into a spray bottle and squirted the liquid all over

Kin's body, after which he directed the fan toward the lizard. After nine hours in a hot room full of motionless summer air, Kin was dehydrated and enfeebled, and by the time Tetsuyuki returned past midnight, his limp body was bent over as it hung on the nail.

Tetsuyuki sprayed Kin's body again and again, and then gave him water with a spoon in his usual manner. Darting his thread-like tongue out, Kin greedily lapped up the water. He regained his vigor about ten minutes after having drunk the water. The ice water that had been sprayed on him dried in the breeze from the fan, but at the same time the vitality of his skin was restored. Strength came back to his limp body, and when he slowly began to move his legs, Tetsuyuki used tweezers to feed him chestnut weevil larvae. Tetsuyuki always felt a moment of relief and happiness when Kin swallowed the first one.

Kin consumed five larvae and took a few more laps of water from the spoon. The movement of the lizard's tongue had become nimbler than at first. As he sprayed Kin one more time to be sure, Tetsuyuki smiled at Isogai. "This is how I wrap up the day."

Isogai, who had until then remained immobile, approached the lizard and cautiously moved his pallid face close to it. Kin began to thrash furiously with his long tail.

"He's afraid because an unfamiliar human is present." Showing no response to that warning, Isogai kept the strange glow in his eyes trained on Kin. Tetsuyuki was spurred by a fear that Isogai might be so overly stimulated by the sight that he would suffer another one of his attacks.

"This is awesome . . ." Isogai's voice was barely audible. Pointing to the black stains on the pillar by Kin's tail, he asked, "What are these?"

"Droppings. I wipe them off every day, but they leave a stain. Someday I'm going to catch it from the landlady."

"Would he let me feed him?"

"Mm, dunno . . ."

Despite his inquiry, Isogai made no move to try feeding Kin. Instead, without saying a word, he cautiously extended his hand and grabbed the head of the nail. Kin writhed violently, but Isogai held fast to the nail.

All at once, the sound of croaking frogs broke out. To Tetsuyuki it was an eerie and repulsive sound, a curse pronounced by bizarre creatures portending misfortune. Isogai attempted to move the nail, and Tetsuyuki hurriedly restrained him. Isogai finally shifted his gaze from Kin to the hands grasping his wrist.

"Pull this nail out!" There was anger in Isogai's voice. "Why don't you pull it out? What does it matter if he dies? This lizard doesn't care if he dies, he just wants you to pull the nail out."

The croaking of the frogs abruptly ceased. The sound of a television came from the apartment next door where the middle-aged woman lived.

"The lizard itself doesn't think it would be okay to die." In an instant, Tetsuyuki's mood had soured, and he glared intensely into Isogai's pallid face. He thought: *It's not as if I nailed Kin to this pillar for a lark or to suit some kind of fancy. You pull this nail out, if you can.*

Taking a crowbar out of the toolbox in his closet, Tetsuyuki thrust it in front of Isogai. "I can't pull it out. You do it, please."

Isogai forced himself to soften the expression on his face, as if trying to make his own anger back down before Tetsuyuki's ire. Like a fretful child, Kin struggled and wriggled, bending his body backward. The sight caused both Tetsuyuki and Isogai to step back from the pillar and finally sit on the floor. Isogai bit his nails in silence.

"Would you like some beer?" Tetsuyuki asked as he got up and went to the kitchen to take some cans out of the refrigerator.

"If I drink alcohol, I'll end up dead," Isogai muttered, staring blankly at the tatami. Then, for the first time, he broke into a smile. "I've had a bad heart ever since I was little, and never knew when I might die. Maybe after five minutes, maybe tomorrow morning. I've gone through life with that constantly on my mind." It wasn't until Tetsuyuki had drunk the last of his can of beer that Isogai continued.

"Even if I'm reborn, I'll probably come back with a heart disease."

"Why's that?"

"If you fall asleep owing money, the debt never disappears before you wake up. I have a feeling that it's like that for me, so it would be meaningless for me to, say, off myself. When I realized that suicide would be pointless, I was left clueless as to what I ought to do. What do you think I should do?"

Tetsuyuki opened the screen on the window overlooking the rice paddy and threw his empty beer can into the darkness, aiming at the frogs. The quiet that ensued filled his heart with an even greater loneliness. "If you die, that's the end. It's impossible to think that there's anything like rebirth." He quickly shut the screen and, clapping with both hands, crushed the mosquitoes that had entered.

"Where's the proof that death is the end? Have you ever died?"

"I don't remember anything but this life. If I had lived a different life before being born into this one, then I ought to be able to remember something of it. There's just this one life, nothing before or after. Death is the end of everything."

"There's no way I could think like that."

Tetsuyuki stood there looking at Isogai, who, meeting his gaze with a determined look in his eyes, picked up a book and threw it at him. Tetsuyuki was taken aback, but caught the volume.

"That book went flying toward you because I threw it. It didn't go flying off on its own. Before there can be any effect, there has to be a cause. That's the basis of physics, isn't it? Is there a single effect in this universe that doesn't have a cause? Does a tree grow where there's no seed? Does a nail all by itself pierce a lizard's back? It's because everything in this world has a cause that there are effects."

Not quite comprehending everything he'd heard, Tetsuyuki stood there with the book in his hands, staring wordlessly at Isogai's lips.

"Why are we humans born into this life with differences from each other? There must be some cause for that, too. So then, that cause must have been produced before we were born, right? Doesn't that make the most sense? Some are born into wealthy families, some into poor ones. Some are born with healthy bodies, some crippled. So then, even though all things have cause and effect, wouldn't it be odd to say that the differences we are born with have no cause? We certainly experienced lives before being born into this one, we just don't remember, that's all. So, I died carrying various debts and then, just like waking up from sleep, I was reborn. But the debts haven't disappeared . . ."

Since he had only one set of bedding, Tetsuyuki spread out the futon for Isogai and, arranging the quilt next to it, lay down upon it himself. Staring at the ceiling, he asked, "How long have you been thinking that way?"

Isogai took off his clothes and, clad only in a tank top and undershorts, sat down cross-legged on the futon. "Since about two years after I started working at the hotel."

Pulling off his horizontal-striped polo shirt had mussed Isogai's usual flawlessly arranged hair. The unyielding professional demeanor that he forced himself to maintain, and which thus appeared to come naturally from within, had disappeared. In its place was a look enfolded in the same kind of fright that Tetsuyuki sometimes saw in his own face when he looked at himself in the mirror.

Seeing Isogai in such a state, Tetsuyuki regretted having brought him home to spend the night. He had wanted to laugh, to gossip about the other bellboys, to criticize the affected expressions the clerks at the front desk adopted toward guests, and to fall asleep in good spirits. Otherwise, the retreating figure of Yōko as she walked away looking more forlorn than usual—and her ambiguous smile as if she were hiding something—would come to mind and he would end up feeling restless.

The frog chorus started up again.

"By that equation, then, even if you die you'll be reborn?" Tetsuyuki wanted to get away from the topic, but was unable to think of anything else to say.

Isogai nodded feebly. "Yeah. I think we die and are born, die and are born, again and again. There isn't an 'other world'; we're reborn in this one."

With a broad yawn, Tetsuyuki rolled over, turning his back to Isogai. "I don't much care either way. I don't feel like discussing such dreamlike stuff seriously. Let's go to sleep." Asking Isogai to turn off the light, Tetsuyuki closed his eyes. He wanted to walk alone down the unlit path and call Yōko. But it was already past one thirty, and everyone at her house would be asleep. As soon as he got up in the morning, he'd call her and arrange to meet somewhere. He became aware that Isogai had remained sitting cross-legged, as still as could be. Isogai made no move to stand up and turn off the light, nor did he lie down to sleep, but just sat there absolutely motionless. Tetsuyuki opened his eyes and looked at Kin, sensing that Isogai was also directing his gaze at the lizard.

He turned toward Isogai and said sharply, "You'd better not do anything to Kin while I'm asleep."

Not taking his eyes off Kin, Isogai muttered, "What do you mean by 'anything'?"

"You know very well what I mean."

At that, Isogai finally stood up and switched off the light. "I'm the one who wants the nail pulled out."

"In that case, why don't you just make up your mind to have surgery? Section Chief Shimazaki said that operations for valve disorders have the highest success rate of all heart surgeries."

Isogai said something in a small voice, but it was drowned out by the croaking of the frogs.

"Huh? What was that? The frogs are so noisy, I couldn't hear."

Isogai put his mouth near Tetsuyuki's ear. "What I'm afraid of isn't an operation."

"What are you afraid of, then?"

"Trains."

This time it was Tetsuyuki who sat up on the quilt, crossing his legs and looking down at Isogai. "How can you cancel the debt of being hit and killed by a train?" Anger had risen in Tetsuyuki's heart, along with a vague uneasiness. "Just because your parents were hit and killed by trains, it doesn't necessarily follow that you will be. Before you seek the help of a cardiologist, you need to go to a psychiatrist. That has priority here."

Tetsuyuki went to the kitchen, opened the refrigerator, and drank a can of beer as he stood there. A stream of sweat ran from behind an ear, dropping down onto his shoulder. He took his time downing the beer, which increased his agony with each mouthful. A large cockroach scampered across his big toe. Even in the dimness, he could tell it was a cockroach.

Taking a damp towel out of the sink, he threw it at the insect, closing off a way for it to run into the main room. The cockroach spread its wings and set off in flight, buzzing once around Tetsuyuki then bumping into his forehead, after which it fell to the floor and escaped behind the refrigerator. Tetsuyuki hurriedly turned on the faucet and washed his forehead with soap.

"What's wrong?" Isogai's voice came from the other room. Tetsuyuki repeatedly washed his forehead, and said as he was wiping it, "A flying cockroach hit me in the forehead."

A muffled laugh came from Isogai. "You're afraid of cockroaches?"

"I'm not afraid of them, except when they fly. I really lose it when one flies and hits me."

"But you're not afraid of a lizard that's been nailed alive?"

Tetsuyuki returned to his futon and turned his back to Isogai, remaining silent as he felt the alcohol beginning to course through his veins.

"This is the first time in my life I've seen something so frightening. Seeing you spray a lizard's body to keep it moist and feed it with tweezers . . . it gives me the creeps. *You* go to a psychiatrist. You may be different from me, but both of us are sick."

"I showed it to you because you said you wanted to see it. If it scares you that this lizard is alive, then get out of my apartment now."

After some silence, Isogai asked, "How long would it take to get to a place where I could catch a cab?" Tetsuyuki replied that it would be a thirty-minute walk to Suminodō Station, but at this hour, he couldn't be sure any cabs would be there.

"Then I have no choice but to have you put me up."

"In that case, please just go to sleep. Right now I don't feel like having complicated discussions about cause and effect, about this world or the other world, or about repeatedly dying and being reborn. I just want to sleep. It's just natural that people die, and it's all the same to me."

Thus reminding his guest that he would no longer respond to anything said, Tetsuyuki closed his eyes. Undeterred, Isogai mused aloud, "I wonder why people die." Exasperated, Tetsuyuki again sat up facing Isogai. "Would you *please* stop talking about that? It's not as if I were the main character in Tokutomi Roka's novel *Namiko* and could make a vow about how I'd be reborn. How would I know why people die?"

"*Namiko*? You know a lot of old stuff, huh?" Isogai's suppressed laughter filled the muggy room.

Tetsuyuki was not amused. Muffling the volume of his own enraged voice, he shouted in a whisper. "If people didn't die, what would become of this world? It'd be repulsive if geezers and grannies 680 years old—or 1,360 years old—were hanging around, and they'd be wishing that they could somehow just die. And besides, if people didn't die no matter what, then they'd lose their fear of everything and just turn into specters consisting of nothing but desire. The world would be a mess, because no one could die anyway. They'd do evil things, taking from each other by force whatever they wanted. Then they wouldn't even be human any longer. Just beasts."

Tetsuyuki felt silly for having gone on about such things and, forcing a long sigh to convey to Isogai that he would absolutely not respond to any further talk, he again lay down.

"My little sister is really a sweet girl . . ." Tetsuyuki ignored Isogai's words and kept his eyes closed. "When my mom died the same way as my dad, I was really worried that my sister would go insane. It's only recently that she's been back to normal." He shook Tetsuyuki's shoulder. "Hey, my sister's a real knockout. There aren't many women as good-looking as she is."

"That's a big brother's blind partiality." No sooner had Tetsuyuki spoken than he thought, *Damn! Now that I've responded, I'll have to play company to his prattle.* But as the night wore on, no further utterances issued from Isogai's mouth.

And then a thought came to Tetsuyuki—that it must be precisely because of the certainty of death lying in wait that human beings know happiness. It seemed to him that it was because of death that people are able to live. He recalled his mother's scent. Pleasant memories of his father while he was still alive surged like waves into the recesses of his heart. He felt enveloped by the palpable warmth of Yōko's smile and by the purity of her body. There came back to him also the sensation of relief he felt when, after returning to his apartment and feeding Kin, he would strip down to his shorts and have a beer. For him, those things could all be called "happiness" and these words formed in his mind: it is because there is death that people feel happiness. It was the first time he had entertained such a thought, and it echoed within him as if some larger-than-life entity had whispered it, revealing the true form of happiness.

And yet he was not able to see it clearly, and the concept emerging in his mind caused the image of happiness to flicker and finally disappear. Past life, next life, past life, next life . . . At first, those words were a flame no bigger than a pinhead, but it gradually swelled into a raging blaze scattering innumerable thornlike sparks. What stoked this inferno was the strange dream that he'd had, a dream that provided the flame from beneath with inexhaustible fuel. The dream that had taken place during a mere forty-minute doze, in which he had gone through several centuries of life and death as a lizard, was pried open as if by the gentle yet tenacious power of a sorcerer's hands.

He was certain that the dream had come to him the night after Kobori, the collector, had come to beat him, bloodying his nose and lip. He groped in the darkness to feel Kin. A narrow thread of light was shining from someplace, illuminating Kin's body. It seemed as if Kin—nailed alive to a pillar—were a messenger that had been sent to him by something. He felt a joy so intense that, in spite of himself, he almost cried out.

But in the next instant, that joy turned into fear: perhaps Kin had been sent to let him know that he would be reborn as a lizard in the next life. An enormous something had carefully placed Kin on the four-inch-wide pillar in the cramped room of that dark apartment in order to serve notice. If that were not so, then a small lizard could not possibly remain alive for several months with its body pierced by a thick nail. Moreover, the enormous something had not only sent him the dream of several centuries of life as a lizard, but had brought to his room this man Isogai, who believed in the existence of past and future lives. As soon as that crossed his mind, he sat up and looked down at Isogai's recumbent figure.

"Even if you're reborn, you won't necessarily come back as human."

"What's wrong?" Isogai was almost asleep and muttered in a muffled voice, sounding rather annoyed.

Tetsuyuki related the dream to Isogai. "But when I awoke and looked at the clock, it had lasted only forty minutes."

"So, this is about a dream?" Isogai rolled over with his back toward Tetsuyuki.

"Even though I had turned into a lizard and gone through centuries of life and death, when I woke up and licked my lips, I was my same old self. Don't you think that's strange?"

"Well, naturally you were the same. That's just a matter of course."

"It's that 'matter of course' that frightens me." Tetsuyuki kept on talking to Isogai, who was craving sleep. "You seem to think that you'll be reborn with a heart disease, and you sensed that your parents would be hit by a train . . . but you might not even be reborn as human. That's even scarier, isn't it?"

Isogai didn't reply. Tetsuyuki was irritated, finding it selfish of Isogai to have brought up such a complicated question in the first place and then ducked out. But out of consideration for Isogai's physical condition, he hesitated to disturb his sleep any further. Isogai said, "I have to leave early. I need to be at the hotel by eight. Tell me how to get to Osaka Station from here."

Tetsuyuki mentioned the train connections, then added that he would accompany Isogai to Osaka Station.

"What will you do if you get to Osaka Station so early?"

Certainly, eight in the morning was too early to arrange a meeting with Yōko.

"I'll just leave your apartment on my own, so you stay in bed."

At length, Isogai's rhythmic breathing indicated that he was asleep. Tetsuyuki wondered if he would have that dream again tonight, and didn't want to fall asleep. He had a feeling that next time he wouldn't wake up but would just remain a lizard forever.

Tetsuyuki kept his eyes open almost until daybreak, but he closed them inadvertently, and fell asleep feeling a slight coolness around his feet and shoulders. It was a little past noon when he awoke. Isogai was nowhere to be seen. Hurriedly washing his face and brushing his teeth, he got dressed and said to Kin, "Wait a bit. I'll be right back."

He raced down the apartment stairs and hurried along the path under the heat of the summer sun. On both sides were vacant lots overgrown with weeds. It was always at night when he walked to the phone booth, so he had not known what lay along the unlit road, and now for the first time realized that it ran between huge empty factories whose rusted steel frames stood at equidistant intervals. On one of them was written in red paint: WE DENOUNCE THE PLANNED BANKRUPTCY OF YAMAOKA INDUSTRIES!

Leaving an observer uncertain whether they had finished

blooming or were about to bloom, some meager-looking sun-
flowers were bent like bows, bearing only a few petals. After
making his way to the phone booth, Tetsuyuki realized that
there was no need to have come so far; he could have used
the phone in the general store near his apartment. Clicking
his tongue, he looked up at the sun and wiped the sweat from
his brow.

It was like a greenhouse inside the phone booth, and the
receiver was so hot that he could barely hold it. Mosquito car-
casses, like leavings from an eraser, were scattered across the
phone book's shelf. Yōko was not at home. Her mother said she
had already left, and might return rather late.

"She's not working during the summer break, is she?"

"That's right, it seems she isn't."

Judging from her mother's tone of voice, Tetsuyuki realized that something was being kept from him. He returned to
his apartment and drank some cold milk. The only thing he
could imagine was that another man was involved. There could
be nothing else that Yōko and her mother would have to hide
from him. He felt sick at heart and restless. Almost unconsciously he filled a cup with water and, with a spoon in one
hand, approached Kin.

"You must be sick of chestnut weevil larvae, huh, Kin?
Wouldn't you like some crickets or caterpillars once in a while
for a change?"

After feeding him weevil larvae until his tongue no longer
darted out, Tetsuyuki realized that he had been offering Kin
his meal with his bare fingers, not using the tweezers at all.

Kin was no longer afraid of him. He caressed Kin's head and lower jaw. Kin showed no resistance, yielding to Tetsuyuki's finger as if he expected it. He felt sad, sad for Kin that he had no choice but to allow a human to caress him. Tetsuyuki opened the closet and took a knife out of his toolbox, intending to kill Kin. If he sliced off its head quickly, the lizard would die without suffering. Tetsuyuki extended the knife toward Kin.

"Kin-chan, in the next life, I'll be a lizard, and I'll probably never again be born as a human. A lizard can't do what it takes to create a cause to be born human. Once I become a lizard, I'll be one forever. Yōko has found another man she likes. It was written all over her face yesterday. She came to see me, but she's a lousy liar. It's going to take years for me to pay back my dad's debts, a little every month. My mom is also having years taken off her life, being pushed around by her whimsical, former geisha of a boss. There's not a single thing to feel good about. When that Kobori gets out of prison, he's sure to come and get back at me. It's hard on me if you're alive. Your staying alive is a way of getting back at me. You and I should both just die."

As he spoke, Tetsuyuki actually began to think of killing Kin, and then dying himself. The stuffy heat in the unventilated room seemed to transform him, moment by moment, into a different person. He felt that the loss of Yōko's broadcheeked smile amounted to the vanishing of any potential happiness for himself. That in itself wasn't a reason to die, and he knew that the misfortunes that beset him would seem trivial compared to the suffering many others endured. Yet he felt a desire to die. The heat, the figure of Kin before his eyes, the already faraway mind and body of Yōko, the paltry sum of the debt . . . all of these things seemed to concentrate in the point of the knife in his right hand, urging him to be quick and decisive.

"Die, you wretched creature!" Kin writhed at Tetsuyuki's screaming, desperately flailing with his legs as if he wanted to climb up the pillar in spite of being nailed down. He shook his head back and forth and wriggled his tail, moving like mosquito larvae in a gutter. Tetsuyuki cried. He didn't want to, but he let himself anyway, and tears gushed forth.

He threw the knife down and ran out of the apartment, down the stairs to the path he had just traversed, fighting his way into a thicket of weeds, stirring up pollen from goldenrod blossoms. Clouds of mosquitoes, flies, and other nameless flying insects rose up, drawn to him like metal shavings to a magnet. The searing heat burned his neck and back.

A grasshopper jumped onto the leg of his trousers, and he gathered it up in one hand. Something bumped into his face, and it seemed to him like a giant, mutant flea. He dived into the thicket in pursuit of that insect that showed such remarkable leaping ability. He got close enough to grab it, returning to the roadway after verifying that it was unmistakably a cricket. With a grasshopper in his left hand and a cricket securely enclosed in his right, he trudged back home, sneezing several times as he went.

"Let's save the tasty one for later." With that, he held the small grasshopper in front of Kin, who took two or three minutes before shooting his tongue out to wrap it around his prize. Putting the cricket into the box containing the weevil larvae, Tetsuyuki took off his clothes, tossing everything he had on into the washing machine, an older model that the owner of an appliance shop had sold to him at a discount. Goldenrod pollen and flying ants were clinging to his forehead and neck, and had even gotten into his ears and navel. Having carefully wiped himself with a wet towel, he began to prepare his meal, clad only in undershorts.

His intention to kill Kin had vanished suddenly, as well as his thought to die himself. In place of those feelings, his entire mind was occupied by a determined resolve not to let Yōko be taken from him. Finishing his meal, he once again gave Kin water, sprayed him thoroughly, and then left the apartment.

As he walked down the road to the station, he recalled his own words to Isogai: "I don't remember anything but this life . . . There's just this one life, nothing before or after. Death is the end of everything." Somehow he felt that the pitiful form of Kin yielding to the caress of his fingertip wordlessly denied that statement.

6

In a dimly lit periphery of the station, near rows of coin lockers where the guardroom of the Railway Public Security officer and branch offices of travel agencies stood side by side, was an area where about fifty red pay phones had been set up.

Tetsuyuki gazed for some time at the throngs of people projecting their words into their respective mouthpieces in that sweltering space. One irate man was shouting at a phone, while a woman laughed as she spoke softly, twisting the cord around a finger. A young man—likely a salesman—was quoting prices for some kind of merchandise to his interlocutor as he studied a pamphlet. A laborer kept dialing a number apparently only to get a busy signal, finally slamming the receiver down and spitting on the ground. To Tetsuyuki the scene spoke of loneliness; this was the noisiest but also the loneliest area in the enormous station. He felt uneasy about calling his mother from a place like this. The back of his polo shirt was wet with perspiration and clung to his skin. The coin lockers, the scores of red pay phones, the people talking to others via machinery, the mid-summer heat . . .

Tetsuyuki escaped down into the central underground arcade and entered a coffee shop. After ordering iced coffee, he dialed the number from the pay phone in the corner of the shop. Cool air, trained directly at him from a large air condi-tioner, felt good for a moment, but soon gooseflesh broke out on his sweat-drenched body.

To Tetsuyuki's question as to why her voice sounded so listless, his mother replied, "A bit of heat exhaustion. This sum-mer's a real scorcher. How are you doing?"

"Yeah, I'm fine. I'm eating three meals a day, and when I'm finished with work I go right home, where I get plenty of sleep."

"Has something happened?" his mother asked after taking a breath.

"No, nothing."

"Would you actually give your mother a call if it were nothing? Maybe you're suffering from heat exhaustion too."

It was only when they had first started living separately that he kept his promise to phone her daily at noon. Then that turned into once every three or four days, and finally only when he had something to discuss.

"Will Yōko be working at the department store again this year?" his mother asked.

"Yeah."

His mother fell silent, and so did he. She mentioned the need to be patient only a bit longer, that next spring they would be able to live together. With that, she hung up. Judging from her manner of speaking, he had a feeling she knew something about Yōko that he did not.

He went to the hotel at three o'clock that day and explained to Section Chief Shimazaki that there was a matter he would unavoidably have to take care of and asked to be allowed to leave at nine, but to compensate he had come to work two hours early. After Shimazaki agreed to his request, he went to look for Isogai, whose time card indicated that he had come to work at eight in the morning, and had just finished at three. Thinking that he might still find him in the locker room, Tetsuyuki dashed through the passageway between the kitchen and the laundry room, with temperatures as high as 140 degrees Fahrenheit in the summer, and found Tsuruta changing into his uniform.

"Has Isogai already left?"

"He left just now. Didn't you see him?" Tsuruta whistled as he arranged his hair neatly with a brush and left the locker room without so much as glancing at Tetsuyuki. He soon returned and smiled at Tetsuyuki. "Excuse me, Iryō!" This was the first time Tsuruta had ever addressed him in such a friendly way.

"Just now, Section Chief Shimazaki mentioned that you'd be hired full-time here next year. Is that true?"

"He has recommended it to me, but I still haven't decided what I'll do."

Tsuruta went on: about how in the first year of employment here they offered 20 or 30 percent more than some other places, but since the base salary was low, raises and bonuses after that would be paltry; about how the hotel industry had grown excessively competitive, resulting in a decrease in guests since last autumn; about how the perversity of the bosses made it an unpleasant and difficult place to work. He urged Tetsuyuki to seek permanent employment elsewhere.

"At any rate, their pay system is underhanded."

Tetsuyuki had been on the job less than five months, but he knew that between full-time employees with only a high school diploma and those who had graduated from college, the gap was considerable in terms of promotions and raises. Tsuruta was the same age as Tetsuyuki, but had only graduated from high school, and was probably worried that if he were hired full-time, after three years or so he would be his superior. Perhaps Tsuruta was concerned about the possibility that Tetsuyuki would make trouble for him by lodging a complaint about his usual behavior.

"Well, I'm ninety-nine percent certain that I want to stay on here." It was really more like fifty-fifty, but he put it that way to Tsuruta hoping to effect a change in him.

"For your sake, I think you'd be better off quitting," Tsuruta said as he closed the door. Tetsuyuki did not care; his mind was totally occupied with Yōko. If she had found a guy she liked better, and if she had already pressed her beautiful body against his chest . . . He was overcome with emotion at the thought, and wanted to sink to the linoleum floor of the locker room, cradling his head in his hands.

That day, all the guests he escorted to their rooms tipped him. That was the first time such a thing had happened, and as he stood in the lobby he pressed his hands against the pockets of his uniform to prevent the abundant coins from jingling.

After finishing his shift, he took the Hankyū Line to Mu-konosō Station, where the clock read 9:40. Tetsuyuki assumed that even if Yōko was working, surely she would be home by now. He phoned her from the station, but she had not yet returned. He walked through the residential area to her house and leaned against a utility pole, waiting for her to return. After about an hour a cab stopped and Yōko got out. Tetsuyuki intently studied the taxi, and was relieved to confirm that no one else was in the passenger seat; Yōko had returned alone. Hurrying toward the house, she stopped in her tracks when she recognized Tetsuyuki.

"Tetsuyuki, what is it?"

"Yōko . . . what's up?" Observing her bearing as she had dashed from the cab toward her house and the expression on her face, he realized that his premonitions had not been mistaken.

"Do you think you'll be able to hide this forever? In any case, you'll have to decide." Yōko just continued to stare at him silently.

"Who is he? Is he a student, like me? Or is he someone a lot older and loaded?" Yōko remained silent. Leaning as before against the utility pole, Tetsuyuki continued his questioning. "When we parted yesterday, did you go somewhere with him?"

"We went to see a movie."

"And then?"

"We went to dinner, and then I came home . . ."

"What about today?"

"We went to Kyoto."

"You've fallen in love with him, haven't you?"

Yōko averted her eyes and said in a small voice, "I thought that if I couldn't marry you, then I would want to marry him."

"Don't confuse the issue. That means that you want to marry him more than me, doesn't it?"

Yōko shook her head. "It doesn't mean that. I just think that if I can't marry you, then I'd want to marry him."

Tetsuyuki wasn't sure he understood what she was saying. He started to walk toward the station. She followed after him.

"How old is he?"

"Twenty-eight."

"What kind of work does he do?"

"He's an architect. This year he's been able to establish an independent practice."

Tetsuyuki stopped and wheeled around. "You see? You'd be a lot better off marrying him!" He spoke with conviction.

"I'm not making comparisons between you and him."

"You just think you're not. But somewhere in your mind, you're definitely making comparisons. And naturally you'll be more inclined toward him. I think that's what will happen."

The two of them went to a small park nearby and sat side by side on swings. After some hesitation he asked Yōko never to see that man again. Granted, Tetsuyuki had no secure employment, and even after graduation he would have to spend several years paying back his father's debts. But he would give everything in him to make certain she would be glad that she had married a man like himself. He loved her more than she could possibly know. He didn't want her to see that guy anymore. His words were firm but delivered in what could hardly have been a more desperate tone of voice.

"I can't make such a promise right now." Enunciating each

syllable separately, Yōko answered weakly and gripped the chain of the swing. Her words fell on Tetsuyuki like a pile driver, burying the calmness he had struggled so hard to call forth.

"Why? Until recently you were in love only with me, right? Why this, all of a sudden?"

"I can't lie to you. I'd hate meeting him if I'd lied and told you I wouldn't. That's why I'm being honest with you. Give me some time to do as I please." Yōko was crying, shaking her head as if in a gesture of reluctance.

"Some time . . . how long?"

". . . I don't know."

Each time a train stopped at the station, the number of people exiting the gate decreased. The voice of a drunk slurring his words as he shouted at them, "Hey, what the hell you sayin'?" gradually faded in the distance.

"You like me, don't you?"

Yōko nodded deeply.

"And you like him, too?"

This time she made a shallow nod, and muttered, "I don't understand my feelings." Tetsuyuki gazed at the garishly blazing illuminated sign on the roof of a love hotel incongruously situated among the condominiums and rental buildings lined up on the other side of the tracks.

"How far have you gone with that guy?"

Yōko looked up into Tetsuyuki's eyes. "We've just gone to movies and dinners together."

Tetsuyuki found it impossible to believe her. He stood up

from the swing and, pointing at the love hotel, asked, "Can you go with me now, over there?" Yōko nodded and stood up.

They crossed the railroad tracks and circled around the south side of the station. Approaching the front of the hotel, Tetsuyuki marched right inside, not slackening his pace. Without saying a word, a reception clerk showed them to their room and then disappeared, closing the door. Tetsuyuki threw Yōko down on the bed. He bit her lips, and she responded in kind, following the same actions and reactions as they had done in his apartment. But this time Tetsuyuki looked down at her steadfastly as she let out only restrained cries of ecstasy, clinging tightly to him. Her eyes opened slightly, and he asked her once again never to see that man. Her body completely given over to Tetsuyuki, she said, "I want to see him, too."

Something like a shudder ran through Tetsuyuki's mind. He barely restrained himself from shouting and, pulling away from her, quickly got dressed.

"You go out first, okay? I'm embarrassed to leave together."

Making no reply to Yōko's request, Tetsuyuki descended the cheaply constructed hotel staircase and paid the fee at the front desk, informing them that his partner would leave in another five minutes.

He ran outside. The warning signal was sounding at the railroad crossing. He bought a ticket, dashed up the stairs to cross over to the platform on the other side, and jumped on the train just before it departed. On previous occasions Yōko had insisted on using a contraceptive device, but today she had taken his fluid deep within her. This evening she had lost her composure and had perhaps forgotten. Or had she done that on purpose? The questions continued to pass through Tetsuyuki's mind as he sat in the train, leaving him totally mystified.

It was 11:40 when he arrived at Umeda Station, and he missed the last train for Suminodō. He hesitated, unsure whether he should go to his mother's place or have Nakazawa put him up, but his feet spontaneously began moving toward Kita Shinchi.

Just before reaching the main avenue in Shinchi, he re-membered Kin: today had been unusually hot and, having had no water or fan to cool him, he would probably expire before morning. He counted the money in his pocket: the fee at the love hotel had been higher than he expected, leaving him with only a little over 600 yen. The taxi fare Isogai had paid the night before was 3,200 yen. With that, he immediately recalled: yes, he had received an unusual number of tips that day, and many hundred-yen coins were still stuffed in his uniform.

He retraced his steps, running through the employees' entrance and the overheated hallway to the locker room. He opened his locker and grabbed the coins from his uniform: thirty-three 100-yen coins, and one 500-yen note. During the more than four months he had been working as a bellboy, this was the first time every guest had tipped him; such a thing was unlikely to happen again. It even seemed almost as if, in order to protect himself, Kin had used some supernatural power to make the guests tip.

The cab he hailed was privately owned, and the cleanli-ness of the seat covers and floor mats signaled the driver's care for this instrument of his livelihood. Tetsuyuki removed his soiled cheap shoes and placed them upside down on the side of the mat.

The driver laughed. "There's no need for you to remove your shoes." Surely he was not able to see a customer's feet in his rearview mirror. Tetsuyuki wondered how he knew that he had removed his shoes, but rather than ask, he simply said, "They're so dirty, it would be a shame to soil your cab."

"I can always wash the floor mat. You're a paying customer. If you always show that kind of deference, you'll never make it through life."

". . . I see."

"To get to Suminodō, I go straight down the Hanna Free-way and past the intersection at Akai, right?"

"That's right. After you pass the intersection at Akai, the turns are rather confusing."

"That area's always getting hit by downpours or typhoons, leaving standing water on the road. Anyway, there's no good storm drainage system. After typhoons there've been two or three times when I've had customers and gotten stuck."

The driver talked on volubly. Responding perfunctorily, Tetsuyuki pondered Yōko's words, uttered even as she was in his embrace: "I want to see him, too." She spoke those words clearly. And yet when she was in his arms, she gave every evidence of her usual affection: not the slightest hesitation, no sign of disgust, responding to his every caress with one of her own. Nevertheless she was drawn to another man and wanted to see him, asking to be left to do as she pleased.

If Yōko were just another pretty face like one sees around town or on campus, then he would surely not be reduced to such a stupor. She possessed a sort of class, purity, and gentleness that is rare these days, and none of that had changed during the nearly three years they had known each other. And one day, suddenly, she took off everything she had on. Didn't that mean she had decided? At that thought, their conversation that same evening in the park and their first time together at a love hotel seemed like an illusion.

He tried to recall the features of the room in the love hotel, but nothing came to mind, not even the color of the bedspread or the curtains, or the pattern of the wallpaper. Only the lingering warmth of Yōko's body enveloped part of his body as if it were a membrane. There were numerous couples on campus, but everyone regarded Tetsuyuki and Yōko as somehow special. He recalled the words of a rugby team member: "It wouldn't matter with other couples, but if those two broke up, I'd permanently lose all faith in the bond between men and women."

"Please turn right on that street just before the traffic light."

"Nara's just over the mountain. Now there are new homes for sale lined up endlessly, but this place used to be the sticks. The next station after Suminodō is Nozaki. Are you familiar with it?"

"Just with the name."

"Just the name? Yeah, you probably wouldn't know anything but the name." With that, the driver began singing to a folk rhythm:

A pilgrimage to Nozaki
On a roofed pleasure boat—
Let us go . . .

"There's a song that goes like that. There used to be roofed pleasure boats from Osaka carrying geisha who'd bring their lunches and make a pilgrimage to the deity Kannon in Nozaki. Now there's nothing in that river but sludge, and factories are crammed along its banks. You'd never get a pleasure boat down it now."

Tetsuyuki paid the fare with more than thirty 100-yen coins.

"What's this? Did you break your piggy bank to pay the cab fare?"

"Something like that." Tetsuyuki returned the driver's affable smile and trudged with heavy steps up the stairs to the apartment. Entering the room and switching on the fluorescent light, he let out a cry: Kin was drooping with his stomach and chin facing upward.

"Kin-chan!" Tetsuyuki poked Kin's nose, eliciting a slight movement of the tail. He was not yet dead. Tetsuyuki rushed to open the windows and direct the fan toward Kin, then prepared some ice water and sprayed the lizard's body with several times the usual amount, so that the chilled water dripped in streams from its tail down the pillar. After five—then ten—minutes, Kin's nailed body was still drooping backward.

Rummaging about in the kitchen, Tetsuyuki finally found a straw. Dipping it into a cup of water while stopping the other end, he pried Kin's mouth open by gently squeezing both sides with his thumb and index finger. He then released the liquid slowly into Kin's mouth. Most did not enter the throat and just spilled out on Tetsuyuki's hand, but a small amount did get into Kin's dehydrated body. At length, the lizard's feet began to move, and its arched body gradually straightened.

It was about an hour before he recovered from his state of suspended animation, and during that time Tetsuyuki never stopped giving him water through the straw, spraying him with ice water, and setting the fan at different angles, rushing back and forth from the kitchen and trying every measure that came to mind. It took another thirty minutes before Kin was able to lap water from a spoon.

"It was miserably hot today, and I was two hours later than usual getting home," Tetsuyuki explained to Kin, who lapped the water but refused the larvae. "Kin, here's a cricket. They're your favorite." During the day, Tetsuyuki had crawled about in a thicket of tall goldenrod and had managed to catch one cricket, which he thrust before Kin's nose, holding it by its long hind legs. Kin just flicked his red tongue, but would not eat the insect. Tetsuyuki determined to stay up until Kin ate the cricket.

"Mr. Iryō!" A man's voice sounded along with a knock on the door. Assuming it must be one of Kobori's henchmen, Tetsuyuki felt the blood drain from his face.

"Mr. Iryō, are you asleep?" It was not a gangster's tone of voice. Tetsuyuki closed his palm around the cricket.

"Who is it, may I ask?"

"Police."

Tetsuyuki opened the door to see the police officer from the other day standing there.

"Sorry to bother you at this time of night."

"Mosquitoes will get in, so please step inside."

The officer sat down on the step inside the door, which Tetsuyuki quickly closed.

"Has anything happened since then? Any visits from that guy's associates or anything?" When Tetsuyuki answered in the negative, the officer took off his hat and wiped the perspiration from his forehead with a handkerchief. "Upon investigating that collector, Kobori, we found plenty of other crimes, as I expected we would: extortion, assault, illegal trafficking in pornographic films . . . he was even working as a trafficker of amphetamines. I'm sure he won't get out for another seven or eight years." Then he furrowed his brow as he stared suspiciously at one corner of the room. "What is that?"

Tetsuyuki had forgotten to cover Kin. Since he had already been seen, there was nothing for it but to tell the truth.

"It's a lizard."

"A lizard . . ."

"It's nailed to the pillar."

"Why?" The officer turned his astonished face toward Tetsuyuki, who summarized how it had happened.

"Is it actually alive?"

"Today was brutally hot, and I got home later than usual, so he had almost died. He's just now recovered."

"This is the first time I've seen such a thing."

"I myself don't understand why I don't just pull the nail out. If I took a crowbar and used a bit of muscle, I could get the nail out. But then I'm afraid he'd die . . ."

The officer continued to gaze at Kin. "My son keeps hamsters. Ever since he was little, he's liked small animals, you know. But he's never wanted a cat or a dog. When he was in elementary school, he kept frogs and bell crickets. And when he was in high school, he saved his New Year's money and bought a baby alligator. Hey, even though it's a baby, it's still an alligator. After about two months, we had to ask a zoo to take it. My son pouted for four or five days and wouldn't say a word to us. He complained that it had cost fifty thousand yen. Now he has hamsters, a pair, so they keep having litters."

After the officer left, Tetsuyuki again approached Kin and held out the cricket that had been in his hand all that time. With a smooth movement of his tongue, Kin pulled the cricket into his mouth. Tears welled up in Tetsuyuki's eyes as he looked at Kin in that condition. He lifted his voice and cried like a child. Were they tears of joy because Kin was still alive? Or tears of sadness because Yōko was attracted to another man? Tetsuyuki himself could not say for sure. As he cried, he caressed Kin's body with his finger, just as he had done during the day. In Kin's throat was a cricket-shaped bulge.

7

After purchasing chestnut weevil larvae at the fishing gear section of a department store, Tetsuyuki took the subway to Honmachi. Ever since having heard from Yōko's own lips that there was another man in her life, he had confined himself to his apartment, missing work at the hotel. He had no idea how many times he had tossed about on the floor, groaning. After twenty days of that he began to run out of money for food, not to mention rent. He called Nakazawa Masami to ask for a loan, lying that he had come down with such a severe summer cold that he had not been able to work. Nakazawa reluctantly agreed.

As he walked down the street lined with office buildings, it began to rain and thunder rumbled in the distance. The momentum of the rain picked up quickly and in no time it was a downpour, roaring as it pelted the road. Walking slumped over, Tetsuyuki became soaked. This rain seemed to herald the end of summer. He longed for autumn to arrive, and resolved that until then—until fleecy clouds again appeared in the sky—he would not see Yōko. By then she would probably have reached some conclusion.

As soon as Nakazawa saw Tetsuyuki soaked to the bone, he switched off his tape deck. "You said you've been fighting a cold. You get soaked like this, and you'll have a relapse." Then, handing over the money he had prepared, he added, "Instead of borrowing from me, you have a devoted lady friend, don't you?"

Tetsuyuki made no reply. Taking off his wet clothing, he borrowed a towel and dried himself off, then asked Nakazawa to put on "Lady Jane."

"You really like that song, don't you? I've gotten so sick of it that I can't even stand to look at the record jacket anymore. Go ahead and put it on if you like." Lying faceup on the bed, Nakazawa pointed to the shelf of LPs, mentioning that it should be the fourth one from the right. Tetsuyuki did not know how many times he had heard "Lady Jane," but listening intently to the saxophone, he thought of his mother, whose life was getting shorter day by day. He glanced over to see a copy of *Lamenting the Deviations* by Nakazawa's pillow, and thought it unsurprising that he would read such a book.

"To you, these hundreds of LPs and that copy of *Lamenting the Deviations* are all the same thing, aren't they?"

"Have you read *Lamenting the Deviations*?"

"I had to read it for my class in Eastern philosophy. If I wrote and submitted a report on it, I could get credit without taking the exam. So I read it."

"Shinran was extraordinary. I've gradually come to realize how amazing he was."

"What was so amazing about him?"

Flipping through the pages of *Lamenting the Deviations*, Nakazawa found and read aloud the following line:

"'Since I could never succeed in any austerities, hell will surely be my final abode.'"

"What's so amazing about that? Reading *Lamenting the Deviations* made me sick of living. It's a collection of words that rob people of their vitality. Shinran was just a loser himself, and his legacy to humanity was that sort of resignation. So the pampered son of a rich guy who will one day inherit this building says 'hell will surely be my final abode.' How ridiculous!"

"You really like taking a dig at me, don't you?" Unusually for him, a hurt expression appeared on Nakazawa's face. The figure of Kin, nailed to a pillar but still alive, suddenly cast a strange glow in Tetsuyuki's mind.

"Did Shinran really even exist?"

At Tetsuyuki's query, Nakazawa sat up. "Are you some kind of idiot? Haven't you read Japanese history? *Lamenting the Deviations* is a collection of Shinran's words, compiled later by his disciple Yuien. Shinran was a priest in the early Kamakura period. He was born in 1173 and died in 1262. As a child, he went by the name Matsuwaka-maru. He studied under Jien, and later became a disciple to Hōnen. Isn't all of that clear enough in the history books?"

"'History,' huh? That can all be fabricated later to suit someone."

"What? So then you're saying that Shinran was just a

figment of someone's imagination? I'd like to hear what basis you have for thinking so."

"Since I reject *Lamenting the Deviations*, I find it strange that this Shinran is so lionized among the half-baked intelligentsia. I mean, isn't he all too human, warts and all? Hōnen, the founder of Pure Land Buddhism, had his ashes strewn in the Kamo River, leaving a command that no prayers be recited. The Pure Land sect desperately needed to create a charismatic symbol. But when you think of how Hōnen died, he couldn't be of use that way."

"There was no need to create a fictional character as a symbol. There was always Rennyo, wasn't there?"

"Exactly! It was Rennyo who invented that fictional character Shinran. Rennyo was a bright guy. He didn't need to be charismatic himself, just invent this Shinran and make an idol of him, and then bask in the charisma himself. That makes Rennyo a politician as well."

"That's an interesting piece of inference. But don't go around saying that to people with a straight face. You'll be laughed at."

"Well, in any case, it's a defeatist religion. In that age someone born a peasant would be a peasant for life with no recourse to anything but a miserable existence and unable to hope for any happiness in this life. Words like 'hell will surely be my final abode' were probably persuasive. So then the idea was popular that if you chant prayers, after death you'll achieve happiness in the Pure Land, which lies innumerable leagues to the west.

When I see people who are leading ordinary lives reverencing *Lamenting the Deviations* and acting as if they really understand it, it makes me angry. It is a hellish book cobbled together from the defiant words of a defeatist with a generous admixture of beautiful passages gushing melancholy. For you it's just a substitute for records and booze. It's a mental ornament, one that allows you to be pleased with yourself. And that's about all that Pure Land thought amounts to."

Nakazawa approached Tetsuyuki and extended his hand. Tetsuyuki immediately understood what was meant, and returned the money he had borrowed.

"Get out! That doesn't seem like any way to talk to someone who has just lent you money. So, I'm a loser . . . For a malnourished guy who looks like death warmed over, your mouth is in good shape, isn't it? At that rate, you should be able to go another four or five days without eating."

Tetsuyuki put on his wet clothes, picked up the box of larvae, and left Nakazawa's room. The rain was still coming down hard. He stood for a while in the entrance to the Nakazawa Second Building, but at length set out, with head bowed, walking toward the subway station. As he walked, he fixed his gaze on the Rolex watch he had borrowed from Yōko. Nothing had entered his stomach since the glass of milk he had drunk that morning, and now it was nearly dusk. Pawning the watch without her permission would make him a thief.

Without hesitating, he dialed Yōko's number from a pay phone by the ticket gate in the subway station. The moment he heard her voice, he felt as if he might collapse then and there.

Promising that he would definitely return it, he asked if he could pawn the Rolex for a short time.

"What's wrong? Don't you have any money?" Tetsuyuki responded that he was short on cash to pay rent.

"Tetsuyuki, you're hungry, aren't you? This is how you talk when you're hungry."

He remained silent as he tried to think of how to explain it away, but he had never once been able to lie convincingly to her.

"They give you dinner at the hotel, don't they?"

"I've been missing work for a long time."

"Where are you now?"

"In Honmachi. I came here to borrow some money from Nakazawa, but ended up offending him and wasn't able to get a loan."

She said that she would leave right away, and told him to wait at the east gate of the National Railways station.

"No, I don't want to see you anymore." Saying the opposite of what he felt, he listened intently for her response.

"I'm heading out now . . . The east gate, got it?" Then she hung up. The very thought that he would see Yōko revived him. But in his mind's eye, the figure of a man he had never seen before appeared next to her. Also he did not wish to appear before her all drenched like a stray dog, pale and unprepossessing. *She'll probably treat me to a meal, and press me to take half—or even all—of her pocket money. But she'll never come back to me. She's still distressed about the choice she has to make.* Tetsuyuki went to the ticket-vending machine and felt in his pocket for coins. From

Honmachi to Umeda was only one fare sector, but after searching all his pockets, he was still 10 yen short. He unconsciously
scanned the area, thinking perhaps he might find a 10-yen coin.

Exiting onto Midōsuji Avenue in the rain, he walked toward Umeda. He purposely walked slowly. If Yōko hurried,
she would arrive at the east gate in half an hour, and if he were
not there she would no doubt take seriously his words "I don't
want to meet with you anymore," and just return home. With
that thought in mind, Tetsuyuki walked ever so slowly. "In that
case, there's no point in walking from Honmachi to Osaka
Station."

Rain was dripping from his earlobes, from the end of his
nose and from his chin, and his handkerchief was as soaked as
the rest of his clothing. After he had passed Yodoya Bridge and
was close to Umeda, a young office worker approached from
behind.

"Won't you share my umbrella?"

"Since I'm already this wet, it wouldn't make any difference," Tetsuyuki said with a smile and a nod, thanking the man.

He smiled back, as if in agreement, and passed on ahead.
If he walked at a normal pace, it would take about thirty minutes from Honmachi to Osaka Station, but an hour had passed
before Tetsuyuki arrived at the east gate. He peered through
the rush-hour crowd thronging the ticket gate, and saw Yōko
standing there. She quickly espied him and came running.

"What happened? You look as if you fell into a river."

"I walked here from Honmachi, without an umbrella."

"Why didn't you take the subway?"

"I wanted to see what it would be like to walk in the rain."

"If you don't get out of those wet clothes, you'll catch a cold."

"I don't have a change of clothes."

Yōko took a handkerchief out of her purse and wiped Tetsuyuki's head and face. Several people walked past casting suspicious glances at the two of them.

"Will you come to our house? You could put on my dad's underwear and clothes."

Tetsuyuki shook his head. "If I went there, even your mother would not be pleased."

Yōko cast her eyes down, then, as if suddenly hitting on a brilliant idea, leaned over and whispered into Tetsuyuki's ear, blushing: "We could go to a hotel, like the last time. And we could stay there until your clothes dry."

"What the hell are you thinking?" He looked at her with both sorrow and agony. "You want to make a fool of me? There's another man you're fond of, but you can still go to a hotel with me? You've come to a conclusion, have you? You'll take me over him? That's not it, is it? You're still dithering. Or no, you're not dithering. You've pretty much made up your mind. You've decided on that architect guy. But you'll still go to a hotel with me? What kind of woman are you, anyway?"

"I just wanted to go there to get your clothes dry, that's all." Looking as if she were about to burst into tears, she turned an upward glance at him, like a small child being scolded by an adult. Of all the expressions she assumed when arguing with him, that was by far the most endearing. "I wouldn't let you do anything else . . . just dry your clothes. I'd bite you if you made any moves on me."

The hot air in the station made his wet clothing feel heavy. It seemed as if he were coming apart, like overripe fruit, but at the same time he felt a chill in the core of his body.

"How many times have you let that guy touch you?"

"I've only met him once since then, and not at all for over two weeks now."

"Why?"

"His parents came to visit and said they wanted me for their son. It seems that starting next year he'll be studying for about five years in America. He wants to take me with him, so apparently his parents want to hurry things. I haven't been able to make up my mind and I think he must have consulted them about the situation."

"Does he know about us?"

Yōko nodded. "He says he wants to meet with you and talk."

"Fine. I'll meet with him. I'm interested in knowing what kind of guy he is. Go call him."

"Now?"

"Yeah, now. He might still be in his office now. Where is his office?"

"At Sakurabashi . . ."

"Hey, that's just a stone's throw from here, isn't it?"

"I don't want to. I really don't. I'm the one who's got to decide, right? And I'm free to decide. What difference will it make if the two of you meet and talk?" Unusually for her, Yōko spoke rapidly and passionately, then grabbed Tetsuyuki's wrist and began walking. His eyes fixed on the nape of her neck, he put up no resistance as he was drawn into the crowd.

"I don't want to go with you into one of those seedy places."

"We could go to a proper hotel, couldn't we?"

It was only when they had arrived in front of a newly opened high-rise hotel that was a business competitor with Tetsuyuki's place of employment that she finally let go of his wrist. Through a large, thick glass panel he watched Yōko as she went inside and spoke with a clerk at the front desk. At length, she motioned for him to come inside. Glancing at him, the clerk handed a room key to the bellboy and said to Yōko: "After you've entered the room, dial number six and a laundry maid will come. Since it's only to dry the clothes, it shouldn't take even twenty minutes."

After they had been shown to the room Yōko sat on the bed and dialed for laundry. Tetsuyuki asked: "Hotels like this won't usually rent rooms by the hour. How did you put your request?" Yōko did not answer. After conveying her order to the laundry service, she hung up and began unbuttoning Tetsuyuki's shirt. In that spontaneous action he sensed unmistakably her love for him. She removed his shirt, undid his belt, and even pulled off his trousers. Yielding to her movements, he gripped her shoulders and obeyed her every command, raising his right foot, then his left. Kneeling in front of him on the carpet, she took off his shoes. Looking at his torso after his attire had been reduced to undershorts, she asked: "Why have you become so thin?"

"Even Nakazawa says that I look like a malnourished Grim Reaper."

"Your face is so lean . . ."

"That's because my heart is lean."

There was a knock at the door. Yōko hurriedly gathered up his clothing and, opening the door only slightly, handed the bundle to the laundry maid. Then she entered the bathroom and began filling the tub.

"Ah, I forgot to hand you my underpants," Tetsuyuki said to her as she came out of the bathroom. She thought for a moment, but answered that if she wrung them out thoroughly and hung them in front of the air conditioner, they would dry in no time.

"Have a good soak in the hot water." After pushing Tetsuyuki into the bathroom, Yōko again picked up the phone and dialed room service, ordering corn soup, minute steak, salad, and coffee.

Warming himself leisurely by soaking in the bathtub as Yōko had told him to do, it suddenly occurred to Tetsuyuki to force her out of her indecision. "That way, I'll either end up losing something that I'll never again have in my lifetime, or I might gain something even more precious." As he sat in the hot water, Kin immediately came to his mind, and he called out, "Kin-chan! I hear that 'Since I could never succeed in any austerities, hell will surely be my final abode.' I'd like to have the author of these words take a look at you, Kin-chan. I'd like him to see you surviving. I'd like to teach him that hell and paradise aren't separate places. You and I . . . everyone—we all bear hell and paradise within ourselves, and we go through life treading a razor-thin line, easily making false steps one way or the other. If he could just watch you for one hour, that would be clear to him."

Then it occurred to him that it depended on how one looked at things; perhaps if Nakazawa were to look at Kin, he would only cling all the more devotedly to every word and phrase in *Lamenting the Deviations*. He was not sure why, but somehow Tetsuyuki sensed that he understood the human mind. And he had come to understand Yōko's mind. With a bath towel around his waist he walked out of the bathroom, changed into a bathrobe, and confronted Yōko.

"I've come to a decision. Today is the last day I'll see you. I surrender. And since I'm the one who has surrendered, you won't have to remain torn any longer. I'm not going to sulk and miss work any longer. I'm going back to work tomorrow. I can live well enough by myself, but what a woman is depends on what a man is. If the husband is wealthy, then the wife is wealthy. If he's a robber, then she is too, whether she likes it or not. It's really like setting stakes in gambling when a woman decides which man to marry, but she ought to have some criteria to see ahead. If you consider those criteria with a cool head and compare me with that other guy, the conclusion should be obvious. I'll make this easy for you and throw in the towel."

Yōko was about to respond but then clammed up, her vacant stare remaining on Tetsuyuki's shoulder.

Room service brought the food Yōko had ordered, and at almost the same time, the dried and folded clothing was also delivered.

"Leave half the coffee, okay? I want to drink some too," Yōko mumbled to Tetsuyuki, who was devouring the meat and salad voraciously. After informing him that the pot contained two cups of coffee, Yōko bit her lower lip.

"You have an eye for people, don't you, Tetsuyuki? You once said of Akagi: 'He looks serious and mature, but he's really like a thieving dog.'"

"I did. And I said things about others, too."

"I used to think it was a bad habit of yours to make such immediate, biting judgments about people, but you turned out to be right. And it wasn't only Akagi; you guessed right all the faults I had never noticed in Akita, Mie, and Mitsuko, too."

"When my dad's business failed and we were left penniless, those who had always called me 'sonny' were suddenly referring to me as 'that idiot Iryō kid.' While there were those kinds of turncoats, there were also some who treated us the same even after we ended up in poverty. People in each of these two types share indescribable facial features, and so when I meet people, the first thing I do is read their faces to determine whether they would turn on me if things went bad, or continue to associate with me regardless. Strangely enough, I turn out to be right. But it's a pathetic ability to have," Tetsuyuki explained after having wolfed down the heap of food and wiping his mouth. Yōko poured him a cup of coffee, then one for herself. After sipping leisurely, she stood up and opened the curtain. The rain had stopped. She looked at a section of the buildings along the street dyed by the faint residue of a sunset glow.

140

"He's still at work." Tetsuyuki stood up and went to stand next to Yōko, who pointed to a street extending due west from Umeda. "You see that newspaper office on the corner by the traffic light? In the Ōkita Building, right next to it, on the third floor, the room closest to us . . . that's his office." No people could be seen, but the light was on in the room she mentioned. "I'll call him now, so you can go meet him."

Tetsuyuki changed back into his clothing. "Let's forget this idiotic nonsense." The moment he looked at her facing away from him as he answered, he was overcome by an almost insane jealousy. Seen from behind, Yōko looked to him like an unbearably sad statue as she fixed her gaze on the lighted corner of the distant building.

"If you say that he's a fraud, then I'll . . ."

"I'm sure to say you shouldn't marry him, that he's showy but worthless. Even if he's not, that's what I'll say. And if that's what I say, then will you come back to me without any reservation? It's up to you to discern what kind of person he is."

"I'm only twenty-one years old. I can't make such a judgment . . ." Yōko was obstinate, and though Tetsuyuki firmly refused, she picked up the phone and dialed the man's office. In a small voice she conveyed to the other party that she wished to meet Ishihama, and that she would be accompanied by another person. With that, she hung up and said: "He's with a client right now, and it will be about another hour before their consultation ends. He'll come to the tea lounge in this hotel at eight o'clock . . ." It was the first time Tetsuyuki had heard the man's name from Yōko's lips.

"I'm going home. I've already decided that I'm throwing in the towel. Looking like Death warmed over, I don't feel like setting myself against an architectural designer who has his own practice. This seems like some kind of attempt to set this Ishihama guy off to an advantage against me."

As he was about to go out, Yōko clutched at him from behind, sobbing and begging him not to leave. Tetsuyuki reluctantly closed the door and returned to the room, remonstrating with Yōko.

"By now, you should already understand your own feelings, shouldn't you? You're ninety percent in favor of this Ishihama, and reserve ten percent for me. And that ten percent consists of a bit of a guilty conscience, along with some sympathy for me. Do you want to marry out of sympathy and spend the rest of your life feeling that you've made a rotten choice?"

Yōko then buried her face in Tetsuyuki's chest and wrapped her arms tightly around him, sobbing. "I love you."

"Enough! You love that other guy too. I don't want to hear it anymore." Even as he spoke, Tetsuyuki could feel that Yōko's nipples pressed against him had become hard, and he pulled away. In that instant, an idea emerged in his mind, a crude whim that filled even himself with disgust. He told Yōko to get naked. She seemed unable to grasp immediately what he meant, but when he closed the curtains, quickly shed his own clothes, and advanced toward her, she shouted, "You fool!" Grabbing a pillow from the bed, she threw it at him, and then fell into his embrace.

While Yōko was in his arms, Kin occupied a corner of his

mind. As if nailed to his heart rather than to a pillar, the lizard goaded his lust into rougher action than ever before, overturning his resolution.

Throw in the towel . . . You think I'll throw in the towel? You think I'll give up? I'll have this woman I've just embraced sit down in front of that Ishihama guy. As poor as I am, as much as I might look like a wretched stray dog, no one knows how I might be transformed a few years or a few decades from now. Not even I can predict that. Will hell . . . surely be my final abode? No doubt, there's a half truth in that. But there's a bigger truth in the other half that remains unknown. On the other side of the ravine, just a hairsbreadth from hell, everything is charged with bliss and limitless joy.

In both body and mind, Tetsuyuki had turned into Kin. *You think I'll give in? I'll show him that I can take Yōko back.* The Kin inside Tetsuyuki was shedding forth dazzling light, enticing the emptiness he had felt toward an apex of joy that was hidden and awaiting.

Tetsuyuki listened intently for Yōko's breathing to subside. When it appeared to have eased off, she moved her lips toward him, then away again. "You fool!"

"Are you really angry?"

"Yes, I am really angry."

"I'm not going to give up on you. I'm going to have it out with that Ishihama."

Yōko smiled. It was a smile like a mother's. Worried about the time, she tried to glance at the clock, but was held in his powerful lock. He was again about to transform into Kin.

143

•

Ishihama, smartly dressed in a well-tailored, showy blue suit, stood up from his seat as soon as he saw them enter the tea lounge, bowing politely to Tetsuyuki, who was six years his junior. There was nothing diffident about his manners, but neither did he display any condescension toward the younger man. Following Yōko's introduction, he produced a business card and, handing it to Tetsuyuki, said, "How do you do? I am Ishihama Tokurō." His countenance, telling of a strong intel-lectuality, barely offset his dandyish attire—which in any other person might be taken as too calculated—from appearing as affectation, instead turning it into elaborate refinement. His tiepin bore a gem—definitely genuine—of the same hue as his suit, and together with the matching cuff links would have cost a few years' worth of Tetsuyuki's income.

"If I wanted to have what you're wearing, on my part-time income I'd have to live like a church mouse for five or six years to afford it."

Ishihama responded impassively to Tetsuyuki's comment. "These things are tools of my trade. If I let my clients detect even a shred of vulgarity in me, they'll soon imagine the same crudeness in my blueprints."

Tetsuyuki became aware of the extent to which Ishihama Tokurō was being considerate toward him. In a case like this, Ishihama was unaware of how offensive his insincere smile was, in spite of his seeming adeptness at care and consideration for

144

others. Not looking at either man's face, Yōko fixed her gaze on the orange juice before her.

"I hear you'll be going to America next year. When, exactly, will that be?"

"I haven't yet set an exact date, but I need to be there no later than the first part of February."

"And you want to take Yōko with you?"

"I'd like to. But she hasn't yet given me an answer." Ishihama kept his eyes fixed on Tetsuyuki, not even so much as glancing at Yōko. Somewhere in the tone of his words "she hasn't yet given me an answer," Tetsuyuki sensed the betrayal of a slight chink in the careful armor of this man's confidence, and determined to strip him naked.

"When I heard about you from Yōko, I thought the odds were hopelessly stacked against me. An up-and-coming architectural designer with a brilliant future against a malnourished student who is hounded by his dead father's debts and who works part-time as a bellboy at a hotel. When I look at myself in the mirror, I'm amazed at how bedraggled I look."

"Not at all. Your eyes have a very striking aspect about them." The tone of Ishihama's interjection definitely did not suggest an idle compliment. But what did he mean by "striking"? Eyes can be "striking" in various ways. But without giving it further thought, Tetsuyuki continued.

"There's no question which of us would be of more benefit to Yōko, and at one point I had given up. But just moments ago, I retracted that decision to give up." After ascertaining that he possessed a degree of poise that surprised even himself, he went on. "For rather a long time now, Yōko and I have had a physical relationship. Even today, until just before meeting with you, we were in bed together naked in a sixth-floor room in this hotel, and even as she was in my arms I gloated to myself as I imagined you walking here triumphantly. If you're the kind of man who doesn't mind that and who will marry Yōko anyway and take her to America, then I'll give her to you with a laugh. But I wouldn't expect a man to be that big-hearted. Such a man would either be a fool or a coward, and though he'd have robbed me of Yōko, yet in the end I'd still be the winner. I'd never forget such a foolish, cowardly man, and he'd never forget my words. No matter how magnanimous he'd be right now—no matter how confident he might be that he's won—the thought would never vanish from his mind that his wife had slept with some guy named Iryō. Mr. Ishihama, if, in spite of all that, you insist on taking Yōko with you to America, I'll bow out of your lives right now, and never again show my face to Yōko. So, what do you say, Mr. Ishihama? Can your intellectuality trump my baseness? Wouldn't you end up always tormenting Yōko about this?"

Ishihama lit a cigarette, then for a long time fiddled with the matchbox on the table, setting it upright and laying it down as he was lost in thought. Yōko remained motionless, her gaze still on the orange juice.

"Mr. Iryō, when I was twenty-two years old I would certainly not have been able to pull off a tactic like this or produce the kind of look in my eyes that I see in yours. I probably couldn't do it even now." With that, he glanced for the first time at Yōko. "But I still can't very well apologize and surrender, because I haven't yet heard Yōko's reply."

"Then why don't you ask her now?"

Ishihama reproved Tetsuyuki's follow-up attack with a smile. "Let us suppose that Yōko expresses a desire to marry me now. In that case, I might answer that I consider my proposal to have been broken, and then she would be the one to be pitied."

Tetsuyuki thought: *At last I have stripped him of his expensive clothing and accessories, and he thought he'd win, and win big.* Then he said: "But you're in a hurry, aren't you, Mr. Ishihama? Since you have to be in America early in February, you can't afford to take your time."

A look of weariness appeared in Ishihama's face. Sensing that a mere few minutes of exchange with him had rendered his rival exhausted, Tetsuyuki pressed Yōko. "Why don't you just give an answer? Such wishy-washiness isn't good in a woman."

At that, Ishihama turned to him with a look of unconcealed indignation. "If you please, that's no way to talk. You sound just like a gangster pimp."

"Well, even if she's a gangster pimp's woman, I'm sure that as long as Yōko accepts, you'd be magnanimous enough to marry her and take her to America."

Yōko suddenly shook her head violently, and both men turned their gaze toward her almost simultaneously. Still staring at the orange juice, she said in a barely audible voice: "I . . . love Tetsuyuki after all."

Ishihama heaved a sigh that could be taken as expressing

either disappointment or relief. "That's regrettable. Well then, I'll withdraw." With that, he stood up. But Tetsuyuki was no longer looking at him; his eyes were intently fixed on Yōko's profile as he tried to fathom what she was feeling. He was not at all certain he had won her back.

"So, tell me, you with your uncanny powers of discerning people's characters . . . Tell me how Mr. Ishihama appeared to you. That was my purpose in having you meet with him. Well, then? If I had married him, do you think I could have been happy?"

"I can't say. Maybe you could have. At least he's not trashy. He's intelligent, he's clean, he has many qualities that ought to be attractive to young women, he's not given to affectation, and he's in good shape. But he's weak against adversity. He tries to live and act too stylishly. Such guys can't handle hardships. Their range of feelings is narrow. I can't say how things will turn out for him ten or twenty years from now, but life doesn't always go smoothly."

"He told me that during hard times I'd be the one he'd depend on for emotional support."

"Having been put in a position where you had to say 'I love Tetsuyuki after all' made you hate me, didn't it?"

"I don't hate you, but I've become afraid . . ."

"In time, that will turn into hatred." With that pronouncement, he left the tea lounge, but then realized he had left the box containing the chestnut weevil larvae on the table. When he returned, Yōko grabbed his arm as he went to pick it up, staring at him intently.

"Do you have enough for train fare back?"

"I have a commuter pass from Osaka to Suminodō, so it's no problem."

"Do you have anything for breakfast tomorrow?"

"No, I don't."

Pulling her wallet out of her purse, Yōko set several 1,000-yen bills on the box of larvae.

"I'll go back to work tomorrow, so I don't need this much."

He put just one bill in his pocket, and when he tried to return the rest, she stuffed the bills into his pocket with her peculiar endearing smile. "Give it back when you've gained some weight."

As he left the lobby, he looked back to see Yōko still sitting in the tea lounge. She had removed her tiny earrings and was staring at them as they lay in the palm of her hand. It occurred to him that in time another Ishihama would probably appear before her, but he felt no sorrow at parting. A strange vitality that had grown out of the lingering aftertaste of the victorious battle caused him to push the heavy glass doors of the hotel open with energy.

But as he walked along, he began to feel shame and asked himself: What's this "powers of discerning people's characters"? He's "weak against adversity," or his "range of feelings is narrow"? I had my nerve speaking of someone that way. "Weak against adversity" or "range of feelings is narrow" describes me better than anyone. And what will happen to Yōko now that she's been left alone? If we part like this, nothing will be recoverable.

Tetsuyuki wheeled around and ran back to the hotel. His

mind full of a premonition that Yōko had just disappeared forever from his life, he looked into the tea lounge with apprehen-
sion. Yōko was sitting there. She looked at Tetsuyuki and her
face flushed a bright red, a reaction he was unable to understand.

"If you had kept me waiting another ten minutes for you to
come back, I think I'd really have begun to hate you. I thought
for sure you'd come back, but my heart was pounding and I
wondered what I'd do if you didn't show up."

"Why did you think for sure that I'd come back?"

"Because you love me."

"It's already over between you and Ishihama, isn't it?"

"Who was it that pulled a dirty trick to end it?"

"That was the only 'trick' I had left to pull."

"There was no need to do that." Waiting until Tetsuyuki
took a seat, she continued. "Didn't you understand that I'd
made up my mind while you were in the bathtub?"

"How should I have understood that? The night you first
told me that you liked another guy, you went with me to a hotel,
didn't you?" Yōko's face again flushed a bright red. Bracing himself, Tetsuyuki said: "Tell me that you want me to marry you!"

"No! I'd die before I'd say that. Instead, I'll have you bow
your head before me and ask me to marry you." Yōko snick-
ered. Putting his forehead down on the table, Tetsuyuki said
in a small voice, "Please marry me." He could feel that he was
bleeding from a small but deep wound in the depths of his joy.
"I've been writhing in agony these twenty days."

He raised his head and noticed that Yōko's smile was somehow melancholy, and he worried that even after his exchange

with Ishihama, perhaps she really had come to love the guy even more.

"I'm sure you won't be able to forget this, Tetsuyuki. And I have a feeling that after we're married, you'll be the one who'll keep dredging up the past. That's because you're never willing to take a back seat to anyone, you have a strong sense of self-esteem, you're given over to jealousy, you're obsessive, and you're intelligent . . ."

"When it comes to intelligence, you have me beat. I'm an idiot. But you're right about everything else. The most that can become of a guy like me is to be a thief or a swindler, the typical sort who make their wives suffer."

The smile disappeared from Yōko's face and was replaced by an expression of obvious sorrow.

"I never imagined that you'd fall in love with another guy. So, to your analysis of my character you'd have to add: narcissist."

"I'm only twenty-one. And I like it when a man makes a fuss over me. Is there anything wrong with that?"

Tetsuyuki realized that this was turning into a serious argument between them, and clammed up. Whenever it seemed that he was about to lose an argument with her, he had until now always kicked her in the shins. Though he thought he was taking care not to go too far, there were two or three times when he raised a blue welt on her, making her refuse to talk to him for an entire day. By trying to kick her lightly in the shins under the table, he was attempting to show his affection for her, but before he could do so, tears welled up in her eyes.

"I'm afraid of you. I'm afraid, but I'll say how I feel anyway."

He expected to hear from her a renewed confession of love for Ishihama, or words to that effect. But that is not what she said.

"You're special to me. I really did develop a fondness for Ishihama, but compared to what I felt for you, I knew from the start that it was of a completely different nature. And I calculated: who will be of greater benefit to me . . . And that calculation gradually caused me to be in love with Ishihama. I'm a woman who can fall in love with a man that way. I'm not the pure and innocent woman you think I am. Now you'll get angry and kick me in the shins, won't you? Well, go ahead and kick. I don't care."

Tetsuyuki could not bear to look at Yōko's weeping face, and dropped his gaze to the table. He felt both chill and exhaustion. The face of the collector, Kobori, flickered before his eyes, as did the double chin of the portly former geisha who was his mother's employer. The debt his father had left behind formed a pitch-black wall in his path. Yōko asked what time it was.

"Ten after nine." Tetsuyuki rose from his seat, and Yōko grabbed her purse and stood up, walking wordlessly across the lobby and exiting the hotel. Thinking that she would probably never return to him, he watched the form of that lovely, graceful creature as she stood at the Hankyū ticket gate and then ascended the stairs to the platform.

As he sat in the dirty train car on the Katamachi Line he bowed his head and with folded arms and tightly shut eyes mustered strength in an attempt to suppress the chills that continuously assaulted him. He wanted money. As he walked shivering along the long dark path from the station to his apartment, the thought never left his mind: *I want money. I want money.*

Climbing the stairs to his apartment, he realized that he did not have the box containing the larvae; he could not recall whether he had left it on the table in the tea lounge or on the rack in the train car. He went up to Kin. "Sorry, but you'll have to go without dinner today. Try to make do with just water." As was his custom, he talked to Kin as the lizard lapped water from the spoon with its long tongue. Like recording the day's events in a diary, Tetsuyuki had kept up this nightly practice for several months. And, much the same as in a diary, untruths were mixed in among the words.

"Kin-chan, I don't care about myself anymore. I'm so exhausted that I'm just hanging on to life by a thread. I don't have the energy to work, and I don't have the courage to be a thief. And just so that I could claim some kind of victory over that Ishihama guy, I ended up ruining Yōko's entire life. When he walked out of the hotel, I felt as if I knew how to defeat an enemy; it was as if my body were on fire. 'This is how you beat them, one by one.' And courage welled up in me. But you know, Kin-chan, a solitary victory is no victory at all. What'll become of Yōko? It stands to reason that she wanted to marry him more than me. But I interfered, and if my interference results in her unhappiness, then it was no victory for me. It was defeat. I talked big when it came to putting down *Lamenting the Deviations*, but I feel a fascination for that book of cheerless grieving."

The moment he said that, he realized that a thoroughgoing

153

nihilism was linked to a certain kind of courage, but that it was not the sort of courage that could elevate a human being. What exactly was this courage that offered no uplift? Tetsuyuki fell into a dull pensiveness as he looked at Kin's motionless body and taut limbs.

He dived into the quilts, which had been left out. Intense chills left his teeth chattering. He fell asleep, listening closely to his own rough breathing. At about three a.m. he awoke in great discomfort. The shivering had stopped, but his head ached and he could tell that he had a high fever. With the light left on, Kin was writhing. Thinking that Kin could not sleep with the light on, he tried to get up but was unable to move. The slightest movement set off intense shivering. His vision was too clouded for him to focus on the nail piercing Kin, and he succumbed momentarily to the illusion that the lizard had regained its freedom and was crawling down the wall, escaping from this cramped apartment to the spacious world beyond. Something irreplaceable was leaving. Goaded by his own sadness, he finally roused himself to get up and turn off the fluorescent light. His entire body again shivered.

Hearing footsteps and feeling a pleasant coolness on his forehead, Tetsuyuki awoke and glanced around. The fluorescent light was on, and the only thing he understood was that it was nighttime. But he had no idea how many hours he had slept. Kin was still nailed to the pillar. A washbowl filled with ice water had been placed next to his pillow. He reached his hand to his forehead to find a chilled towel placed on it, then twisted around to look into the kitchen. Yōko, her back toward him, was peering into a pot. He gazed at her intently. She turned around, shut off the gas, and sat down at his bedside.

"Is it night now?"

Yōko nodded in reply, and said as she turned the towel over, "You still have a high fever."

"Was it yesterday, or the day before, that we met?"

"Yesterday. What time did you go to bed?"

"Before eleven, I think. I woke up once in the middle of the night, but I've been asleep ever since."

Counting on her fingers, Yōko said with a smile, "Then you've slept twenty hours."

"Why did you come to my apartment?"

"You left something in the hotel yesterday, didn't you? A little box in department store wrapping. When we parted I forgot to hand it to you and ended up taking it home with me. I wondered what was in it, and can you imagine how I screamed when I opened it?" Tetsuyuki laughed. "So, this evening I went to the hotel where you work in order to hand this disgusting package to you. When they told me you were still off and hadn't contacted them I got a bit worried. You said, didn't you, that you were going to return to work today?" Tetsuyuki extended his hand and stroked Yōko's hair. "I borrowed a key from your landlady and . . . didn't you hear my scream when I came in?"

Together they looked at Kin. Yōko explained that when she saw the lizard nailed to the pillar her feet began to shake and did not stop for a long time, and that since Tetsuyuki's breathing was so rough it seemed he might die any moment, she lay down beside him and felt with her hand that he had a high fever. When Tetsuyuki complained of thirst, she brought him some water.

"Can you get up?"

"Yeah, I think so."

"There's a clinic just a seven- or eight-minute walk from here." At Yōko's adamant insistence, Tetsuyuki let himself be taken to the small clinic with only one elderly doctor, who told him that it was a case of influenza and gave him an injection and medicine to take, adding that he would need complete rest for two or three days. When they returned to his apartment, Yōko told him to change into his pajamas, and it was only then that he realized he had been sleeping all that time in his street clothes.

As he was undressing, Yōko sighed. "It's because you got so drenched in the rain."

"But I soaked for a long time in the tub at the hotel . . ."

He had no appetite at all but, sitting upright on the futon, sipped the rice porridge and nibbled at the fried egg she had prepared for him. As he ate, it occurred to him that, while he hadn't swallowed any food for an entire day, Kin had gone even longer without anything. In fits and starts, he described how the lizard came to be nailed to a pillar in his room. After hearing everything, Yōko was lost in thought for a while.

"Tetsuyuki, why don't you get out of this place and move somewhere else?" She mentioned that there was a vacancy in a tidy apartment complex near her home.

"The deposit and rent for a place in your neighborhood would be three or four times what it is here. I don't yet have that kind of money."

"You and your mother could live there together, couldn't you?"

Tetsuyuki shook his head. He was haunted by the thought of not knowing when an accomplice of that collector might show up. He never wanted his mother to go through that kind of bitter experience again. If she were to be threatened by collectors daily the way she was, then she would surely lose her mind. He was about to explain all of that to Yōko, but when he opened his mouth, words unrelated to his thoughts came out instead.

"Just forget about me. Let's agree never to meet again." He was surprised at his own words. His hand, as if of its own accord, took the Rolex off his wrist and placed it in Yōko's lap.

"Why?"

"I've gotten so that I don't care about anything. Not about you, not about this lizard, not about school or graduating . . . I don't care about anything." As he spoke, he gradually came to feel that way. Even if only for a moment, he felt hatred toward Yōko for having shifted her affections to another man. And he harbored anger toward Kin for stubbornly clinging to life as if in some sort of vengeance against him. He wanted money and hated his poverty. Inside of himself, Tetsuyuki shouted all of these things.

"Those are all lies. When your fever goes down, you'll be sure to apologize to me. After all, you love me . . ."

Tetsuyuki looked her in the eyes. No words could have calmed his agitated mind more than those, and the fact that Yōko could deliver them without the slightest pretentiousness or perturbation filled him with immeasurable joy. She had him take his medicine and lie down, then covered him with the quilt.

"It isn't safe around here at night. And a lot of country thugs and small-time gangsters hang out in the shopping arcade near the station. You ought to borrow the landlady's phone and call a cab to take you back."

Yōko carried the pot and dishes to the kitchen and ran some water.

"I'll stay here tonight. Before you woke up, I called home from the pay phone over there at the general store."

"You told your mom that you'd be staying in my room?"

Yōko nodded as she wiped her hands. "My mom was furious, and screamed, 'You get back here!' But when I told her that a guy with that high a fever wasn't going to turn into a ravenous wolf, she reluctantly gave in. When I asked her to tell Dad some suitable lie, she said, 'You're a fool. An intelligent woman thinks of love and marriage separately.' That was her sermon, but she seems to know everything that's going on."

"Everything?"

"Everything." Yōko's eyes sparkled as she sat down beside him. Tetsuyuki reached his hand from under the quilt, groping his way to the innermost recess under her skirt. Pinching his arm, she said with a look of exasperation as she fell against him, "You won't turn into a wolf, but you will turn into a snake, huh?"

But the raging fever prevented Tetsuyuki from turning into either a wolf or a snake. The weight of her body made it difficult for him to breathe.

"I won't touch you anymore, so please, get back a bit. I can't breathe."

Giggling, Yōko leaned on top of him all the more.

"Give that lizard some larvae and water."

Flustered at Tetsuyuki's request, Yōko pulled away. Straightening her disheveled hair, she cast a look at Kin. "I couldn't . . . do something like that."

"But Kin hasn't eaten for two days."

"No, I couldn't bring myself to touch those things."

"Just grab them with tweezers and hold them up to his nose. He'll eat them by himself. And you can give him water with a spoon."

"You should be able to do that much yourself."

"With a fever like this I don't have the energy to get up."

"And yet you were able to walk to the clinic."

At Tetsuyuki's repeated urging and with an expression as if she had just been sobbing, Yōko put some water in a spoon and, standing as far away as possible, held it out to Kin. The lizard appeared to be very thirsty and lapped it up greedily. During all of this, a thin sound like a scream leaked out of her mouth. Tetsuyuki closed his eyes, and in his ears that voice took on a sort of sensual beauty. And as he listened, Kin seemed like some kind of extraordinary being. At the same time, he realized that Yōko was also an extraordinary creature.

8

Tetsuyuki placed the two bags of an elderly German couple in the entrance to their guest room. The luggage was so heavy that he wondered what could possibly be in it. He bowed and was about to leave when the wife grabbed his elbow with her soft hand.

Neither of them could speak English, but with exaggerated gestures asked him to wait a moment. He had never received a tip from a foreign guest. Foreigners who visit Japan have all been thoroughly instructed by the guidebooks that tipping is not necessary and never offer so much as a 100-yen coin.

The white-haired husband and wife were small of stature and gentle of countenance. Discussing something in German, the two of them fumbled about in their pockets, opened their wallets, and shrugged their shoulders with embarrassed looks. She took a 10,000-yen bill out of her wallet and said something in an apologetic tone. Judging from their exchanges with each other and from the expressions on their faces, Tetsuyuki realized that they wished to give him a tip but unfortunately aside from this bill did not have suitable small change between them and were at a loss what to do. Waving his hand, he smiled and used the only German he knew.

"Danke schön!"

Then he bowed again and left the room. The husband followed after him, mimicking walking unsteadily carrying two bags. He brought Tetsuyuki to a halt with a hand on his shoulder, then hurried by himself toward the elevator. It seemed he intended to break the 10,000-yen bill at the front desk. Tetsuyuki declined to accept the money, explaining in his imprecise English that the kind thought was sufficient reward, that carrying bags was his job, and that no tip was necessary. Taking the bill from the old man's hand, Tetsuyuki folded it in two and returned it to the man's coat pocket.

But the old man was obstinate and waited for the elevator to arrive, indicating to Tetsuyuki to remain there. His wife then came out of the room and said something to him, to which he grunted a reply and put an arm around Tetsuyuki's shoulders, speaking to him in German. The wife smiled at Tetsuyuki. He recalled that one of the cooks down in the kitchen had spent three years working in Munich and, motioning for the elderly couple to wait in their room, got on the elevator. He opened the door to the basement kitchen and looked about for Nabeshima. Their busiest hours had ended, and the cooks were leaning against wooden crates and walls, smoking. He found Nabeshima sitting by an enormous refrigerator, leafing through a weekly magazine.

"Some German guests I showed to their room tried to

detain me, but I couldn't understand a word they were saying.
Could you come interpret for me?"

A good-natured man, Nabeshima sometimes secretly
passed on to Tetsuyuki cake or roast beef that guests had left
untouched.

"Just leave it to me." He got up and followed Tetsuyuki.
The German couple were still waiting for Tetsuyuki in the
hallway. Nabeshima conversed with them for a long time, then
turned toward Tetsuyuki with a smile.

"They had requested an interpreter, but due to some slip-up
at the tour agency, they won't get one until the day after tomorrow. They want you to be their guide in Kyoto tomorrow, and
will give you a hundred U.S. dollars for your trouble."

"Me? But I don't understand a word of German!"

"It seems they don't mind that. They've really taken to you."

"Even so, if we can't communicate, I can't be their guide."

Nabeshima and the German couple again negotiated. The
three of them laughed and turned to look at Tetsuyuki.

"They say they'll just follow your lead, and even if you can't
understand each other's words, you'll be able to communicate
by spirit. They say 'This young man's honest. We feel at ease
with him.'"

The next day Yōko planned to come to his apartment—the
one day of the week he could hold her in his arms. But a hundred U.S. dollars amounted to a third of his monthly part-time
income, and he would be able to afford a Christmas present
for Yōko: the silver bracelet she had been wanting. He wasn't
very familiar with the layout of Kyoto and asked if he might

invite someone who knew the city well to accompany them. Nabeshima relayed the question to the couple, who immediately gave their consent.

"Is this person who knows Kyoto well a man or a woman?" The question appeared to be Nabeshima's own, reflecting his personal curiosity.

"A woman."

"Is it the girl who sometimes comes to the back of the hotel?" A smile spread on Nabeshima's hardy face. Tetsuyuki answered in the affirmative, taken aback. He had assumed that no one saw them. Nabeshima talked to the elderly couple, and the three of them again laughed, turning to Tetsuyuki.

"He said, 'It appears he's going to bring his girlfriend along. If he says she knows Kyoto well, who could doubt it? We'll make sure not to disturb the two of them.'"

With Nabeshima interpreting, they determined the time and place to meet. Then with a smile and a wave the couple disappeared into their room.

"This is perfect. Tomorrow's your day off, isn't it?" Nabeshima asked as he put his white cap back on in the elevator. Then he went over the plan once more, adding that tomorrow morning at nine o'clock, the German couple would be waiting by a mailbox and public phone down the street to the right of the hotel entrance.

"If you went to the lobby to meet them, there'd be all kinds of gossip. The employees in this hotel are all pretty conniving."

"I hear there are tensions in the office. Is it like that in the kitchen, too?"

"Cooks are all craftsmen of sorts and a lot of them have their idiosyncrasies, especially the section chief. He wears his ten years of training in France like a badge of honor and lords it over everyone from dawn till dusk. One guy who studied with him in France received some kind of fourth-order medal, and since he didn't get one he's been in a bad mood for some time now."

"So then, getting a medal is that big a deal, huh?"

"As you get older you lose your sex appeal, but you have as much money as you need. All that's left is a thirst for honor and recognition." Then with a look of indifference he added: "That old guy is especially critical of me. He insisted that the essence of cuisine is in France, and asked me if I went all the way to Germany and spent three years just to learn to make Vienna sausages. I've heard plenty of boasting from that age-spotted face of his." He got off the elevator and opened the hallway door to the kitchen. "Hey, whatever you do, don't even think of working full-time in a hotel like this."

Tetsuyuki returned to the lobby and assisted in attaching tags with room numbers to the Boston bags of a party of tourists. He recalled his father's advice a month before he died. "You never know what life has in store for you, but if you're going to spend it as a salaried worker, make sure it's with a major corporation. If that doesn't work out, then work in a government office. If you can't get a job with either one of those, then any company will do, but just work conscientiously for ten years or so and save money until the right time comes along, and then start some business.

"If you're able to work with a large corporation or in a government office, then stay with it no matter what. The wind doesn't always blow from the same direction, and someday it will surely come your way. There are always those who quit, thinking, 'The boss is bullying me' or 'I'm not really suited to this work,' but no matter where they end up, it turns out that they're bothered by the same things. And so they go from company to company and just end up as a salesman with some piddling outfit. Then, when they figure out that they've blown it, they're already in their late forties and no longer worth much.

"But there's the old saying: 'Selling baking pans is also my business.' If you can't secure employment with a large company or a government office, then any small business will do. Just study and prepare to become lord of your own castle. A ramen shop will do, or even dealing junk. Just keep cultivating your own small plot. That's the only secret to living, I can say with conviction after seventy years of seeing all kinds of people and having faced one setback after another." He held and rubbed his son's hands after muttering these last words, which rang now in Tetsuyuki's ears.

"I don't like to sound preachy, but just think of this as a sort of pompous last will and testament. There are people out there who have courage but lack endurance. And there are those who have hope but no courage. And some have as much hope and courage as anyone, but give up at the drop of a hat. Then there are lots who go through life enduring everything, but never rise to any challenge. Courage, hope, patience—only those who keep holding on to all three of these will achieve their potential.

If one of them is lacking, then no end will be reached. I had courage and hope, but no patience. I was unable to wait for the right time. I couldn't stick it out until a favorable wind blew my way. Someone who possesses all three of these qualities is the most fearsome of all. No matter he turns into a beggar or is sick and at death's door, he'll always crawl back up to the top."

His father's words rang true. Courage, hope, patience—these three words, trite as they may sound, presented him with a challenge. Repeating them in his mind, he lifted the heavy tagged bags and headed toward the elevator to take them to the guest rooms.

Tetsuyuki had taken the exam for employment in major companies and government offices, and three days ago he'd received the notification that he hadn't passed. The moment the elevator doors closed, he resolved to take Section Chief Shimazaki's advice and seek permanent employment at this hotel. He called out "Kin-chan!" and Kin immediately appeared in his mind's eye: shining, his small, frigid eyes turned toward Tetsuyuki. What was Kin if not an embodiment of these three words? Then what was the nail that pierced his torso? As he was absorbed in these thoughts, the elevator stopped and a couple entered: a man who could be called elderly, and a woman about Yōko's age.

"The meat today was kind of tough."

"And the consommé was salty, too," the woman responded. Having worked as a bellboy since spring, Tetsuyuki could immediately tell that such couples were not parent and child.

•

At 8:45, Tetsuyuki went to the place Nabeshima had mentioned. Although it was a Sunday, the street was crowded. Yōko sprang out of the throng, trying to surprise him.

"Did you eat a good breakfast?" she asked. Tetsuyuki was fond of Yōko's morning fragrance. The scent she exuded when she was asleep—after all artificial fragrances had dissipated—was at times like that of an osmanthus blossom, at other times that of straw after it had soaked in the sunlight, and at still other times simply that of a woman's body.

"I did exactly as you told me. I heated some milk, had bread and butter with cheese, and a whole tomato, too." He took in Yōko's fragrance as he answered.

"After I talked to you yesterday, I got out my German–Japanese and Japanese–German dictionaries. And I borrowed these from my dad." She excitedly showed him a volume titled *Easy German Conversation*.

"I wanted to see you, and at the same time I wanted the hundred-dollar guide fee, so without thinking I let it slip out that I'd bring along a friend who was familiar with Kyoto. Is it really okay?"

"Two years ago I toured Kyoto with a friend, so I know my way around there."

At exactly nine o'clock the elderly German couple came. Both were wearing brown overcoats and olive-green hats which, though different in shape, appeared to be from the same set. Tetsuyuki pointed at Yōko and said, "Yōko," and then at himself and said, "Tetsu." He thought "Tetsuyuki" would be too difficult for foreigners to remember.

Nodding, they repeated their names and shook hands. As they stood there in the street, Yōko leafed through the Japanese– German dictionary she had brought and pointed to the word for "train." The German couple began to discuss something between themselves, and then said something to her slowly. She was able to catch the word she had pointed to, along with "taxi."

"They seem to be asking which would be faster, a train or a taxi."

"The train would be faster. We could take the Hankyū Line to Kawaramachi, and then take a cab from there. It would be both faster and cheaper. Tell them that."

"You think I can say something like that?"

Yōko pointed to the word in her dictionary for "train," and started walking ahead. At the ticket counter, the wife handed her big leather wallet to Tetsuyuki, who took out the necessary amount and made the purchase. They boarded the special express bound for Kawaramachi, and Tetsuyuki quickly secured seats for the couple. With Tetsuyuki in the seats behind them, Yōko opened her *Easy German Conversation*.

"I wonder if this has any phrases asking people what they want to see." At length Yōko found something suitable and pointed that section out to the couple. They responded with the same words at the same time. Then, remembering that neither Tetsuyuki nor Yōko understood German, they began leafing through Yōko's German–English dictionary. First, they pointed out the word meaning "garden," and next the adjective for "quiet."

"Hmm, a quiet garden. Are there any quiet gardens in Kyoto on a Sunday? All of them would be crawling with tourists."

Yōko thought for a while. "Oh, yes, there is one."

"Where? Any temple that charges money to show its garden would be filled to capacity on a nice day like today, especially since the autumn leaves are at their best."

"It isn't a temple. It's an ordinary house. An elderly woman in her eighties lives there alone." She went on to say that it was close to the Shūgakuin Imperial Villa, and that when she had toured Kyoto two years previously, she happened to go past it. It was such a magnificent, elegant building in the pure Japanese style that she peered inside, and the woman who lived there invited her in and treated her to tea and sweets. Yōko sent her a thank-you note and then later New Year's greetings, and always got a reply.

Arriving at Kawaramachi, Yōko found a public phone and dialed the number. Tetsuyuki and the German couple stood off to the side, avoiding the crowd and watching Yōko. Whenever their eyes met, the couple would smile gently at Tetsuyuki, who would return the look.

Yōko came running up to them. "She said we're welcome to come by."

"Won't it be an imposition?"

"She said that she didn't have anything on hand that would likely suit German tastes, but that we shouldn't hesitate to come by."

Tetsuyuki hailed a cab and urged the couple to get in.

"There's also a house within the garden, a splendid, small retreat that looks as if Prince Genji might steal in for a visit."

They passed the Shūgakuin Imperial Villa and came to an

intersection where Yōko told the driver to turn right. Alongside a stream of clear moving water, the road sloped uphill gently. A forest of chestnut and oak trees stretched out before them, and they saw nothing that looked like human habitation. Yōko had the driver stop in front of a grove of tall bamboo.

"This is it? There's a house here?"

"It's inside this grove. The bamboo serves as a wall."

To pay the taxi fare, the wife again handed her wallet to Tetsuyuki, who had the driver write a receipt just to make sure, and handed it back to her along with the change.

Along the way to Shūgakuin they had seen several old temples that seemed likely to attract the attention of foreigners, but the couple showed no particular interest in them and made no comment. Tetsuyuki felt something slightly suspicious about their lack of interest, but as they followed Yōko along the winding path through the bamboo grove where countless bright rays of light filtering through the leaves created geometric patterns, they would occasionally come to a stop and talk in low voices. Each time, Tetsuyuki and Yōko would also come to a standstill and wait for them. A large gate with a tiled roof opened and a gaunt elderly woman with a half-coat over her kimono stepped out. She wore small square glasses and, appearing to be rather unsteady on her feet, used a cane. Yōko rushed up to her. "We're sorry to impose on you like this."

"Not at all! Mine is a lonely life, with guests coming around only about once a year. I was happy to hear from you and have been on pins and needles since your call." Her build was that of an old woman, but there was something bold and energetic about her manner of speaking. Yōko introduced her to Tetsuyuki and the German couple.

"I'm Sawamura Chiyono. Welcome to my home."

When she introduced herself by name, Tetsuyuki realized that he did not yet know the German couple's name. He opened the conversation book and showed them the phrase "What is your name?" They also seemed to have realized that they had not yet told anyone their names, and introduced themselves to Sawamura Chiyono as they shook her hand. Tetsuyuki did not catch their first names, but understood their last name.

"I believe they are Mr. and Mrs. Lang. Neither Yōko nor I understand German, but their last name sounds like Lang. At any rate, I'd like to introduce Mr. and Mrs. Lang."

"Please, make yourselves at home," Sawamura Chiyono said to the foreign couple and showed her four sudden guests inside. Her Kyoto accent was clipped, and sounded slightly unnatural.

"Aren't you from Kyoto?" Tetsuyuki asked.

"I've lived longer in Tokyo, but sometimes I do try to use Kyoto dialect."

Just as Yōko had said, among the ancient pines and dwarf chestnut trees could be seen a one-story mansion appearing to cover more than seven thousand square feet which, with its stucco walls and thick cypress pillars, created an imposing scene in spite of its simplicity.

"The garden covers more than eighty thousand square feet. I prefer a garden in which trees and flowers grow as they like, but my late husband had gardeners come from a great distance to design it in the style of Kobori Enshū. Beyond that elevation in the lawn there is a pond in the southeast section, and they built a tea hut to the side of it. Since my husband died no one uses it, and now I just take naps there."

Seemingly oblivious to the fact that her listeners were unable to understand Japanese, the old woman talked on and on to the properly dressed foreigners, who were seven or eight years her junior.

The husband opened the German–Japanese dictionary and pointed to the word "temple." Tetsuyuki shook his head and, finding the words for "this is her house" in the phrase book, pointed it out to them. This elicited an exclamation of admiration from them. When they reached the front door after walking along the round stepping stones, their edges encased in moss, Mr. and Mrs. Lang called to Tetsuyuki to stop and handed him an envelope. It was apparently the guide fee they had promised him, and so he thanked them and put it in his pocket. It felt rather thick for a single hundred-dollar bill, and it occurred to him that perhaps they had included a little extra.

Two maids were waiting at the front door. One was a plump woman over fifty, the other a young woman of about eighteen or nineteen with a somewhat somber expression. Sawamura Chiyono invited the four of them to go inside, but Mr. and Mrs. Lang conveyed through gestures the desire to see the garden.

"They must want to be alone and take their time," said Sawamura Chiyono and, turning to the servants, she added: "Show them to the tea hut. From there they can look out over the pond, and the view of momiji leaves falling on the stone lantern is really nice."

Tetsuyuki showed Mr. and Mrs. Lang his watch, and conveyed through gestures and words from the dictionary that it was now past ten, and they should return to the house by noon. They nodded demonstratively, and shook hands again with everyone.

Birds were alighting here and there in the spacious garden to forage on something or other, and black-eared kites were flying up from the area around the tea hut. After Mr. and Mrs. Lang disappeared over the knoll, Yōko and Tetsuyuki were shown inside.

"Thank you for your annual New Year's card." The old woman bowed her head slightly, peering into Yōko's face as the younger of the maids helped her to sit down on a cushion. "You seem to have matured a lot since I first met you."

"You, too, seem to be in good spirits. You look a lot younger than before."

At Yōko's words, the old woman waved her hand covered with small age spots and said: "I try to be careful, and walk as much as I can, but even so my legs have gotten weak." In the tokonoma alcove was a scroll painting of two cranes standing in a field of snow and a white ceramic vase with a single camellia of the same color. Yōko looked at Tetsuyuki and a short laugh escaped as she cast her eyes down, thereby communicating to the old woman what she could not have said in words. Was that on purpose or did it just come out without thought? Tetsuyuki could not tell, but feeling the gaze of the old woman, he could not very well laugh back. But neither could he think of anything to talk about, and just fumbled about in his pocket for a cigarette.

Yōko said, "The Langs are lucky, aren't they? No matter

how much they might have searched in Kyoto, they'd never have found a splendid, quiet garden like this."

"A while ago, I mentioned my late husband, but he wasn't really my husband," Sawamura Chiyono said, addressing Tetsuyuki. "I won't mention his name, but the man who built this house had a wife and children in Tokyo . . . not to put too fine a point on it, but I was his mistress. For about the last three years of his life he hardly ever went back to Tokyo, and just spent all his time here."

"I see . . ." was Tetsuyuki's only response as he listened to the old woman.

"And so when he died, there was real trouble. After all, this much land and this mansion were involved. His family in Tokyo insisted that they should of course inherit it, and took the matter to court, but his will clearly stated that the land and house in Shūgakuin were to be left to me. But acquiring this much presented other problems. The inheritance taxes came to a staggering amount, and I even considered just turning it over to his family. However, a friend reminded me that if it became impossible to manage the place, I could always just sell it."

Suddenly changing the topic, she added in a lowered voice, "It's really wonderful that a couple who have been together so long as that can go on a trip abroad." She looked back and forth at Tetsuyuki and Yōko and smiled. When Tetsuyuki pulled the pack of cigarettes out of his pocket, the envelope from Mr. Lang came out with it. Feeling it again, it somehow seemed even thicker.

"Mr. Lang promised he'd give me a hundred dollars, but this envelope is way too thick." Yōko looked at it and said, "Maybe it's ten ten-dollar bills." Tetsuyuki broke the seal and looked inside. There were far more than ten, each one a crisp hundred-dollar bill.

"What can this mean?" Tetsuyuki placed the contents of the envelope on the table and, glancing at Yōko and the old woman, counted the money. "It's more than two thousand dollars."

Yōko looked again inside the envelope and found a sheet of thin paper, folded in four, covered with small writing in German.

"Mr. Lang handed you the wrong envelope with this in it."

Tetsuyuki thought it impossible that he could mistake an envelope containing more than twenty hundred-dollar bills for a thin one with only one. He glanced at Sawamura Chiyono, who was looking at the wad of bills with the same suspicious look on her face, and their eyes met. After looking at each other for some time, Tetsuyuki hurriedly stood up. Simultaneously the sound of the old woman's call for the maid rang throughout the quiet mansion.

Tetsuyuki ran down the long hallway on its well-polished floorboards and dashed out onto the garden path without even putting on his shoes. The grass of the low-cut lawn stabbed the soles of his feet as he ran over the gently sloping green hillock with all the speed he could muster. Startled wild birds flew up in a frenzy, rising into the skies with their cries congealing into a mass of sound. The tea hut by the southeastern pond came into view. The pond was softly gleaming, casting reflections that looked like yellow clouds on the walls and small shōji windows of the hut. Before reaching the hut, he stumbled and fell over, taking a hard hit to his abdomen.

"Mr. Lang!" he called in a loud voice and, opening the sliding door of the hut, dived into the four-and-a-half-mat room. A gentle light from two windows of differing sizes above the entrance and from the low window above the floor on the north side flooded the simple, east-facing room. Sitting side by side with their legs stretched out, the German couple turned their pallid faces toward Tetsuyuki and hurriedly stuffed into their pockets something they had been holding in their hands.

"What were you intending to do? If you want to look at the garden, then you ought to open the windows. What was it that you just hid in your pockets?"

Tetsuyuki's Japanese was of course unintelligible to them, but they were both silent as they fixed their strangely serene gaze upon him. Gone were their former smiles, the blood appeared to be drained from their cheeks, and they were as listless as invalids who had given up all hope. Their blue eyes trembled somewhat as they stared at him. He thrust his open hands in front of them as if to demand that they surrender what was in their pockets, but they did not make the slightest move, and only continued to stare intently at him.

At length he heard footsteps running toward the hut: Yōko and the middle-aged maid who had shown the couple there. As soon as the maid ascertained that they were all right, she dashed off back toward the mansion. Yōko assumed a formal sitting position by the low window on the north side and said to Tetsuyuki, "Why don't you sit down too?" He opened all three of the hut's windows. Supported by the young maid and with the help of her cane, Sawamura Chiyono was descending the grassy knoll. Behind them was the middle-aged maid with the envelope in hand.

"As soon as I came into the hut, the two of them quickly hid something in their pockets. I've told them to hand over whatever it was."

Sawamura Chiyono silently placed the envelope containing more than two thousand dollars before the Langs.

"It's too bad we can't communicate at a time like this," she muttered to no one in particular, and then addressed the young maid. "Have Mr. Kumai come. If he's not at home, call him at his office. He said he would be at his office Sunday to tie up some loose ends." Then, as the maid was about to leave, she added, "Explain the circumstances briefly, and request that he come right away. Don't dawdle, be off, quickly!" she commanded in a sharp tone of voice. Then she beckoned for the middle-aged maid.

"It's been a long time since we made tea here. Build a fire, and bring that red raku tea bowl. It's in the cupboard in my room."

After the two maids had gone, Sawamura Chiyono went before the tokonoma and picked up an incense burner.

"Kumai is the nephew of the late master of this place. He's on his own now, and runs a small trading company, but before that he worked for a commercial firm in Germany for seven years, so he'll have no trouble conversing with these two."

"I'm sorry to have put you to such trouble."

Sawamura Chiyono responded to Yōko's dejected utterance with a smile. "There's no need for you to apologize." She drew herself up to a rigid pose and fixed her eyes silently on the Langs. Then she added, "There is no one here who needs to apologize."

The middle-aged maid brought live coals and a kettle filled with water.

"Let's burn just a bit of incense." At this suggestion of Sawamura Chiyono's, Tetsuyuki closed the windows and urged the Langs to face the kettle. They meekly complied.

"I received this incense as a gift a long time ago. It's a highly prized variety known as Mandarin Orange Blossom."

Seated to administer the tea ceremony, Sawamura Chiyono straightened her back and for a long time looked at the kettle. Tetsuyuki knew nothing about tea, but he sensed that the ceremony that was about to be performed would not be her attempt to soften the hearts of the Langs; nor would it be a means to convey how she felt to people from an alien land.

The slight scent of Mandarin Orange Blossom wafted through the room. Tetsuyuki felt certain that what the couple had been holding in their hands was poison, and that if he had arrived even a few minutes later, they would already have taken it. With a start, his eyes darted around the room. He was seized by the thought that even in this room Kin was nailed fast to a pillar. Sawamura Chiyono drew the red tea bowl up beside her and took a tea caddy out of a bag. Only Yōko had learned the ceremony; the other three were unfamiliar with the proper manners, and clumsily drank the warm, green, frothy liquid.

When they were finished, Sawamura Chiyono said drily, "How dreary! I've never experienced a more cheerless tea ceremony. It will no doubt make death seem very attractive, won't it?" Then, heaving a sigh, she added, "These two were not able to die here, but they will no doubt carry out their plan someplace else. This was a farewell tea ceremony."

"Why do you think so?" Tetsuyuki asked, but Sawamura Chiyono did not reply. Tetsuyuki handed to the Langs the envelope, which had been left lying on the tatami. Mr. Lang took out one of the bills and placed it on Tetsuyuki's lap. The young maid's voice came from outside.

"Mr. Kumai is here."

"Please show him in."

A short, round-faced man of forty-four or forty-five whose bearing revealed that he was a "mover and shaker" assumed a formal sitting posture in the entrance to the tea hut. Sawamura Chiyono handed him the slip of paper covered with small German writing, which she had not put back into the envelope but had instead stuffed into her obi. While Mr. Kumai was running his eyes over the note, Mr. and Mrs. Lang looked at each other nervously, then suddenly turned toward the four Japanese with a determined look on their faces.

"Let me tell you exactly what it says." Mr. Kumai spoke in a measured voice, dropping his eyes to the note.

"'I, Friedrich Lang, and my wife, Bebel Lang, apologize

for creating such trouble for the kindhearted Japanese people whose names we do not even know. Please inform the person noted below of our deaths. He is our son. Please use this money for the cremation of our remains. If it appears that our son will not come to Japan, then we humbly request that you send our ashes to the address below. According to the laws of your country, an autopsy may be required, but we attest herewith that death was caused by potassium cyanide, administered by our own hands. It was by our own mutual agreement that we took this poison. Our determination to die followed many long conversations. We agreed that we wanted to die in a quiet, incomparably beautiful place somewhere in the Far East, and accordingly sold our home and its furnishings, along with our automobile and some jewelry. This yielded a rather large sum, but we gave a third of it to two friends who were in need of money, donated another third of it to our church, and used the remainder for our travel expenses. The $2,500 in the envelope is all that is left of our money. Please use it to dispose of our corpses. Once again, we sincerely apologize for creating such trouble for kindhearted Japanese people whom we do not even know. May God bless them with eternal happiness.'"

After listening to the end, Sawamura Chiyono—erect with her chest thrown out, her shoulders and the hairline above her collar projecting a vigor that belied her more than eighty years—stared silently at the kettle in front of her for what seemed an eternity. Suddenly she smiled. It was a smile that at first glance could be taken as one of a gentle and compassionate elderly person, but to Tetsuyuki it appeared as the reverse side of an incomparably ominous and cruel malicious-ness. He shuddered as he waited for the words to issue from her mouth.

"They've already died. The two of them have achieved their desire here in my tea hut. Tell them so."

Kumai conveyed her words in German to the Langs. For a while, they were lost in thought, and seemed not to have understood what she meant.

"I think that tea is a ritual for gazing on life and death. Tea may also be the same as the God you both believe in. Tea is also a religion. While in the tearoom, both host and guest are dead. When they leave the tearoom, they are alive. And so, when you leave here, you must live whether you like it or not."

The Langs listened intently to Kumai's fluent German. It was difficult to tell whether the elderly Western couple comprehended the meaning of Sawamura Chiyono's words, but Mr. Lang occasionally nodded as he listened.

"Let's go back to the house. Mr. Kumai, get them to talk in more detail about their circumstances. Just as people might suddenly want to die, so might they also suddenly want to live."

With Sawamura Chiyono's unsteady steps supported on both sides by Tetsuyuki and Yōko, the three of them left the tea hut. Wild birds came circling back and were chirping here and there on the lawn. Around the stone lantern the deep scarlet leaves of the momiji were falling, illumined by sunlight filtering through the trees. When they came to the highest elevation in the garden, Sawamura Chiyono muttered, "Shall we bask in the sun?" and, sitting on the grass, rubbed the foot that was aching. Then, as the three of them looked at the tea hut, she said, "I met that man about fifty years ago, at a tea gathering."

"By 'that man,' do you mean your husband?"

She tittered slightly at Yōko's question. "Not my husband, my *patron*. I was thirty-two at the time. He lavished money on wonderful tea utensils for me, all very famous pieces: pots, tea bowls, tea ladles, kettles . . . The studded kettle that I just now used was one of those. But he didn't know a thing about tea. Oh, he had a lot of knowledge of Sen no Rikyū and the tea masters of that age but . . . I've never seen anyone less adept at tea itself. He used to talk as if anyone who has had the slightest dealings with tea will of course wonder why Sen no Rikyū took his own life, as if anyone who doesn't talk about such things couldn't have a real love for the art. He was like that, and so was I. There were various theories: that it was a disguised reproach to Hideyoshi, or that it was intended as a challenge to him . . . But recently—or rather, about two years ago—I finally came to understand."

Her strange faint smile reappeared in Tetsuyuki's mind. He didn't know the first thing about tea. Regarding Sen no Rikyū, he knew only the facts that he was a tea master during the age of Hideyoshi, and that he committed suicide, yet he found himself wanting to hear what she had come to understand about Rikyū's death. But she only gazed silently with narrowed eyes at the shimmering pond. As Tetsuyuki was about to open his mouth, Yōko asked, "Why did Rikyū die?"

At that, Sawamura Chiyono began to talk. "Do you suppose that Rikyū was afraid of a poor peasant upstart like

Hideyoshi, no matter how much power the latter had in the realm? He must have regarded Hideyoshi with disdain. One morning about two years ago, I woke up at a dreadfully early hour and for some reason wanted to make tea. The maids were still asleep, so I had no choice but to make the fire myself in the tea hut. I've forgotten which utensils were there except for the tea bowl: the same red raku—from the sixteenth century—that I used just now. Sitting in the formal position in the tea hut before dawn, I stared inside that bowl and wondered: for sixty years from the time I was twenty I had studied tea, and what had I seen in it? At that moment, the tea suddenly appeared as green poison. Or, perhaps rather than poison, it appeared as death itself. There was death, and I was living right beside it. Together with that thought it occurred to me that Rikyū must have realized the same thing. Within the tea bowl is death, and one drinks it and has one's guests drink it. There is no way a tea master like Rikyū with his long experience could not have understood that; that is, the secret of death. After all, at some point or other tea had definitely become a religion for him."

With that Sawamura Chiyono broke off and was lost in thought. She continued in a quiet tone.

"But that must have been something he couldn't talk about. So perhaps there was no way for Rikyū to verify the secret of death he had come to comprehend except by dying himself. That was the only means he had to bring his art of tea to perfection. Hideyoshi's command that he commit seppuku was merely a convenient excuse for him. He didn't care about the countless military commanders who had drunk his tea and then gone out to die in battle. Rikyū died as a testament of something that approximated his own inexplicable realization of what death is. I'm certain that must be why. That winter morning before dawn two years ago, when I saw death inside that red tea bowl, I earnestly thought so. That's why I take naps in the tea hut. That way, I come to understand more fully. When I'm asleep, that's death. When I'm awake, that's life. But both are my same self. Life and death, life and death, life and death . . . By dying, Rikyū attempted to ascertain that . . ."

As if embarrassed that she had forgotten herself and been carried away by her impassioned speech, she glanced at Tetsuyuki and Yōko and laughed. Her laugh made the tea hut where the Langs were together with Mr. Kumai seem like an elegant, roofed tomb.

Tetsuyuki recalled his strange dream in which he had turned into a lizard, dying and being reborn again and again over hundreds of years. That dream was strongly connected to Sawamura Chiyono's reasoning, which could be taken either as erudition or as self-righteousness. It occurred to him that it was time to bring to a conclusion this caring for Kin, which had already turned into a daily routine.

He noticed that the branches of the hackberry and sweet acorn trees surrounding the garden were waving, each time scattering their leaves. Next spring, on a day when vernal warmth filled heaven and earth, he would pull the nail out. If he did it now, Kin would be unable to withstand the cold with a fresh wound, and would likely die.

The door of the tea hut opened and the Langs emerged along with Kumai.

"What time is it now?" Sawamura Chiyono asked.

"Almost twelve."

"I went ahead and ordered some Kyoto cuisine from a restaurant. They should be delivering it about now. Perfect! The boxed lunches from that place have suitable portions, and are very good. They should be just right for Mr. and Mrs. Lang."

She stood up, brushing bits of grass from her kimono. The Langs stood next to each other, looking out over the surface of the pond. Kumai walked up the slope and handed to Sawamura Chiyono two small white paper packages.

"It's potassium cyanide."

"I'm surprised you got them to hand it over."

"I told them that, if they were so inclined, there are any number of ways to die, but that I could not let them leave the tea hut with that in their possession," Kumai explained as they walked toward the house.

"Did you ask about the reason?"

"They have one son, an attorney in Munich. They bought a house in a town about a hundred kilometers away and began their retirement living on a pension. Mrs. Lang said that their son's wife hates her, and Mr. Lang said that his son hates him. Even though they live only a hundred kilometers away, these two years their son has not come to see them once. They just take care of matters by phone. I'm sure they each have their own excuses, but I couldn't very well probe further, so I quit asking."

"Things like that happen in every country," Sawamura Chi-yono remarked.

"Whether his wife would go first, or he would, there's no way to know, but in either case the one left behind would be lonely. He said that they couldn't bear even to imagine such sadness."

"Write a letter to his son. If he's an attorney, money shouldn't be a problem for him. Say, 'For such and such reasons, your parents tried to end their life in Japan. What do you intend to do about it?'"

"Well, if you insist, I can write something right away . . ."

"But there's nothing else we can do, is there? They gave up their house and all their property, and set out on a journey. All they have left is a little over two thousand dollars, not even enough to buy return tickets to their own country. And even if they do return, they have nowhere to settle down except at their son's place."

Listening to this exchange between Kumai and Sawamura Chiyono, Tetsuyuki suddenly recalled the words the old woman spoke in the tea hut: "These two were not able to die here, but they will no doubt carry out their plan someplace else. This was a farewell tea ceremony." But in spite of that, she was trying to prevent these two foreigners from dying. He felt a kind of eeriness about what she had said, and about Rikyū's thoughts on death. The maid announced that the meal had been delivered.

"I'll go call them." With that, Tetsuyuki set off at a trot toward the pond. At the sound of footsteps, the Langs looked around and gave what sounded like an apology. Using gestures, he communicated that the meal was ready. The Langs looked at each other. There was a note of contrition in their voices as they said, "Danke, danke schön!"

Sitting around a low table, the Langs looked at the Japanese food and asked what things were.

"How to say kōya-dōfu?" Kumai cocked his head. Sawamura Chiyono smiled and said, "I guess there's nothing to call it but freeze-dried tofu." At the end of the meal, the maids brought in sliced melon. For a long time, Kumai was engaged in conversation with the Langs.

"'After making so much trouble for you, you have treated us to such wonderful Japanese cuisine. We were not able to die. God no doubt did not permit it, and so we certainly won't be able to attempt it again. Please do not worry about us anymore.' That is what they said." After Kumai relayed their words, Sawamura Chiyono stared at her melon, then lifted a spoonful of it to her mouth. "Ask them how they'll return to their country." The Langs made no reply. Sawamura Chiyono suddenly raised her head and gave them a sharp look.

"How very sad! Why must life end up so sad? What have they lived this long for?"

Kumai relayed what she had said. Mr. Lang loosened his tie and began speaking in a calm tone of voice, with Kumai providing simultaneous interpretation.

"I wonder the same thing. When I retired and purchased a small, comfortable house in the country, I assumed that a new life was about to begin. But then, what is a 'new life'? The thought that I was a creature of the past took root in my heart. I came into this life in a poor family. I graduated from high school and became a printer. Then there was the great war, and I fought against French and British troops. I could never verify it with my own eyes, but the bullets I fired no doubt killed several people. Germany lost, and a long and difficult period ensued. In the meantime, I became acquainted with my wife, and we began to live together. At length, the printing company where I had been employed was reconstructed and I returned to work there. For ten years my hands were always pitch-black from setting type, but finally machines deprived me of my job. I demanded that my beloved son become either a doctor or a lawyer. I wanted him to have work that only a human being and not a machine could perform, work that would command respect. My son rebelled, saying he wanted to become a chef. But I would not allow it. We tightened our belts on my meager salary and engaged a private tutor for him. Now that I think about it, I marvel at how docile he was. He didn't like it, but he fulfilled my dream. But it was my dream, not his. When he brought his girlfriend to meet us, neither I nor my wife liked her, but I thought I should at least grant him the freedom to choose his own wife. It appeared he was suited neither to the work of an attorney nor to his wife. My son was too virtuous and gentle of character to perform the work of a lawyer, and it damaged his spirit. The hysterics of his beautiful but vain and extravagant wife led him to excessive drinking. Each time he consumed liquor, he would scream furiously at me that even now he wanted to become a chef. When he didn't drink, there was no way he could bring himself to shout like that. One day, I said to him: 'Let's not see each other anymore.' At the time

I really meant it. He stopped coming to see us. By then, we were already seventy-six years old. There was no 'new life,' and no way to seek one but to die. At some point, we began to think that way. This past spring, two of my friends from my childhood died at about the same time. That urged me to do something. There are lots of lonely old folk and they're just waiting. I began to be afraid of waiting. Rather than wait, I wanted to go on my own accord. My wife was afraid, but I persuaded her. 'We've lived long enough. Whichever of us goes first, the remaining one will just face loneliness, and that's even more frightening.'"

Tetsuyuki thought about the frail constitution of his own mother, who about now was probably cleaning the restaurant, and did not realize that he was being addressed by Sawamura Chiyono until Yōko nudged him.

"Please call the hotel and inform them that the Langs will be staying in Kyoto tonight. Rather than returning to the hustle and bustle of Osaka, they'll relax here this evening." With exaggerated gestures, Mr. Lang declined her offer, but she replied with a smile. "Since you've put us to great trouble, you're obliged to do as I say." Only then did he dejectedly droop his shoulders. Tetsuyuki sensed that it would be better to return to the hotel and explain the situation directly to Section Chief Shimazaki, and suggested this to Sawamura Chiyono. She conceded. "It would be a bother for you, but that would no doubt be best."

Tetsuyuki and Yōko went down the slope from the front gate and hailed a taxi. Once inside, Yōko languidly pillowed her head on Tetsuyuki's shoulder. The scent of her usual perfume now smelled like sunshine. He wanted to embrace her so badly he could no longer bear it, and evoked the usual code the two of them employed at such times.

"Kin-chan is calling."

He thought she was sure to put him off, accusing him of being out of his mind. But she muttered, "Mm, all right," and grasped his index finger.

"As long as we're back in Osaka by nightfall, it should be okay, huh?" Yōko also clearly indicated her desire, her glum countenance and the deliberate lisping of her words notwithstanding.

Beyond the street-front buildings the neon-lit tower of a love hotel left one wondering what colors it must project at night onto the roadside trees and roofs of houses. Tetsuyuki told the driver to stop.

"Didn't you say you wanted to go to Kawaramachi?" The driver deliberately slammed on the brakes and glared at Tetsuyuki through the rearview mirror.

"Sorry, I suddenly remember that a friend's house is in this area," he said to vindicate himself as he paid the fare, thinking at the same time, *It's the customer's business where and when he wants to get out.*

Why must people be so brutal? The street was filthy and noisy, and everyone was irritable and short-tempered. The driver clicked his tongue to show his annoyance as he handed over the change, and then drove off at breakneck speed. The driver's decidedly unhappy face emblazoned in his mind's eye, Tetsuyuki glanced at Yōko.

"I feel exhausted. Somehow, everything has become repulsive to me."

"Didn't you just say that Kin-chan is calling?" Bathed in the autumn sunlight, Yōko's face appeared more beautiful than usual. What was this strange wholesomeness her features possessed? At the same moment this thought came into his head: he had no confidence in his ability to make her happy.

"In the middle of the day like this, you won't like people seeing you come out of the hotel, will you?"

"Well, no, but then there's not enough time to go to your apartment."

Tetsuyuki looked down silently at the scattered leaves around his feet. Yōko whispered, "Kin-chan is calling," and pulled him by the hand. Following along the wall of a temple, the street turned to the left and led directly to the entrance to the hotel. Across the street, several boys of junior high school age were playing on roller skates. One of them spied Tetsuyuki and Yōko and began to jeer, "Oh, they're going in! They're going in!" As they entered, they could hear shouts peppered with obscene words. A man appeared, muttering, "Every time customers come, those kids taunt them like that." Leaving Tetsuyuki and Yōko there in the entranceway, he went out front.

"Hey! Get out of here!"

"We can play wherever we want!"

Hearing the footsteps of the man in pursuit and the sound of fleeing roller-skaters, Tetsuyuki and Yōko smiled at each other.

"Sorry to keep you waiting," the man said as he returned and set out two pairs of slippers. "Until six o'clock the price remains the same no matter how many hours you stay. We offer three courses: for three thousand yen, four thousand yen, or five thousand yen. So, which would you like?" He explained in a lively tone of voice, as if he were a merchant in a fish market bargaining with customers, "The four-thousand-yen room comes with its own bath."

"Well, then, we'll take that one." After Tetsuyuki stated his choice, the man called out in a loud voice, "Show these guests to a four-thousand-yen room!" They thought that perhaps an usher would appear at such a signal, but the same man brought a key from the reception desk and pressed the elevator button. When they entered the room, he knocked on the mirror in the bathroom, then on the wall, and took down a framed cheap art reproduction.

"There are no peepholes, so don't worry about that." Then he took out a business card on which was printed an unusual name: Mata Kitarō. (Meaning, you've come again, haven't you?) Tetsuyuki stared at the characters.

"How are these characters read?"

"Mata Kitarō."

"Huh?"

"The name is Mata Kitarō."

"That isn't your real name, is it?"

"Of course not. If I had really been given a name like that, I'd resent my parents." He smiled congenially as he left the room. "Please come again."

Tetsuyuki kept staring at the business card with knitted brow when he heard Yōko's suppressed giggle near his ear. Controlling her laughter with both hands over her mouth, she fell back on the bed. Joining in the hilarity, Tetsuyuki fell over on top of Yōko. He asked her to get in the shower with him. Still laughing, she refused, saying that it would wash out the curls she had set in her hair. He persisted: she could just take care not to get her head wet. Her glee suddenly stopped and, with eyes only inches from his, stared silently for a long time. Wrapping both arms around his head she asked quietly, "What's to become of me?"

Indistinct voices, reverberating in such a way as to leave the direction of their source obscure, filled Tetsuyuki and Yōko with a sort of sadness. The heat in the room, so high that they were perspiring, preventing their anxiety from taking shape in words.

"I don't know. I don't even know what things will be like an hour from now." He finally managed to get that much out, and leaned his forehead against her neck.

"I wonder . . . if a woman marries, maybe she has to throw all caution to the wind, not really caring what he's like." With that, she drew her lips close to him, then pulled back, asking, "Are you strong?"

"I'm weak."

Yōko again drew her lips near. They covered his with a pleasant, tumbling sensation.

"Can you live to an old age?"

"I have a feeling that I'll probably die young."

"Are you good at making money?"

"That's what I'm worst at."

"Will you cheat on me?"

"I might."

Yōko sensed that he was not merely joking, and stood up. "It's hot."

"Of course it is. This is a place for getting naked."

"You've come again, haven't you?" Yōko mumbled as she went into the bathroom. Her figure as she took off her clothing was projected onto the frosted glass, and at length he could hear the sound of the shower. Tetsuyuki shed his clothes and went into the bathroom, where he gazed to his heart's content at her naked body as she tilted her head backward under the water. The cramped bathroom was soon steamed up, and spray from the stream beat against and ran down Tetsuyuki's face and chest. He reached out and grabbed her by the waist, turning her to face him, then massaged the stiffness in her muscles.

"I have moles," she said, putting her arms around his neck after he had lathered her body.

"I know. There's one on your butt, and a big one on your stomach."

Yōko shook her head and said that there was one in a very embarrassing place. The steam of the shower had already taken the shape out of their hair. They both sat down on the tiles under the shower stream. Tetsuyuki lathered every part of Yōko's body, washing each part again and again with the palms of his hands. No matter where his hands explored, she did not recoil, but just clung to him tightly. He released himself from her arms and sat cross-legged, placing both hands on the tiles and praising her beautiful body. Yōko listened, leaning to the side and with hands also on the tiles.

He asked her to show him the mole in the embarrassing place. She had to open her legs and bend back as far as possible, but she did as he asked. Steam and water running down her body alternately hid and revealed it. To Tetsuyuki, it looked like one of Kin's tiny, blinking eyes. He closed her legs and embraced her.

"Actually, I'm strong," he said. Yōko nodded.

"I'll live to an old age."

"I have a knack for making money."

"I'll never cheat on you."

Yōko nodded at each declaration. Yet it was Tetsuyuki who was being caressed, both physically and psychologically, and so it was after they had gotten into bed. He poured his whole heart into performing the few sexual techniques he knew, but felt that it was he who was the recipient, though Yōko remained passive with her eyes closed.

Several hours later, they both recalled the Langs at the same time. During their ecstasy they had forgotten about the life drama they had just witnessed. As they lay in spent embrace they thought of the depressing sadness that constantly flitted through their rapture. Why sporadic gloom during such supreme bliss?

He concluded that it certainly owed to his poverty. Even after graduation and employment, more than half of his meager salary would disappear in repayment of his father's debts. Despite that, Yōko had accepted his command and assumed that posture in the bathroom. No doubt she would blush and shed tears every time she recalled it. What did that mole mean to her that she was willing to show it to him? Why had she loosened up so much as he was lathering her body in the shower? And why had he felt so caressed by her, though he was the one moving and she was still?

His mind's eye saw the long way from Osaka Station to his apartment: the crowded, bright brick-red train to Kyōbashi; from the platform at Kyōbashi Station, caked with a thick film of sputum, phlegm, and vomit mixed with cigarette butts, mud, and dust, descending the stairs to the platform for the Katamachi Line; the sewer ditches and construction sites visible from the window of the well-worn and metallic-smelling old car; the sound of cranes; the oil film and methane gas spreading over the ditches; the dirty fluorescent lights blinking at Suminodō Station, a place that felt alien to him no matter how many times he got off there; the smell of garlic always wafting around the shopping arcade where country toughs hung out; the stand-up bars where someone would always be babbling in his cups; the toy store; the pack of mangy, stray dogs; the railroad crossing; the smokestack of the public bath; the single path that was either cold or hot; the laundry waving on the drying platforms of housing complexes all of the same shape; the metal stairs; and his own room: his own room, where Kin was waiting. Tetsuyuki held tightly to Yōko.

"My hair's a mess. My mom is sure to be suspicious."

"You could just tell her that it rained only in Kyoto." Yōko giggled as she rearranged her hair in front of the mirror.

When they went down to the front counter, the man said, "Oh? You're leaving already? Until six o'clock, it's the same price no matter how long you stay." With an ambiguous smile on his face, Tetsuyuki handed over the money.

"When I was young, I'd have kept a knockout like this young lady for a good five or six hours." Then he went outside and beckoned to the two of them. "There's no one out here. You can leave without embarrassment."

At the corner, Tetsuyuki and Yōko looked back. The man suddenly raised his hand and bowed his head. "Please come again."

"If we come back to Kyoto, let's really come here again."

"With a hair dryer and curlers in hand . . ." Yōko responded, blushing.

After hearing Tetsuyuki's explanation to the end, Section Chief Shimazaki lowered his voice. "Well, this has turned into a fine mess." He called the front desk. "Please get me the extension for the front-desk manager." The receiver pressed to his ear, Shimazaki nodded a few times as if to say, "Leave it all to me."

"Is Section Head Imoto on duty today?" Shimazaki asked the person in charge at the front desk, then, covering the mouthpiece with his hand, he explained to Tetsuyuki with a wink, "Imoto came here when I did. He can be trusted to keep a secret." When Imoto came to the phone, Shimazaki asked him to come by to discuss an urgent matter. Section Head Imoto appeared immediately. He had the serious, honest face of a country school principal and possessed the greatest language aptitude of anyone in the hotel, his facility with English and French such as occasionally to earn the straightforward praise of foreign guests. He pondered the matter for a while, then went out of the office. When he returned, he announced, "Mr. Lang paid in advance for tonight." Then, taking a puff on his cigarette, mumbled as if weighed down by anguish, "I'll refund the charges for tonight. Under these circumstances, they'll need to reduce any expense possible. I have an eighty-eight-year-old mother who doesn't get along well with my wife. I'm embarrassed to say so, but last month she decided on her own to enter a rest home in Nishinomiya. It's a private establishment with good facilities, not gloomy or anything like that. In a way I feel relieved, and in a way I feel very unfilial."

As Tetsuyuki went out from the employee exit behind the building and headed for the coffee shop where Yōko was waiting, Shimazaki caught up with him and tapped him on the shoulder.

"About permanent employment . . . I'd like to have your answer soon."

"I've decided to take you up on your kind offer."

"So, you've decided, have you? Good. Now, just leave everything up to me." Shimazaki beamed and bustled back to his office. *But, ten years* . . . Tetsuyuki thought to himself. He would work hard for ten years, save money, and then start some business of his own, just as his father had said. He had no idea what kind of business he was suited for, or how much capital it would require, but Yōko's mysterious caresses a mere two hours ago had emboldened him.

At a telephone in the coffee shop, Yōko informed Sawamura

Chiyono of the arrangements made at the hotel. She returned to the table with a dejected look on her face.

"What's wrong?"

"They decided a letter would take too long, so they made an international call to Munich."

"Will their son come to pick them up?"

Yōko shook her head. "The son said to let them do as they pleased, and then curtly hung up."

"So then, he's telling them just to go ahead and die?"

"Mrs. Sawamura seemed a bit surprised by that too. What should I do? After all, I'm the one who took the Langs to her house to begin with."

There is really such a thing as a son who could be indifferent to his aged parents after they had gone to a foreign country, attempted to poison themselves, and lacked the money for a return trip? Tetsuyuki conjectured that Mr. Lang must be concealing the real reason for the discord between himself and his son.

"She said they called at two thirty. Since the difference between Japan and West Germany is about eight hours, it would have been about six thirty in the morning there. Even so, from his manner of speaking the son seemed to be quite drunk. Mrs. Sawamura said that they'd try calling again after a while."

"No matter how drunk he might be, a call like that from Japan should sober him up."

Making no reply, Yōko fingered her curlless hair and said in a barely audible voice, "I'm tired."

"Go home and have a good rest. I'll see you to the station."

"Then you'll go home too, won't you?"

"I'll try going to my mom's place. We've only talked on the phone, and I haven't seen her in a long time. Today's Sunday, her day off."

Once she had gone through the ticket gate and climbed the stairs to the platform, Yōko came rushing back, insisting stubbornly on going with him. It had, in fact, been a long time since his mother and Yōko had seen each other.

The Yūki restaurant was a considerable distance, on the western end of the main road in Kita Shinchi, far from the Midōsuji Avenue area. Most of the clubs and eateries clustered in Kita Shinchi were closed on Sundays, and were it not for the rancid odor of offal crammed into plastic buckets, the place could seem like a ghost town. Occasionally one might find a young man properly dressed in a jacket and expensive tie standing idly in front of some shop. Without exception, they all possessed comely features, but slight mannerisms betrayed decadence and self-indulgence. A light was on in the second floor of Yūki. Staring at that light, Tetsuyuki thought how he would like to live together with his mother as soon as tomorrow. As long as one or the other of them exercises intelligence, a mother-in-law and her daughter-in-law ought to be able to live together amicably. He expressed this thought to Yōko.

"I'm very fond of your mother."

Of course, at the beginning no mother-in-law and no daughter-in-law intend not to get along, so why do so few of them live harmoniously under the same roof? Tetsuyuki mused that it was all due to the elemental core of that creature called woman.

Tetsuyuki knocked on the door of Yūki. A second-story window opened, and his mother poked her head out.

"Good evening!" Yōko smiled and waved unreservedly as if greeting a close female friend.

"Oh, Yōko, it's been a long time since I saw you!" Smiling exuberantly, his mother closed the window and soon they heard her unlocking the front door. Tetsuyuki could tell, by her movements through the frosted glass, just how pleased she was by their visit. As soon as she saw Yōko, a questioning look appeared on her face.

"What happened to you? Your hair . . ." Then she led them to her second-story room.

"Excuse me for a moment. I'll bring some tea." With that, his mother went downstairs.

"See, I told you! All because of you, I have this hair that makes me look like a ghost." Yōko pouted and glared reproachfully at Tetsuyuki.

"I never told you to get your hair wet in the shower. That's something you chose to do."

"Yeah, but at the time, I just felt like throwing all caution to the wind."

"It's all Mata Kitarō's fault. He put you in the mood." After that slipped out, it occurred to Tetsuyuki that it might actually be true. The wretchedness of the love hotel in that section of downtown Kyoto, the momentary sadness when they entered its front door, the good-natured drollery of its manager, and the frightening speed with which the human heart can change as a result of trivial matters—what an absurd thing it is to go through life dominated by such an uncertain heart. In Tetsu-yuki's mind this thought was accompanied by the image of Kin with his tail writhing back and forth.

"Don't sit over there. Come and get warm under the ko-tatsu." Entering the room with a tray bearing a teapot and cups, Tetsuyuki's mother urged Yōko to make herself comfortable. Yōko asked where the bathroom was, and after making sure that she had gone down the stairs, his mother poked him on the head.

"Men are always in a hurry, aren't they?"

"What are you talking about?"

"About how perfectly set hair should end up so straight. Yōko isn't the kind of girl who would ever go out without set-ting her hair nicely."

"It rained." Led on by his mother's gentle tone of voice, Tetsuyuki answered with a smile.

"A sudden rainstorm?"

"Yeah."

Yōko returned and began sipping her tea. Tetsuyuki told them that his employment had been decided.

"When?" Yōko asked, surprised.

"A little while ago. They'd offered it to me some time ago, but I wasn't able to make up my mind. Anyway, I've got to set sail, so it doesn't matter which port I leave from. So when the section chief pressed my for an answer today, I made up my mind."

" 'I've got to set sail, so it doesn't matter which port I leave from' . . . now, there's a showy expression." Chided by Yōko, he laughed with embarrassment. With a serious look on her face, his mother congratulated him. Since he had last seen her, his mother was thinner and she seemed pale. After much hesitation, Tetsuyuki brought up the matter of having her live with them. Yōko again mentioned the tidy apartment she had talked about before with Tetsuyuki.

"It's actually more of a two-story town house than an apartment. Downstairs there is a six-mat room and an eat-in kitchen. Upstairs there are three-mat and six-mat rooms. It has a bathroom, and it's about a five-minute walk from my house."

Smiling slightly, Tetsuyuki's mother asked, "Yōko, are you really going to marry Tetsuyuki?" Yōko nodded, but his mother shook her head.

"If I were your mother, I'd be dead set against it. For the next two or three years, we'll be paying off the debts his father left behind, and until we do that, marriage is out of the question. Our family consists of one mother and one child, we have no home, just a lot of debts. I would never let my daughter marry into a situation like that, and I'm sure your parents wouldn't either."

Yōko was about to say something when Tetsuyuki's mother cut her off. "Even if you make the decision now, in two or three years' time you might find someone else you like." Tetsuyuki and Yōko glanced at each other in silence. "And you can't imagine how thrilled I'd be to have a daughter-in-law like you, but such feelings are not the only basis for a marriage—we can only really be linked by karmic fate." At that point she paused and, tilting her prim face—the face that still suggested what

Tetsuyuki's father often said without exaggeration when he was drunk, "When your mother was young, she was a real beauty"—mumbled to no one in particular: "Everyone uses the word 'fate' without much thought, but it's a mysterious thing."

Yōko's nose was beginning to redden. Tetsuyuki, who knew that was a herald of her tears, felt eager to say something, but no words came out of his mouth. Yōko drooped her head and cried, barely audibly. Tetsuyuki thought that his mother's words had doused the flame of courage Yōko had mustered, but such was not the case.

"Without telling anyone, I went ahead and rented that place. I've paid both the deposit and rent. After graduation, Tetsuyuki and I will both work, and the three of us will live there."

This time, Tetsuyuki and his mother looked at each other with open mouths. "Where did you get the money for the deposit?" she asked.

"I added my money from part-time work to what I've saved since junior high school, and borrowed the rest from a cousin in Yokohama." Yōko's answer was delivered in a quivering voice, ending in muffled sobs and difficult to understand. Tetsuyuki's mother bent forward and wiped Yōko's tears with her handkerchief. Yōko raised her face and, with eyes closed like a child, allowed her face to be wiped.

"I'm glad I didn't have a daughter. You never know what they'll go and do when they grow up." With that, Tetsuyuki's mother stood up and, taking a savings passbook out of a dresser drawer, showed it to them. She had nearly 700,000 yen in her account.

"How did you save so much?"

"My net monthly pay is 110,000 yen, you see? But I don't have to pay for rent or food, so I've been able to save 100,000 yen each month."

"So then, you live on 10,000 a month?"

"Sometimes customers tip me. Some of them slip as much as 10,000 or 20,000 yen into the sleeve of my kimono." She shrugged. "I've always been good at squirreling money away . . . Such a quantity of tears!" Speaking as if in praise, she again leaned forward to wipe Yōko's face. Yōko giggled, but still kept pouring out tears endlessly.

Tetsuyuki's mother went along to see Yōko to the station. After parting at the ticket gate of the Hankyū Line, as he was walking alongside his mother Tetsuyuki recalled the blue eyes of Mr. and Mrs. Lang. These several months—or rather these several years—he had never run that desperately. Even during a tennis match he had never chased the ball with such heroic resolve. He was glad that he had made it in time to stop them. He did not want them to die. On no account should he have allowed them to die. His mother suddenly stopped walking, and Tetsuyuki stopped and looked at her.

"She's had a privileged upbringing, but I think that even to-morrow she'd be able to put off a bill collector." At his mother's words, Tetsuyuki's face brightened and he turned to her. "Any bill collector who encountered tears like that would hightail it."

9

By the time November came around, Kin would no longer eat anything. Tetsuyuki took *Reptiles of Japan* out of his bookcase and read the section "Keeping Lizards." A point of caution on raising them indoors stated that in place of sunlight an infrared lamp should be used; otherwise, they would lose appetite. He thought he had committed all of that to memory, but it had slipped his mind. It also stated that during the winter one feeding per week is sufficient.

Two weeks had passed since Kin stopped eating. Tetsuyuki thought perhaps he was just tired of chestnut weevil larvae and tried giving him ants or spiders he found in the weeds growing thick behind the building, but Kin would just blink and not open his mouth.

Having purchased an infrared lamp at a department store, as soon as he finished his shift Tetsuyuki hurried back along the cold path in the deep of night and immediately trained the light on Kin. Then an idea came to him and he took out a ruler to measure Kin's length: he was about one centimeter longer than the day he first appeared before Tetsuyuki.

"Kin-chan, you were still just a kid when I drove that nail through you." For nearly half an hour he continued to talk to the lizard in a soft voice. Like keeping a diary, it had become a daily routine for him to relate to Kin the events of each day and to talk about his own state of mind. The shabby attire of the laborer accompanying his child in the train and the awkward manner in which he had shown affection . . . The wealthy-looking woman in Osaka Station whose profile somehow suggested a lack of vitality . . . The spitefulness of the front-desk manager . . . The overbearing guests whose manner of tipping made him want to throw it back at them . . . The look that woman who worked at the grill would give him from a distance, and how it did not just seem to be his vain imagination . . .

And just as in a diary, fictionalizing was mixed in with his words. When he became aware of these embellishments, it seemed as if he were improvising a novel, assaulted at times by feelings of sorrow, elation, or anger.

"If I didn't have Yōko, maybe I'd have fallen for that woman at the grill. She moved to Osaka from Shimane Prefecture right after graduating from high school just to work at that hotel. Today, on the sly she brought me a steak fillet in piecrust that the cook had mistakenly made too many of, wrapped hidden in a napkin. I completely understood her motive, but still asked, 'Why are you bringing me this?' 'The cook gave it to me.' But that doesn't amount to an answer. Even so, I know exactly why

the cook gave it to her. She's too pretty to be working as a waitress at a grill. With a little polishing, she'd be a real knockout."

Tetsuyuki shut off the infrared lamp, thinking that sudden
long exposure might not be good for Kin. "Before I go to bed,
I'll turn it on for another ten minutes."

He spread out his futon and stared at the research materials
for his graduation thesis piled on the desk. The day at the end of
summer when he walked down Midōsuji Avenue through a violent downpour, getting soaking wet, suddenly came to mind, as
did the evening scene where he heard from Yōko's own mouth
of the existence of another man in her life. Yōko, who had been
meeting with that architectural designer Ishihama, mumbled
words that Tetsuyuki had not forgotten: "If I can't marry you,
then I'd want to marry him." And there was another suspicion
that stubbornly smoldered in his mind: Yōko denied it, but did
she really not have a physical relationship with that Ishihama?

Even though they had met many times since then, and
even as their love had increased and they had made seemingly
unbreakable promises to each other, that suspicion would suddenly well up. Though that incident was supposed to be behind
them, it could still generate incurable jealousy. On those occasions, he would think of Mr. and Mrs. Lang. It had no relationship to them, but every time jealousy and suspicion darkened
his mind there would arise in his thoughts the countenances
of that elderly German couple—expressing at the same time
resolution and helplessness—who had chosen a tea hut in the
quiet and elegant garden of a foreign land as their place to die.

"I wonder how those two are doing. Their son ended up

coming to Japan to pick them up, but I can't imagine that he's now living together with his parents in harmony in Munich. Human beings are all petty when it comes to feelings, and they won't let bygones be bygones, no matter how small the matter. But you're the same, too, aren't you, Kin? You haven't forgiven me, have you?"

Though he had just uttered the words "petty when it comes to feelings," when he thought of Yōko's having even briefly shifted her affections to another man, Tetsuyuki lost all sense of reason and, manipulated by that emotional scar, would imagine her naked in Ishihama's embrace.

"I'm a man, so I understand how other men's minds work, especially toward women. He put on the airs of a gentleman, but am I supposed to believe that he never laid a finger on Yōko when her feelings were inclined toward him? She'd rather die than admit it, though."

He again switched on the infrared lamp, and while Kin basked in it, he thought of the words he would like to hear from Yōko's mouth that would clear her of the suspicions he harbored. But he instantly realized that any words would be powerless: if you doubt, then any words are unbelievable, and even in the unlikely event that she were to confess to having been in Ishihama's embrace, he still would not be able to leave her.

Kin drank some water, but would not eat anything that night either. Tetsuyuki changed into his pajamas, turned off the light, and got under the quilts. As he looked at the faint glow from the curtains of the back window, a certain strategy occurred to him: he would get revenge on her. He would make her experience the same grief he had been feeling. He would torment her by creating a drama of his own affections shifting to another woman. An image flashed before him of a country girl, aware of her own beauty, whose ample, captivating breasts could seriously draw him away if he were not careful.

The next day, Tetsuyuki went earlier than usual to the employee cafeteria, because he knew that the grill cook, Nakae Yuriko, ate her dinner there an hour earlier than the other employees. Along with the other grill employees, Yuriko had finished eating and was washing the dishes. Having heaped rice into a plastic bowl, Tetsuyuki took one of the plates of side dishes set out near the sinks and whispered so that only Yuriko could hear, "Thanks for yesterday."

Yuriko nodded slightly, taking care that her coworkers not notice. Tetsuyuki motioned to her, then, setting his dish and bowl down on a table, left the cafeteria in the direction of the laundry room. He asked Yuriko, who came trotting up after him: "What time are you off today?"

"I came in early, so I'll finish at eight."

"Then I'll be waiting at the north entrance of Osaka Station at eight thirty."

". . . Why?"

Not giving the obvious response to her question, Tetsuyuki went on. "I'll wait ten minutes, and if you haven't come, I'll consider myself stood up and leave."

With that, he returned to the cafeteria with a quick pace. Picking with his chopsticks the sparse meat, carrots, and onion out of the sauce consisting more of clumps of starch than anything else, he downed his meal and then went up to the lobby to stand in his prescribed place near the front desk.

Most of the employees knew that next spring he would graduate and begin work as a permanent employee. Tsuruta, who until now had shown a spiteful attitude toward him, did a complete turnaround and began paying him compliments, sometimes even giving him cigarettes he had won at pachinko.

When Tsuruta returned to the lobby from showing some guests to their room, Tetsuyuki asked: "Please let me off early at eight. An uncle of mine is ill, and it seems he only has another two or three days. I'd like to meet with him while I still can." He had an aunt, but no uncles.

"That's going to be a bit of a problem. Today, we have two groups arriving: one American and one Taiwanese. But under the circumstances, I suppose it can't be helped." Tsuruta really did seem to be at a loss, but agreed anyway. Then, still standing abreast, he moved closer to Tetsuyuki and said, "Starting next month, Isogai will be moved to the general affairs office."

Tetsuyuki had been thinking that he should pay a get-well visit to Isogai, who had been suffering from his bad heart condition and had taken nearly a month off work.

"Is he better now?"

"Probably a bit better than he was. But in moving him to General Affairs, the management must have determined that work as a bellboy was too demanding physically."

It occurred to Tetsuyuki that perhaps Tsuruta would then be promoted to head of bellboys.

"Actually, in terms of years of service, he shouldn't have

been made head, but they made him head in order for him to avoid strenuous work."

"Who has the most years of service?"

"I do." The expression on Tsuruta's face seemed to say that the headship should have been his, but he had yielded it to sickly Isogai.

"Yes, but Isogai is older than you, isn't he?"

"True, but he was hired later." Then, twisting his acne-scarred face into an obsequious expression, he whispered, "You know, Iryō, you and I are the same age, so we ought to stick together after this."

Tetsuyuki thought to himself, *Don't worry. Even if I become a regular employee of this hotel and occupy a position above you, I won't repay your bullying.* Then he said, "No matter if we're the same age, you'll always be my senior." Pleased at that, Tsuruta smiled and gave Tetsuyuki's shoulder a congenial pat.

At seven thirty, a large tour bus arrived and seventy Americans crowded into the lobby. Tetsuyuki busied himself with the task of efficiently unloading the heavy travel bags from the bus. Foreigners' luggage—especially that of Americans—was always heavy, and although they lifted them easily with one hand, at first Tetsuyuki was barely able to move them with both. By now he had learned the knack of it—or perhaps he had developed a bit more strength in his arms—and he was able to take care of the luggage much more quickly than before.

At eight on the dot, Tsuruta informed him of the time. He changed his clothes and headed to the north entrance of Osaka Station. Standing by the stairs leading to the ticket gate of the

Hankyū Line, he waited for Yuriko. An elderly man with large rosary beads wrapped around his neck was dancing to the peculiar rhythm of what seemed to be some kind of sutra. Hardly anyone paid attention, but just gave him a glance that registered neither pity nor surprise.

The man suddenly pointed at Tetsuyuki and shouted, "You are a kindhearted egoist." He began to approach as if wanting to say more. Pretending not to have heard, Tetsuyuki escaped inside the station. He looked back to see that the man had abandoned his pursuit and was again dancing in the same place as before. Taking care not to be noticed, Tetsuyuki stealthily returned to wait and saw Yuriko coming toward him over the crosswalk.

"What time do you have to be back at your dormitory?"

"The curfew is ten, but nobody keeps it."

"Nobody?"

"Yeah. The caretaker shuts the gate and goes to bed. But it's easy to get in and out by ducking under the shrubs, and we've secretly hidden a master key to the front door in three places."

"In three places?"

A vaguely coquettish smile—one she would definitely not show at work—had gradually stolen over Yuriko's face. "All of us are accomplices in this crime."

"I see. So I guess you all colluded to make three copies of the master key?"

Walking abreast, they descended into the subterranean mall. As they were making their way through the crowds Tetsuyuki began to regret having put this strategy into action, sensing that this was likely to take a much more troublesome course than he had anticipated. He had no idea what kind of religion influenced the man he had just encountered, but it was amazing how accurately the guy had described his nature: "You are a kindhearted egoist." That was right on target; there could have been no more accurate analysis. But he sensed that within that brief phrase lay countless invectives: petty punk, hypocrite, show-off, coward, dimwit with balls smaller than a mite's, idiot who is easily blown about by anger, pain, jealously, and disappointment . . .

Tetsuyuki realized that his feelings of revenge toward Yōko were born from his own makeshift sense of self-esteem. He loved her deeply and more strongly than ever even as he walked with Yuriko. But for that very reason he wanted to inflict brief torment on Yōko. The words she spoke on that day when he confronted Ishihama in the tea lounge of the hotel were justifiable: "I'm only twenty-one. And I like it when a man makes a fuss over me. Is there anything wrong with that?" Now if she were to have those same kinds of words thrown back at her, even if she recognized that her partner's excuse was justifiable, she would know how depressing and wounding they were. *So, I'm a 'kindhearted egoist,' huh?* Tetsuyuki muttered in his mind with self-scorn. Then it occurred to him that Kin probably also held the same estimation of him.

Tetsuyuki and Yuriko went into a coffee shop. At first, she seemed awkward and ill-at-ease, but as they exchanged rambling chatter she loosened up. When he asked her if she would like to go see a movie on her day off, she nodded slightly.

"When is your next day off?"

"Day after tomorrow."

Friday, the day after tomorrow, he had three classes he absolutely had to attend. But two of those were with Yōko, and if she saw he was absent, she would probably ask some other male student to answer the roll call in his stead. She always did that for him. As he so conjectured, he looked at Yuriko, who suddenly appeared grave and aloof, nervously gazing down at her coffee cup.

Now that he had a closer look at her, he could see that she possessed far more beautiful features than he had noticed with the stolen glances at her from the entrance to the grill or in the hallway. Her eyes had a brownish cast, and her nose was well defined. Once in a collection of photographs from the Silk Road he had seen a picture of a Chinese girl who had a slight admixture of Western blood, and Yuriko reminded him of that image. As they talked, he learned that she had been orphaned when she was in middle school. She explained that her mother had died when she was five years old, and that her father was killed by a tornado.

"A tornado?"

"Yeah, a tornado. Behind the paddy, there was a shed for insecticide and fertilizer. A typhoon was approaching, so Dad went out to drive stakes to keep the shed from falling over. And then a tornado rushed in and smashed the shed to pieces, and a splinter of wood pierced his neck . . ."

"The typhoon hadn't hit yet, had it?"

"It hadn't, but a tornado suddenly formed. From the window I watched as it advanced directly toward the shed where Dad was."

"Any brothers or sisters?"

"No, none." She mentioned that her father had remarried three years after her mother died, but no children came. "I couldn't stand my stepmother, and she didn't seem to like me either. After I came to Osaka, she went back to her parents' house. I've never so much as sent her a postcard, and have heard nothing from her either."

"You don't look like a farm girl from Shimane Prefecture."

"Why's that?"

"Because you have the face of someone with some Russian ancestry: light-skinned, well-defined features, and very pretty."

It had not been meant as a compliment; Tetsuyuki simply spoke his mind. Yuriko's eyes moistened, and her gestures meant to conceal her pleasure only made it all the more obvious. This aroused his desire, and it occurred to him that, if he wanted to, she could be his in a few more hours. But he smothered his desires. Yuriko was simply a prop in his strategy, to be used as well as any woman other than Yōko. As such thoughts ran through his mind, Yuriko broke the silence.

"Farm girls from Shimane would be furious to hear you say something like that."

"Why?"

"Because that's like saying that there are no beauties among them."

Having agreed to meet at the same coffee shop two days hence, they parted at the intersection of two subterranean arcades.

He arrived at Suminodō Station forty minutes earlier than

216

usual. Ordinarily, he boarded the 11:03 train bound for Shi-jōnawate at Kyōbashi, and immediately called Yōko from the pay phone in front of the station at Suminodō. But he decided that, for the time being, he would not place those calls, which her mother had dubbed "scheduled service." The first matter of business for him was to take a suspicious course of action and raise doubts in her mind. Tomorrow at the university, she would probably ask why he hadn't called, and he would tell her in an unnatural tone of voice something that would be an obvious lie. For example, that the pay phone was broken, or that he didn't have any change on him. Yōko would be sure to think: "If the pay phone in front of the station was broken, there's one in the shopping arcade, isn't there? Or one just before you cross the tracks, or one in front of the little grilled chicken shop just beyond that? And if you don't have small change, you could just use the change machine by the ticket-vending machines in the station. Isn't that what you always do?" And maybe she wouldn't just think those things; she might say them in reproach. If she did, then he would again assume an unnatural expression and make an excuse. Just as he had sniffed out the existence of another man in her life by observing her behavior, she would also be filled with the same kind of anxiety. Tetsuyuki turned down the dark country lane, blown by chilly winds, and arrived at the lane lined with jerry-built two-story houses.

When he turned on the light, Kin thrashed his legs about. For a few minutes this morning before setting out, Tetsuyuki had trained the infrared lamp on the lizard, and it seemed that perhaps Kin had regained some strength. He patted Kin's head.

As he switched on the lamp again, there was a knock at the door. Tetsuyuki tensed.

"Yes?" Gooseflesh down his spine had become a conditioned response for Tetsuyuki when he heard a knock at the door in the middle of the night.

"This is Kurachi, from next door. Sorry to bother you so late." It was a thin, female voice. Tetsuyuki stuck his head out the kitchen window. His neighbor who lived alone again apologized for troubling him at such an hour, but wondered if he could lend her a hand.

"What is it?"

"My refrigerator tipped over, and I can't set it back up by myself."

Tetsuyuki turned off the infrared lamp and stepped out in front of the woman's apartment. She was so thin as to arouse pity, walked with an awkward gait, and both wrists were swollen and bent. Her neatly arranged room was filled with the smell of medicinal infusions. A white cat was curled up on a red cushion.

She had purchased a new cupboard and wanted to put it where the refrigerator was, and to move the refrigerator over beside the stove. But the wheels on the bottom of the refrigerator were rusted and would not move, and as soon as she gave it a strong push it ended up tipping over. It wasn't very large, and Tetsuyuki was able to set it up without her assistance.

Bending over and pushing it from the bottom, he moved it next to the stove. While he was at it, he also moved the cupboard to the refrigerator's former place. Blinking her beadlike eyes, she thanked him profusely. Though he demurred, she poured a cup of tea, brought out some cookies, and placed them on a round table. Tetsuyuki reluctantly sat on the cushion she set out for him and sipped the tea, but did not touch the cookies.

"What Chinese medicine are you making an infusion of?"

The woman responded that she had been suffering from rheumatism for nearly ten years. She asked where he was from, apparently supposing that he had moved to Osaka from the countryside in order to attend college.

"I was born and raised in Osaka."

After some hesitation she asked as she looked at her pet, "Has my cat ever relieved itself in your room?"

"In my room?"

"During the summer, I sometimes saw my cat coming out your back window. It seems that it got in by following the water pipes from my apartment to yours."

Last summer, seeing how desiccated and wilted Kin looked, Tetsuyuki sometimes left the back window open. Even if a thief broke in, there was nothing worth stealing anyway.

"No, nothing like that ever happened." The moment he answered, he realized that the cat had entered his room aiming for Kin. As far as he could recall, he had left the back window open about twenty times, and each time Kin was no doubt paralyzed with fear. That thought made his heart feel heavy.

Returning to his room and switching on the infrared lamp, he glanced up at Kin, about even on the pillar with his own head. The cat no doubt jumped many times, aiming for the lizard, and probably even tried climbing. Inspecting the pillar closely, there remained definite claw marks. In his absence, Kin, unable to move and helpless, endured persistent attempted assaults by a cat. How terrified he must have been. The words of that man at the station came to mind: "You are a kindhearted egoist." Those words turned into a shower of accusations raining down on him. The terror Kin must have felt resonated in Tetsuyuki's heart, turning him into a lizard nailed to a pillar.

That white cat slipped in through the back window, and Tetsuyuki struggled, trying to flee, but was unable to move. The cat's claws reached almost to his tail. Digging its claws into the wood, the cat climbed after him, sliding down and then repeating its attempt. After the cat gave up and left, Tetsuyuki despised the guy who had nailed him there, who had left him there like that and given him food and water, which he had no choice but to accept. He thought of himself suffering from thirst and fear in this suffocating room, and yet unable to die. Why was he alive?

Coming back to his senses, Tetsuyuki opened the box of larvae. Kin finally ate one.

"I'm going to save you if it's the last thing I do. When spring comes, I'll pull that nail out. You might die, but I'm going to pull it out. If you die, you'll never come back as a lizard. Next time, you'll be reborn as a human."

Tetsuyuki meant every word of what he said, though it espoused neither logic nor any scientific principle of the genesis of life. Only a vague sense of the mysteriousness of life produced in him that absurd conviction, one that told him of the existence of a thick nail piercing his own back.

Images of his mother, Yōko, Isogai, Yuriko, the lady next door, Mr. and Mrs. Lang, Sawamura Chiyono . . . all emerged in the back of his mind. And all of them were smiling at him with nails piercing their backs. All of them were suffering from these nails but knew of no way to pull them out, and moreover were afraid of the pain if they *were* extracted. A sense of nihilism and resignation sapped all of his energy. Sluggishly he spread out his futon and lay down in bed without even brushing his teeth. He turned off the infrared lamp, and then the light in the room, mumbling to himself a few phrases from *Lamenting the Deviations*, which so infatuated Nakazawa:

> "Since I could never succeed in any austerities, hell will surely be my final abode.
>
> "We, who are so completely in the thrall of our passions, cannot free ourselves from the cycle of birth and death through any sort of austerities. Amida took pity on us, and the intention of his Original Vow was to bring buddhahood to the wicked, and thus the wicked who plead for his grace are the real reason for the Vow to bring salvation.
>
> "But even if we are reluctant to part from it, when our bonds to this earthly existence are severed and we are bereft of all strength, we shall go to that Pure Land. Amida takes special pity on those who feel that they are in no rush to get there."

"So, 'I could never succeed in any austerities,' huh? I'm one of 'the wicked who plead for his grace,' huh? So he 'takes special pity on those who feel that they are in no rush to get there,' huh?" Tetsuyuki was not able in these phrases to sense any encouragement to live. If one peeled away their veneer, even words that at first spoke to a perfect enlightenment seemed to be only the sophistries of someone who has given up on life. Tetsuyuki harbored a hatred for whatever incited people toward death. *In that case, there'd be no point in struggling to live. We should all just die, shouldn't we? And what exactly is 'that Pure Land'? Where is it? Show it to me. Even if you went to the far reaches of the universe, would you find such a place? It's right here inside me. I've seen it many times. No matter how many times I try to escape, no matter how many times I die, I can't go beyond this universe.*

Tetsuyuki had once seen on television a well-known intellectual who claimed that *Lamenting the Deviations* had given him the wherewithal to go on living. But no matter how he tried, Tetsuyuki was not able to sense any spirit in that man, who seemed somehow enervated and not at all happy. Hadn't resignation simply replaced a desire to live? What a string of words it was that so enchanted intellectuals! And all concealing poison that ultimately entices one toward death!

He considered the feelings of nihilism and resignation that he himself harbored and resolved to live. The Kin that inhabited his heart shone bright gold. He wanted to see Yōko. He longed for her body, and wanted to quit this ridiculous farce he had started. He groped his crotch and began to indulge in masturbation, playing with himself for a long time. His masturbatory fantasy did not include Yōko, but rather the nude pink body of Yuriko, which he had never seen.

The next day, Tetsuyuki was on campus. When he threw a teasing smile at a familiar couple snuggling up to each other on the no longer green lawn under a single duffel coat, he heard Yōko's voice. He looked about, but she was nowhere to be seen. Unusually, there was a large number of students around then. No doubt many were seniors who had rarely been on campus and were coming up against graduation, so they could not afford to miss more lectures and had begun to show up en masse. He turned toward the main gate, glancing at the closest building, housing the Engineering Department.

He again heard Yōko's voice calling his name, and looking at the expression of the couple sitting beneath the duffel coat, a smile spread across his face: Yōko was hiding behind them. He hurriedly extinguished his smile and walked across the lawn to address the lovebirds.

"Hey, what're you doing inside that coat? It must be some indecent act."

"We're just holding hands," the female student responded.

"Well, that already amounts to having sex."

The male student responded with a laugh. "I think the one who's hiding behind us and sweetly calling out 'Tetsuyuki!' is even more indecent."

Yōko stood up from behind them and knocked the guy on the head with her textbook. She pressed against Tetsuyuki's arm, wrapping hers around it.

The male student gibed, "Hey, you two look as if you already have two or three kids."

"A virgin can't have kids, can she?" The couple burst out laughing at Tetsuyuki's riposte.

As they walked off arm in arm, just as expected Yōko asked, "Why didn't you call last night?"

Tetsuyuki deliberately looked in another direction. "I didn't have any ten-yen coins."

"You could have gotten change, couldn't you?"

"I only had a thousand-yen bill with me. I asked for change at two or three stores, but they all refused."

"I stayed up until two o'clock waiting. After all, you've never failed to call . . ."

"Yes, I have. Those several weeks during the summer . . ."

Yōko released her arm from his and stood still. "Why say something like that?"

"I wanted to call, and went up and down the shopping arcade. Everyone had an attitude as if to say, 'If you'll buy something, I'll give you change.' That got under my skin. I was about to buy some gum or something, but gave up on that idea." As he spoke, Tetsuyuki renewed his resolve to stop this silly charade, and turned toward her to apologize. But Yōko's eyes were unexpectedly full of indignation.

"What's that supposed to mean, 'those several weeks during the summer'? Why are you bringing that up now?"

Why did Yōko flare up at the mention of those several weeks? It must be because there was something between her and Ishihama that she refused to admit. That thought made him abandon his resolve. *I'll create several blank weeks, then.*

Without saying a word, he entered the building of the Literature Department and climbed the stairs to the classroom. Yōko, likewise silent, climbed the stairs five or six steps behind him and took a seat far from his, though they always sat together. She was wearing a light blue dress. As the lecture was nearing its end, a slip of paper from her was passed down the row: "Are you hungry?" When he went without eating, his nerves would be on edge, and he had frequently lashed out at her, saying unreasonable and selfish things.

And here she was extending an olive branch. All he would have to do was smile and nod at her, and this petty skirmish would be over. And he wanted to do so. And yet the fact that she was so much more fixed on those "several weeks during the summer" left him unable to abandon his suspicions.

Instead of nodding at her with a smile, he stood up and exited the classroom, his face turned away. Expecting her to come running after him, he descended the stairs and passed through the dimly lit hallway to exit the building. As he approached the main gate he kept his ears pricked, but was unable to discern anything like her footsteps.

He arrived at the hotel, and even as he was changing into his uniform—even as he was carrying luggage and showing guests to rooms—he rehearsed in his mind words he had hurled at Ishihama, and the expression on that man's face. "Even as I had

Yōko in my arms, I gloated as I imagined a guy name Ishihama walking triumphantly toward the hotel. But he was probably gloating in his own mind as he listened to what I said, thinking 'What a stupid jerk! I've already had plenty of fun with Yōko's body.'" Those imagined words felt very real, as if an actual human voice were assaulting his eardrums. He ended up passing Yuriko several times without so much as glancing at her. It wasn't that he hadn't noticed her; he was trying to act indifferent. He had lost the composure to respond to the signals she was sending.

About an hour before his shift ended, he stepped out of the hotel and called three friends from a pay phone, asking them to answer the roll call for him at tomorrow's lectures. All three asked why he did not have Yōko do it. He replied that it would be found out if he always had her do it, but that didn't really amount to a reply, because she always asked those three to answer the roll call for him anyway.

When Tetsuyuki returned to the front desk of the hotel, a middle-aged guest was grabbing Nakaoka by the lapels and shouting in a loud, angry voice. He was well dressed and wasn't under the influence of alcohol, but from his language it was obvious that he was a gangster. That guest had arrived just past eight, accompanied by a young woman. It was Tetsuyuki who had shown them to their room, so he knew that the man had made a reservation two weeks previously, and that at check-in he had written the woman's name as "wife: Mitsuko." He also knew the man's address and occupation. And he also knew that all of it was false. Tetsuyuki had gotten so that he could tell at a glance whether or not a couple was actually married. Where he had written his address, what was supposed to have been "To-kyo, Itabashi Ward" contained a mistaken character, and was "Sakabashi Ward" instead. Moreover, no real gallery director when shown to his room would say of the 3,000- or 4,000-yen reproductions hanging on the wall: "These are some very fine pictures you have."

In the lobby, a crowd of guests had come to a standstill with stunned looks on their faces, and so the manager rushed up, say-ing politely that he would like to discuss the matter in the office.

The man boomed out in an even louder voice, "Seems this hotel has some thieves on its staff, doesn't it?" He claimed that after finishing his meal at the grill, he returned to his room to find that one of his three pieces of luggage was missing. "The hotel has a master key that opens any room, right?"

Since Tetsuyuki had begun to work there, this was the third time a gangster had used the same trick to extort money from the hotel. Receiving a meaningful glance from the man-ager, Tetsuyuki went to the office of the guest room manager on the twelfth floor and, picking up a master key, then stood in front of the door to the man's room. A woman's voice answered his knocking.

"The gentleman who accompanied you said that you are missing a piece of luggage. May we please come in and check?"

"I don't have anything on right now. If you're going to check the room, I want you to do that later when he's here."

Tetsuyuki waited for the plainclothes guard employed by the hotel. He soon came, and, smiling, whispered to Tetsuyuki that he had ascertained that the two of them had gone nowhere but the grill after checking in. "This is an old trick they're using." With that, he used the master key to open the door quickly. Panicked, the woman tried to slip into the bathroom, but the guard caught her by the arm.

"What're you doing, bursting in on a woman who's alone? I'll call the police!"

"This man is a detective."

At Tetsuyuki's explanation, the woman shot back, "Then show me your identification!"

"If we don't find the missing luggage in this room, then I'll be happy to show it to you." With that, the guard went into the bathroom and pounded the ceiling with the back of his hand. After pounding a few times, he grabbed the woman by the hair. "That was damned naïve of you to try a trick like that. If you're going to practice extortion, how about thinking of something more original?"

In a corner of the bathroom next to an opening for ventilation there was a passage—ordinarily covered by a panel fastened with four screws—large enough for a person to crawl in and make repairs. Using a screwdriver, the guard removed the panel and reached in, pulling out a hidden black leather attaché case. Calling from the telephone next to the bed, Tetsuyuki informed the front desk.

"Let me tell you for your future reference: for this kind of extortion, you can't cut corners. Pretend that you're just going out somewhere, put the piece of luggage in a paper bag or something and go get rid of it, far away. If a guest did that to us, there'd be nothing we could do about it, since we're in a service business. Of course, it would make us look bad in front of other guests and would hurt our image, but it could be smoothed over with polite words and chump change. The longest anyone's ever gotten away with cheating us has been six days. Amateurs like you wouldn't last two days."

Snickering, the woman threw herself on the bed and lit a cigarette. The guard had to keep watch over her until the real police arrived. Leaving the door open, Tetsuyuki returned the master key to the guest-room manager and went down to the front desk. The lobby had returned to its usual peaceful state. A newlywed couple, drinking orange juice costing 1,200 yen per glass, was gazing at a small Japanese garden with an artificial stream and waterwheel outside the window.

"It won't always be idiots like the ones today. There's no telling what kind of ingenious trick someone might think of. Take plenty of caution with a guest that seems suspicious," Tetsuyuki overheard the manager warning the staff at the desk. Appearing to have had his necktie tugged rather forcefully, some long welts had risen on Nakaoka's slender neck. In an ill-tempered tone of voice, he called for Tetsuyuki.

"A little while ago, a woman came to see you. Since we were in the middle of all that, we sent her away, but it creates a problem when bellboys meet with their friends at the front desk. If it's an urgent matter, please have them come to the office through the rear entrance."

"Was she wearing a light blue dress?"

"I didn't notice what she was wearing, but I think it was light blue."

Since the police had arrived, Nakaoka went into the office, rubbing the welts on his neck. Tetsuyuki could picture Yōko's dejected face as she left the hotel and walked toward the ticket gate of the Hankyū Line. That one line she had written on the scrap of paper came to his mind, words so brimming with love that it made his heart ache: "Are you hungry?"

He tried to crush his feelings of jealousy. Just as she had said, it would be strange if a young woman were not moved when a handsome man makes a fuss over her, wouldn't it? Is there something wrong with that? And even if Yōko was in Ishihama's embrace many times during that void of "several weeks during the summer," what of it? She's no saintly woman. "What a petty, base person I am to dredge up what I should have just let go, and to be consumed by this sinister desire for revenge."

He glanced at the clock. Nearly forty minutes had passed since the commotion with the gangster. Maybe Yōko would be arriving home about now. That thought made him restless. Dashing out of the hotel, he entered a phone booth. But he had used all his change to call his three friends, and didn't have a single coin left. Smoothing out a 1,000-yen bill he ran toward a tobacconist's shop. As he was running, the thought flashed through his mind: *She knows me so well, yet she could still let her feelings shift to another man! Even as I was so tormented by that, every day I rode that dirty train back to a room inhabited by a lizard.*

At that thought he stuffed the money back into his pocket and turned around. The tremendous honking of a taxicab resounded in the night street. The extremely irate driver honked incessantly. To Tetsuyuki, it was like a factory's siren, signaling the end of his work for the day.

In a bookstore next to the coffee shop where he had agreed to meet Yuriko, Tetsuyuki leafed through the pages of various magazines. He felt it a bother to have to go to a movie with her, and he was uncertain how he should deal with her afterward.

"I don't mind if you glance through something, but I can't do business when people stand here and read entire issues the way you do." The proprietress of the bookstore was addressing a high school student in another section of the store who was absorbed in a manga book, but her words prompted two or three college students to leave also. Tetsuyuki likewise returned the magazines to the rack and exited. It was already more than a half hour past the time they were to meet.

He reluctantly pushed open the door of the coffee shop and recognized Yuriko's bowed profile, which reflected an image of loneliness and helplessness and caused some agitation in his mind. What agitated him even more, however, was the expression of unfeigned joy and relief on her face the moment she looked up at him.

"I had to cut three classes today, so I've been making phone calls to friends to ask them to answer the roll call for me. That's why I'm late. Sorry . . ."

"I was thinkin' you'd be a no-show." It was the first time Tetsuyuki had hear her speak in her home dialect. Realizing that herself, she covered her mouth and blushed.

"Why? I'm the one who invited you, so of course I'd show up."

Yuriko added some milk to her untouched coffee, which had grown cold, stirring it with a spoon.

"You don't add sugar?"

"That's right."

"Because you don't want to gain weight?"

"Yeah." Then Yuriko mentioned that it was her day off, but asked what he had arranged.

"I'm still just a part-timer, so I can take days off when I want. Tsuruta will get on my case about it later, though."

Lowering her voice, Yuriko informed him that Tsuruta would soon be forced to quit. In the basement of the hotel there were five exclusive shops specializing in imported goods. From about a year ago, French handbags and Danish silverware had been disappearing. Of course, the showcases were locked even when the shops were open, and at closing time the glass doors were also locked. And yet goods were disappearing, not in large quantities, but in small amounts and over time, so that the owners were not at first aware.

But when they checked sales receipts against their inventory, it became apparent that seven or eight items that had not been sold were missing from the showcases. If it were only one shop, the employees there might come under suspicion. But since all five shops had suffered loss, it was obvious that the criminal was among the hotel employees, the conclusion being reached that an outsider would naturally steal a large quantity all at once, not one thing at a time over an extended period.

232

Thus the hotel management checked its employees' attendance book against the dates when the items seem to have disappeared, and Tsuruta's name came up as the one on night duty at those times. All this came to light five days ago, and Tsuruta was on night shift tonight.

"Tonight, from about two a.m., guards will be hiding out in the basement."

"Who told you this?"

After some hesitation, Yuriko answered. "Nakaoka, at the front desk. He's an upperclassman from the high school I went to."

"That's not the only reason, is it? He's in love with an underclassman from his high school, and she's well aware of it. That inspires me all the more to contend with a rival." It was a mystery even to Tetsuyuki why such insincere, honeyed words should slip so casually from his lips. He realized what a bind it was putting him in, but he let slip out another phrase as if he were some kind of genius at womanizing. "This is no time for something so idle as watching a movie."

A smile so slight one would need to strain one's eyes to see it was playing on Yuriko's lips. Tetsuyuki was somewhat surprised to sense that she probably had carnal experience with men, but this also brought a strange feeling of relief. What was the quickest way to make Yuriko—this woman possessing both earthiness and a peculiar seductiveness—yield to him? He stood up, paid for the coffee, and then went out into the subterranean mall. A casual remark Tsuruta had made to him about six months ago came to mind.

"That idiot Nakaoka! Whenever he's on night shift, he puts me on the same shift too. Then he has me keep watch on the front desk while he goes to take a nap for two or three hours. And if I refuse, he'll dump all kinds of grueling work on me."

With a start, Tetsuyuki asked Yuriko, "It was a year ago that things began to turn up missing, wasn't it?"

"Yeah, that seems about right."

"But how far back did they check the attendance book?"

"Hmm, he didn't mention that . . ."

Yuriko was surprised when Tetsuyuki bought tickets at the movie theater, but she followed him inside and sat next to him. The movie had been heavily advertised, but it turned out to be nothing more than a trivial love game among American adolescents. Pretending to need to use the restroom, he went to a pay phone next to the concession stand and called Tsuruta.

"You're on night shift today, aren't you?"

"Yeah, that's right."

"You once mentioned, didn't you, that whenever Nakaoka was on the night shift, he made you work it too?"

"Yeah, but not tonight."

"After making you change your schedule and work on the night shift, did he ever treat you to meals or take you out for drinks?"

"What's up? Did something happen that you're calling me all of a sudden and asking off-the-wall questions?"

Tetsuyuki said he would explain everything tomorrow, and pressed him to answer.

"Well, he took me out for a drink two or three times."

Reminding Tsuruta never to tell anyone about this conversation, Tetsuyuki added, "No matter what errand Nakaoka gives you, you absolutely must not go down to the basement tonight." Tsuruta kept asking why, but he finally sensed the gravity of the situation from the tone of Tetsuyuki's voice.

"Okay, I won't go down to the basement tonight. I don't know what this is all about, but I'll do as you say. But tomorrow you've got to explain all of this to me."

With that, he hung up. Judging from Tsuruta's reaction, Tetsuyuki was certain he was not the culprit. As he sat in the smoking area, the thought came to him that this affair was about to become more complicated. It was unlikely that Nakaoka would ever again steal into the import shops in the basement, and the hotel would settle the matter by paying for the stolen goods rather than reporting it to the police.

But whether the ruse used by that gangster last night, or Nakaoka's scheme to set Tsuruta up as a criminal—both were childish. People end up making fools of themselves as soon as they let their fears run ahead of them. It was odd that even Nakaoka, reputed to be a prodigy among the younger employees, did not understand that if Tsuruta were to be arrested tonight by a guard lying in wait, it would rather serve to expose his own guilt.

At first, Tsuruta would be treated as guilty, but after hearing him out and once again checking the attendance book, Nakaoka's name was bound to come up. And if they checked it back thoroughly to a year ago rather than just six months, then Tsuruta's name would vanish and Nakaoka's would remain.

As he was pondering these things, it occurred to Tetsuyuki that perhaps Yuriko and Nakaoka were in a deep relationship, and that moreover Yuriko knew of Nakaoka's guilt. Or perhaps the two were complicit in the crime. If that were the case, then what was the meaning of the look she gave him? The lustful feelings he had felt for her vanished without a trace.

Tetsuyuki tried mapping out in his mind the factional strife within the hotel as far as he had been able to grasp it. The company president was already seventy-nine years old, and was for the most part confined to his home in Ashiya as his chronic ailment of sciatica worsened. According to rumors, a replacement would be appointed at next year's stockholders' meeting. There were two vice presidents, and both were his sons, but the president did not have much confidence in the business acumen of the elder of the two, and wanted to be succeeded by the younger one, who had more of a knack for practical affairs. Ever since summer a bitter battle had ensued behind the scenes between supporters of these two. Most of those occupying the senior positions were on the side of the younger brother: the manager, Imoto, the head of personnel, Shimazaki, head of dining services . . . all directly connected with the practical affairs of the hotel. Opposing them, such parties as the chief of the business office, the chief of the general affairs office, and the like were carrying the banner of support for the older brother. Tetsuyuki sighed and stood up, recalling that he had once heard Tsuruta say, "Nakaoka works at the front desk, but he's the pet of the head of the business office."

"I get it. Nakaoka isn't so stupid that he'd pilfer bracelets and handbags." Tetsuyuki unconsciously mumbled these words aloud. Was it a big gamble to wave a flag of righteousness at the stockholders' meeting after piling up black marks against responsible parties in the faction supporting the younger brother? Well, that was the only hand they had left to play in order to make the older brother president, Tetsuyuki told himself. He thought that glance of Yuriko's was probably suggested to her by Nakaoka. If it could be shown that someone whom Section Chief Shimazaki had recommended for employment without even being formally tested for the position—who before even formally being employed—had seduced a female employee, then it would disgrace not only Shimazaki but those over him as well. And if a bellboy were committing theft and gangsters were extorting money, then the responsibility would lie with the manager.

Tetsuyuki returned to his seat.

"What's wrong? You were gone a long time, weren't you?" Yuriko asked in a low voice. Keeping his eyes on the screen, Tetsuyuki leaned over to Yuriko's ear.

"I just called Tsuruta to warn him not to go down to the basement tonight, or he'll fall into Nakaoka's trap. And Tsuruta warned me not to get carried away and touch you, or I'd fall into the same trap."

The image on the screen was reflected with distortion in both of Yuriko's eyes. Grabbing her by the wrist, Tetsuyuki hurried back to the bench in the smoking area.

"I don't care if it spoils my chances for employment at the hotel. I feel I'd like to take you to some cheap hotel and sleep with you, but do you think Nakaoka is going to marry you? You made a bad bet. You'll let a milksop like Nakaoka have his fun with you, and then you'll be dumped."

Yuriko glared at him for an uncannily long time, finally saying, "I have no wish to marry Nakaoka. I'm the one who's having fun with him. If that weren't the case, then I wouldn't have told you what's going to happen tonight."

Ignoring her, Tetsuyuki began to walk down the hallway of the theater. Behind him came Yuriko's voice, "I've really come to like you."

Unfazed, he continued walking.

"I'm going to go to the hotel right now and tell everyone that you raped me." Tetsuyuki came to a standstill and turned around. "Even if it's a lie, everyone will believe me because I'm a woman."

"I'm not bluffing. I really don't care if it turns out that I can't get hired there." Tetsuyuki was overcome with a strange sense of wretchedness as he spoke those words.

"I really do like you, and I was waiting for you to ask me out. That has nothing to do with Nakaoka. He knows nothing about our date today."

Tetsuyuki was about to respond, but just said "Goodbye" and walked out of the theater. A gentle rain was falling. Perhaps Yuriko really meant what she said. But the more he sensed that she meant it, the more his feelings for her withered. And so did his feeling that she had been nothing more than a prop in his scheme for revenge on Yōko. And so did his fear that one misstep might have resulted in a new object of his love.

238

That night, Tetsuyuki took the Hankyū Line to Mukonosō Station. He was so impatient that he misdialed three times, and finally said to Yōko, "I surrender. There's no way I could ever claim victory over you."

"Where are you now?"

"At Mukonosō Station."

Five minutes had not passed before he saw her running toward him.

"What do you mean that you 'surrender'?" Yōko asked as she tried to catch her breath.

"I was fighting a unilateral war."

"With . . . ?"

"With myself."

Yōko took him to the two-story house she had rented, unbeknownst to her parents. Both the bathtub and the toilet had been polished to a shine, over the windows were hung curtains she had sewn herself, and a small chest of drawers had been placed in the upstairs six-mat room. Yōko crouched down behind him.

"Say you're sorry!"

"What for?"

"For dredging up that stuff about the summer . . ."

"No."

"Why?"

Tetsuyuki brought her around in front of him and, with her in his embrace, lay down on the floor as he pressed her to talk. "You explain to me everything that happened during those few weeks of the summer. How many times did you meet with Ishihama?"

"Two or three times."

"That's all?"

Yōko nodded.

"And it's true that nothing went on between you?"

Suddenly shaking her head furiously, she pushed him away and, retreating to a corner of the room, tears welled up in her eyes.

"I don't like you when you ask me things like that."

"Because there's something you don't like to be asked about?"

"Idiot!"

"Well, then tell me in a way that will persuade me."

"No matter how many times I say it, you won't give up."

"Then nothing went on between you?"

"Nothing!"

"I don't like the way you say that. As if you find saying it a bother. How about putting your heart into it when you say it? This is the only thing you're inconsiderate about."

"Nothing went on. We didn't even hold hands."

Tetsuyuki got down on all fours and, like a puppy, nestled his head against Yōko's breast.

"I have a feeling that even after we're married, you're going to keep bringing this up." Mumbling those words, she began to bite his lips.

10

The New Year arrived. Many families were spending the holiday in the hotel, and both the full-time and the part-time bellboys were on duty, lodging in the napping room between December 30 and January 3. There were no vacancies, and the grill, the coffee shop, the bar, and the room service staff were all frenetically taking orders and working longer hours than usual.

In the early afternoon of January 3, Tetsuyuki finished carrying all the luggage of the guests who checked out en masse. Returning to the bellboy room, he found Tsuruta indicating by the way he held the cigarette in his mouth how impatiently he had been waiting. Motioning for him to come closer, Tsuruta's eyes glinted as he whispered in Tetsuyuki's ear. "They've decided to fire that bastard Nakaoka."

Taken aback, Tetsuyuki gave Tsuruta a hard look. He grabbed him by the sleeve of his uniform and pulled him to the passageway between the kitchen and the laundry room.

"Did you blab? You promised to keep it a secret, didn't you?" Tetsuyuki was suppressing his anger. It was, after all, only his personal inference that Nakaoka was the probable culprit, and he had reminded Tsuruta never to tell anyone about it.

"Yeah, but there was no way I could avoid talking about it, was there? You'll be all right, because you had nothing to do with it. But I was under suspicion. The only way I could defend my innocence was to have them check the attendance record once more. Your suspicions turned out to be right. My name was cleared, and Nakaoka's was the only one remaining. It was a lifesaver. Without that, I'd have remained under suspicion and would've lost my job here. That idiot Nakaoka! He got what he had coming."

To be sure, Tsuruta's excuse was reasonable, but Tetsuyuki somehow felt like a criminal as he leaned against the overheated concrete wall of the passageway. His forehead was perspiring. Tsuruta continued.

"That bastard Nakaoka was cocky at first. Even when he was being grilled by the head of personnel and the manager and had the attendance book shoved in his face, he was cool as a cucumber. I suppose he thought the fatso party would come to his aid."

Of the company president's two sons, the elder was corpulent while the younger was tall and lean, and so in private the employees referred to the two factions as the "fatso party" and the "beanpole party."

"The beanpole party pulled off a major stunt while Nakaoka was in a situation where he couldn't get in touch with anyone in the fatso party. The beanpole phoned the fat guy's home, and placed the call directly himself. They had pressed the beanpole, saying that Nakaoka had confessed that the fatso put him up to it, and asked, 'Is that true?' But he replied that his older brother couldn't possibly do anything like that, and if it were true, the hotel would have no choice but to request that the police conduct a thorough investigation, and brace itself for the disgrace to its reputation. And this was the fat guy's measured response."

Rivulets of sweat were running down Tsuruta's forehead. As if he were a cop who had busted a criminal, he continued. "'We can't very well keep a thief like that. Let's sack him. What possible reason would exist for me to have an employee enter my own hotel and steal goods from a shop? Nakaoka's not only a thief, but appears to be insane as well.' And so that was the end of the Nakaoka affair."

"You're really in on all the details, aren't you? How is it that a bellboy like you knows all the dealings of the top brass in this company?"

Looking up at Tetsuyuki, Tsuruta twisted his lips in a laugh. "Since you helped me out, I'll tell you, but don't mention this to anyone." Thus prefacing his remarks, he proceeded slowly. "I have a very surprising source of information."

"Who?"

"Yuriko, the grill girl."

"Yuriko!"

"I've slept with her many times," Tsuruta said with a note of pride, then added, "but she's this to the head of the business office, who's with the fatso party." Tsuruta extended and retracted several times the pinkie he thrust in front of Tetsuyuki's face——a suggestive gesture. "You pretty much get what I mean, don't you?"

"Get what?" Tetsuyuki asked indifferently. He no longer cared. He just wanted to get out of that hot passageway as soon as possible.

"That the head of the business office only pretends to be with the fatso party, but is really a spy for the beanpole party."

Tetsuyuki thought to himself as he smiled at Tsuruta: *This guy may look like a dope, but he's pretty shrewd.* So then it was Miyake Minoru, the good-looking head of the business office, who deserved the greatest credit for getting the idiots of the fatso party to approve of the execution of this childish plot, using roundabout means to make Nakaoka into his stooge and putting the beanpole party in control to determine the next company president. *Even this guy is able to understand that much.*

Tsuruta was puzzled by Tetsuyuki's silent smile. "What's so funny?"

"No matter which way this turns out, there's no more hope for your career advancement."

"Why's that?"

"Yuriko's the kind of woman who'll sleep with anyone: with Nakaoka, with you . . . and with the head of the business office, who knew a long time ago that she was sleeping with Nakaoka and you. And that's why he devised this tactic of turning Nakaoka into a thief and then casting suspicion on you. Even if Yuriko was nothing more than a convenient receptacle for his physiological discharge, she's a cute and charming receptacle. Miyake is human and male, so there's no way he could be free of jealousy toward you and Nakaoka. The whole scenario has become clear to me. At this year's stockholders' meeting, the beanpole will become company president, and in time Miyake will be promoted to a suitable position. But you'll be a bellboy until you retire."

As he watched Tsuruta's face gradually grow rigid, a strategy came to Tetsuyuki's mind, though he had no idea whether it would work.

"Miyake's a fool too. A guy who has a wife and children yet gets involved with an employee of his own company—a young unmarried woman at that—and then at the end of this bed talk blabs about the beanpole party's game plan . . . Doesn't he understand that if this were to get out, no matter how he had distinguished himself as victor in the factional warfare, he wouldn't be able to remain in this company? If the fatso party got wind of this, in spite of its confidence about winning, the beanpole party would be tossed out of the ring at the last minute."

His inchoate rage turned into a malevolence that wished to see both of them—Tsuruta, who was right in front of him, and Miyake, who was no doubt gleeful about the success of his tactic—vanish from this hotel. Tetsuyuki did not stay to see the effects of his words, but proceeded down the dimly lit passageway.

His anger gradually came to be tinged with a bit of sorrow. When for the first time in five days he changed from his uniform into his own trousers and sweater, he found himself feeling pity for Yuriko, whose peculiar "feminine aspect" could only be described as pathological. Nevertheless, he set off to meet Yōko, who was waiting at the ticket gate of Osaka Station, with a strange cheerfulness of heart.

"You've never been on time, have you?" Unusually for her, Yōko kept on sulking. In the train car on the Kanjō Line, she took a registered-mail envelope out of her purse and held it out.

"Your portion is in here too, but I'm not going to give it to you anymore."

"What's that? What do you mean 'my portion'?"

"Who knows?"

"I was only ten minutes late. Don't get so bent out of shape."

"If I keep you waiting ten minutes, you go on sulking for about an hour."

In order to humor her, as he grasped the strap in the railcar, Tetsuyuki pressed his elbow against her breast through her coat and put on a pleased expression. "You'll be staying tonight, won't you?"

"Don't do such obscene things in public!" But the end of that reproof was mixed with some laughter. Once again she took the registered-mail envelope out of her purse and handed it to him. The sender was Sawamura Chiyono. "It's New Year's gift money, for both of us. It came this morning, and I immediately phoned to thank her. But no matter how many times I called, the line was busy. As soon as we get to Suminodō I'll try again."

Enclosed were two gift envelopes each containing 20,000 yen, and a letter written in brush calligraphy:

Lately I have been finding it very troublesome to see people, and even when guests come by I pretend to be out. Are both of you well? Even though I've become misanthropic, I've wanted to do something for people, and have been giving away things that have been valuable to me. Please accept this without reservation. I tried to think of what would be good to send to you, but was unable to come up with any ideas. Please use this to enjoy some good food or something.

"Wow, that's forty thousand yen between the two of us! Hey, tomorrow when we go to Osaka, let's have Matsuzaka beef at the grill in the hotel. We could order some expensive wine too . . ."

"No." Yōko snatched the envelope from Tetsuyuki's hand. "We're going to put this in savings. We need to pay back your father's debts as soon as possible, don't we?"

Tetsuyuki could not say anything in response. With pursed lips he gazed at the passing scenery outside the window. After some time an idea occurred to him.

"Maybe we should consult with someone versed in legal matters. I got absolutely nothing from my father as inheritance. Am I really obligated to pay back money I never borrowed? Just because I'm his child, I shouldn't have to cover his losses. I inherited no property, just debt. Could there be a dumber idea?"

He had decided that after winter break, he would try asking

a professor in the Law Department. As soon as they arrived at Suminodō, Yōko went into a phone booth. In the meantime, Tetsuyuki purchased the grocery items she had scribbled on a note: two cuts of steak, salad oil, butter, potatoes, cabbage, onions, mayonnaise, carrots, coffee beans and a stand for drip filters. Though his shopping took a rather long time, Yōko had still not come out of the phone booth.

Just as he was approaching the booth with a large bag of groceries she came out and stood still, a blank expression on her face.

"They said Mrs. Sawamura died last night."

"Died?"

"The wake will be held tonight." She took the registered-mail envelope out of her purse and inspected the postmark: it was stamped December 30. "They said she suddenly began to be in pain last evening and was taken to the hospital in an ambulance, but passed away around ten o'clock."

For a long time, the two of them stood still on the street in front of the station, a place brimming with sunlight but swept by chilly winds. As if by tacit agreement, they both started walking, passing through the shopping arcade and crossing the railroad tracks.

"She was well along in years . . ." Tetsuyuki felt a certain disappointment that Sawamura Chiyono did not die in the tea hut she had erected in the middle of that spacious garden. He had perceived from her manner of speaking that she wanted to die there, and had a premonition that her wish would probably be fulfilled. "I think that tea is a ritual for gazing on life and

248

death." Tetsuyuki was strangely able to recall clearly phrases from her unsolicited life story. "While in the tearoom, both host and guest are dead. When they leave the tearoom, they are alive . . . I take naps in the tea hut. That way, I come to understand more fully. When I'm asleep, that's death. When I'm awake, that's life. But both are my same self. Life and death, life and death, life and death . . ."

Upon entering the apartment and locking the door, Tetsuyuki and Yōko embraced and locked their lips in a seemingly endless kiss.

"How is Kin?" Yōko asked in hoarse voice.

"Still alive."

"For a while at least, huh?"

"I'll pull the nail out of him on April twelfth." Though he was not conscious of it, that was a year and a day after Tetsuyuki had, in this room where darkness had slipped in, unwittingly driven a nail through Kin's back. It was also the day he had embraced Yōko's naked body for the first time in the spring light.

"Why April twelfth?"

Tetsuyuki did not respond to Yōko's question. He himself did not understand why he had chosen that day. Instead, he said, "We ought to go to the wake tonight."

Yōko wordlessly slipped off her coat and began preparing dinner in the kitchen. Tetsuyuki lit the heater, then glanced at Kin's motionless body. In that instant, an unforeseen notion took on the form of words, casting a strange illumination in his mind.

"Over the two days of April eleventh and twelfth last year, I drove a nail into two living creatures." He turned around and looked intently at Yōko's back, and she seemed small, helpless, yet at the same time presented a vivid image. He felt a deep love that transcended lust and mere attraction, but in which there was also a glint of anxiety.

He quietly approached her, wrapped his arms around her waist, and rubbed his cheek against hers.

"Let's go to the wake. If we leave here before six, we'll be right on time. And after we've left Mrs. Sawamura's house, let's stay in the 'You've Come Again' Hotel. I can pull the nail out of Kin, but I can't pull it out of you." Yōko turned to face him, a redness in her eyes. She tapped his neck lightly with the handle of the knife. Apparently she had taken his words in an obscene sense.

After their meal, Tetsuyuki changed into his pajamas at Yōko's urging, and slipped under the futon she had spread out for him. Over the past week, he had averaged only four hours of sleep each day. She sat down next to his pillow. He slipped his hand under her skirt.

"Again?" She stopped his hand. "If you do that, you won't get any sleep." Though reproving him, when he promised not to make any indecent movements with his fingers, she relaxed her legs with a half-doubting expression on her face.

"I wonder who'll come into possession of that enormous mansion."

As he thought about how to respond to Yōko, Tetsuyuki fell asleep.

He slept until nearly five thirty, and it was just before nine o'clock when they arrived at Kawaramachi in Kyoto. In the vicinity of the Shūgakuin Imperial Villa—in front of a bam- boo thicket that hardly suggested a residential area—paper lanterns bearing a family crest had been set out, indicating that a wake was being held. Several cars were parked on the road beside the river. As they got out of the cab and approached the gate, both realized at the same time that they had forgotten their juzu prayer beads. Tetsuyuki had arranged that on the following day a fellow student would lend him notes from sev- eral classes to prepare for the upcoming graduation exam, and Yōko had planned to act as tour guide of Kobe for an aunt and uncle who had taken advantage of the New Year's vacation to visit the Kansai area. Thus neither would be able to participate in tomorrow's funeral ceremony, but at Osaka Station they had purchased an envelope for condolence money and had in- serted 10,000 under both their names. They were in a hurry and had completely forgotten to purchase juzu.

Yōko whispered, "What shall we do? We can't go into such a formal gathering without prayer beads."

"It can't be helped. We can't turn back now. We'll just have to tell them that we were out when we heard of Mrs. Sawa- mura's passing, and that coming here directly, we were in such a hurry that we forgot them."

As they opened the front door, a monk was just leaving. The familiar middle-aged maid saw him off, then returned and thanked them with a polite bow for having come from such a distance. As they walked down the long corridor, she continued.

"All of her relatives live far away and have not yet arrived. The only ones here now are her friends and Mr. and Mrs. Kumai."

In the large Japanese-style room in which Mrs. Sawamura's remains had been placed, only five friends were sitting in silence, an all-too-melancholy sight for the wake of the owner of an enormous mansion.

Some time after Tetsuyuki and Yōko had offered incense, one of those friends in attendance addressed Mr. Kumai—the only relation present—saying they were elderly and did not have the stamina to remain at the wake through the night, and asked to be excused. Bowing deeply, Mr. Kumai thanked them for their participation. The five friends then stood in front of the coffin, pressing their hands together reverently. One of them, an elderly woman, placed her hand on the small hinged door on the lid of the coffin to view the face of the deceased, but Mr. Kumai stopped her, explaining in a calm but overpowering voice:

"I'm truly sorry, but before her demise the departed expressed her wish that her face not be viewed by anyone." After the five friends left, only Mr. and Mrs. Kumai, Tetsuyuki, and Yōko remained in the room.

"We're sorry for imposing on you the last time we came."

Mr. Kumai responded impassively to Yōko's apology. "I think I should also inform Mr. and Mrs. Lang of my aunt's passing. Though it was none of my business, their son rather angered me. He did come to pick up his parents, but was very curt with us, and it was difficult to tell whether his greeting to my aunt was intended as an expression of gratitude or a complaint that she had been meddlesome. He did not have a proper spirit about him."

"I received New Year's gift money from Mrs. Sawamura.

It came this morning, and when I tried calling to thank her, I was surprised to hear that she had passed away last night . . ."

Mr. Kumai responded to Yōko. "She had had a cold for about twenty days, and had been coughing constantly. I told her she ought to see a doctor, but she laughed it off, saying that she had no fever and felt fine. Yesterday evening, the sound of something breaking came from her room. When the maid went to check, she was crouching down on the floor in agony. The maid said that her lips were pale. She appeared to be conscious right up to the time she was loaded into the ambulance, because she said something to the maid."

"What did she say?"

Mr. Kumai shook his head at Tetsuyuki's question. "It was difficult to make out, and the maid couldn't understand it. From then until the time she expired, she never regained consciousness. The doctor's diagnosis was heart failure."

Tetsuyuki glanced at Yōko, and was met with a doubtful look. Mr. Kumai had just said to the elderly woman who was about to look at Sawamura Chiyono's face that, before breathing her last, she had said that she wanted no one to see her face after her death. Apologizing for not being able to attend the funeral ceremony, Tetsuyuki explained the reason.

"You've gone to the trouble of coming to the wake, so please do not feel obligated," Mr. Kumai said with a bow. Mrs. Kumai—beautiful, but with a mien that somehow suggested daggers—kept looking intently at Yōko, or training her eyes on Tetsuyuki's threadbare jacket or the black tie he had just purchased in Kawaramachi.

From outside the room, the maid announced relatives. "They have just arrived from Kanazawa." Mr. and Mrs. Kumai stood up and hurriedly exited. As the sound of footsteps receded, Tetsuyuki approached the coffin.

"Tetsuyuki!" Yōko's voice was lowered as she tried to stop him, but he opened the small hinged doors on the coffin and pulled the white cloth back. He broke out in gooseflesh and almost let out an involuntary cry. What he saw was not the fair-skinned, refined, calm and self-possessed Sawamura Chiyono he had known in life, but rather a hideous dead face with blackened skin, whose features were grotesquely distorted in agony. The right eye was shut tight, but the left eye was wide open. The proof that it was not indeed someone else was a small brown mole next to her lip and the peculiarly well-shaped ridge of her nose that was all that remained of the beauty of her younger years.

"Tetsuyuki!" Yōko again called out in a small voice. Footsteps could be heard approaching through the long corridor. Tetsuyuki quickly replaced the white cloth, closed the hinged doors, and returned to his seat. His fingertips were trembling and his heart was pounding wildly. Mr. and Mrs. Kumai entered accompanied by three male relatives. Availing themselves of that opportunity, Tetsuyuki and Yōko took their leave of the Sawamura residence.

"That was kind of a creepy wake. It seems a bit strange that it should be such a lonely affair, with so few people . . ." Yōko commented inside the cab, giving Tetsuyuki's wrist a firm squeeze. "I was really nervous not knowing from where in that huge mansion someone might enter that room."

"Yeah, but you thought it was odd too, didn't you, Yōko? What Mr. Kumai said to that old lady. And it didn't hang together with what he said later."

"Mmm. And then, my heart was really pounding while you were looking inside the coffin . . ."

"My hair was standing on end."

The neon sign for the hotel came into view and they had the cab stop. They both fell silent as they walked along the dark street. The chilly wind typical of winter in Kyoto made their faces grow taut. The square electric sign proclaiming VACAN-CIES was making a creaking noise as it shook in the wind. The owner of the hotel remembered Tetsuyuki and Yōko. With a smile and mannerism more suited to an eager street vendor than to the owner of a love hotel, he said, "Welcome! I'm glad you came again."

"We'll be staying here tonight."

"Guests to stay the night! Usher them to their room!" The owner called commandingly in a loud voice as if addressed to a steward, but like the time before, showed them to their room himself.

"It's pretty cold out tonight, isn't it?"

"Yes, indeed."

"You two are already engaged to be married, aren't you?"

"How did you know?"

"When you've been in this business as long as I have, you pick up on things like that. There are all kinds of couples that come here: some I can tell are both married with families, or that this young woman doesn't realize she's come here with a gangster . . . there are those kinds of couples." The owner explained as he filled the bath for them, then added, "There is no breakfast service for guests who stay the night. We don't have the staff for that, so we can only offer coffee, toast, and a fried egg. Will that be all right?"

"Yes, that's fine."

"What time shall I bring it by?"

"At ten."

"Breakfast at ten! Check!" Raising his voice like a cashier, the owner exited the room. Tetsuyuki and Yōko looked at each other and smiled.

"Looking at that guy energizes me."

It occurred to Tetsuyuki that both times they had come to this hotel were days when they attended on matters of life and death: the previous time was after Mr. and Mrs. Lang's attempted suicide, and today it was after Sawamura Chiyono's wake. Tetsuyuki stood there in his shabby old coat, musing idly. Yōko unbuttoned his coat, buried her face in his chest, and sighed deeply.

"What did Mrs. Sawamura's face look like?"

After some hesitation, he lied. "She looked beautiful, as if she were alive . . ."

"Then why did it frighten you so much?"

"Well, that's obvious, isn't it? I had no idea when Mr. Kumai would come back, and he had told both of us in no uncertain terms that he didn't want to show us the face."

"I wonder why."

"I don't know, but it doesn't matter, does it?"

They bathed together, cavorting with each other in the tiled tub. With his palm, Tetsuyuki traced the contour from her waist over her buttocks, his favorite part of her body. Then he said in as cheerful and unaffected tone as possible, "What's this? A yawn? I'm not going to let you get any sleep tonight."

"No, I'm going to bed."

They dried each other with the towel and lay down naked on the bed until they cooled down from the bath.

". . . it hurts," Yōko whispered in his ear.

"Where?"

". . . my nipples."

The overture was coming from her, but it was not a call for ecstasy. Tetsuyuki perceived it as rather like a child's presuming upon an adult's indulgence. He turned off the light and began whispering sweet nothings, using every phrase he knew to declare his love for her. At some point they coupled, and at some point they finished, ending in such gentle rapture and peace that Tetsuyuki was soon able to begin again.

Several hours later Tetsuyuki awoke, startled by a dream in which he emerged from water only to have someone force his head back into it. He turned on the small lamp by the bed and checked the clock: five a.m. Taking care not to wake her, he brushed Yōko's hair away from her face and looked at her sleeping profile. She was sleeping on her side, her naked body facing him. He breasts appeared very constricted, squeezed between her arms, and he carefully moved her top arm to her side. It took rather a long time before one of her nipples—the one that had been crumpled under her arm—returned to its original shape, and its amusing movement brought a smile to his lips. Yōko also appeared to be having a dream; her lips were making short movements, like those of an infant sucking its mother's breast, even making a slight sound. Tetsuyuki carefully covered her breasts with the quilt and traced the parting of her lips with his index finger. The sucking sound increased, then suddenly stopped.

Tetsuyuki began to comprehend what sort of thing love between a man and woman is, why it is both resilient and at the same time fragile. He vowed that he would never again mention her having once shifted affections to another man, but even as he pledged to himself, he realized how doubtful his resolution was. Even so, he was confident that they would make a very fine married couple. He felt both regret and horror at the thought that her body, lustrous and supple, would someday inevitably disappear from this world, but for that very reason he was drawn to serious reflection about what happiness was, and he felt a renewed drive to turn himself and those he loved toward this happiness.

He was unable to get Sawamura Chiyono's hideous dead face out of his mind. She had such a calm and collected attitude toward life and death, speaking of such matters with a sort of lofty, religious enlightenment. So why did she have such a horrifying visage in death that those paying their condolences were forbidden to look at her? What was it that she said to her maid as she was dying? Did she actually believe her own stated view on life and death? Wasn't it really not a matter of enlightenment, but rather of her own final pride, her last pretense of self-importance? Tetsuyuki compared her face in death with that of his father. His father's was beautiful, peaceful even.

While alive, his father was always being deceived, but had never deceived anyone. He had been betrayed and had lost a great deal, but had never robbed anyone of anything. He had done no wrong, and one could even say that it was because of his honesty that his business failed. And yet didn't he win at the game of life?

Tetsuyuki had no idea what kind of life Sawamura Chiyono had led, but perhaps the abundant and tranquil life of her later years rested on a foundation of the misery of countless other people. No matter how she tried to conceal such things or to dismiss them as belonging to the past, her deeds had blackened her face in death and distorted it, causing one eye to open wide. Yes, that must be it. Unable to take her magnificent mansion or her elegant garden or her famed tea utensils with her, Sawamura Chiyono had set out on a journey accompanied only by her horrifying face. Isn't the face of a dead person the ultimate indication of the unconcealable character of a person? Lost in his thoughts, Tetsuyuki had forgotten about the movements of his own index finger. Yōko's entire body jerked in a sudden spasm. She turned her sleepy eyes to Tetsuyuki.

"You mustn't play such tricks . . . not while I'm asleep." She moved his hand over to her shoulder and appeared to fall asleep again, but at length asked with her eyes closed, "Can't you sleep?"

"I can't."

"That happens when you're too tired."

"It's because my nerves are exhausted. I think I'll have some beer."

The room was so heated that Tetsuyuki was thirsty. He took a can of beer out of the refrigerator and drank it sitting on the bed. Lying prone, Yōko gazed at him, resting her chin in her hands. After two or three sips, Tetsuyuki turned her face up.

"Let me nail you again. Then I'll be able to sleep."

"Can't you put it in a way that sounds more romantic?"

She shifted her body to receive him. His plea of wanting to be able to sleep had just been an excuse, but after sex and beer he actually did fall into a peaceful sleep.

It was around noon when Tetsuyuki and Yōko returned to Umeda Station on the Hankyū Line. They entered a coffee shop on the fifth floor of a building in front of the station, and as soon as they sat down, Yōko said in a hushed voice, "I think it would be great if I could get pregnant."

Tetsuyuki understood immediately the meaning behind those words. Sooner or later he would have to meet with her father and secure his permission for their marriage, something the old man had absolutely no intention of giving.

In the four or five times they had met, it was obvious from her father's bearing that he was not well disposed toward Tetsuyuki. His was a tone of voice and an expression that differed qualitatively from the unpleasantness that is not uncommon in fathers toward men who come to take away their daughters. To

Tetsuyuki it seemed like nothing but undisguised contempt, and he reciprocated with the same feeling.

What was wrong with the fact that his mother worked in a small restaurant in Kita Shinchi? And what was wrong with the fact that he worked as a bellboy while attending college? What was wrong with the fact that he and his mother had been saddled with his father's debts? Tetsuyuki thought that way even as he recognized how a father must feel when sending his daughter off to be married; it was only natural that Yōko's father should disapprove of someone like him. But her father did not just disapprove of him; he despised both him and his life's circumstances. As soon as he graduated, Tetsuyuki planned to thank Yōko's father profusely, and then declare his intentions clearly.

"But if he still refuses to give me your hand, what then?"

"Even if I were pregnant?" Yōko giggled. "If that happened, I'd have to give up on Mom and Dad. But a parent absolutely wouldn't refuse in that case."

Tetsuyuki grimaced at her resoluteness. He sensed something for which he was no match.

She changed the topic of conversation. "It's about time you started putting serious effort into your graduation thesis. I've already written twenty pages."

"I'll start on mine tomorrow."

"What's the topic?"

"Why Kin-chan is still alive after having a nail driven through him."

"Stop it. It'd be just like you to write about something like that. And if they wouldn't let you graduate with that . . ."

"I'm just joking. I couldn't turn a difficult topic like that into a thesis, now, could I? There'd be no topic more impossible for me."

"I'm really exhausted." Yōko's smile was mixed with embarrassment.

"How many times do I have to tell you? It's a hundred times more exhausting for a man than for a woman. I had to be in full command of my intellect and vitality, moment by moment either being wounded or exulting in victory, putting on an act or becoming desperate . . . All you had to do was take it easy and sit there."

"You put on acts? Ugh, that's disgusting. So, what kind of acts do you put on?" Yōko moved her face closer, her expression not concealing her amusement.

"I couldn't mention something like that."

"Keep on acting, okay? Even after you've become an old man. I'll get tired of you the minute you stop acting."

"If I get to be an old man, it'll be too late for acting." Even as he answered, it occurred to Tetsuyuki that some mutual acting would probably be necessary in their lives.

Yōko opened her purse and took out the envelope she had received from Sawamura Chiyono. For a while she was lost in thought, but then said as she pulled a loose thread from Tetsuyuki's jacket and disposed of it in the ashtray, "I've been acting too."

Tetsuyuki was silent. It struck him as not at all strange that, when they were both naked, Yōko too might be "acting" in her own way. But the words she enunciated clearly and distinctly were very different from what he anticipated: "To be quite honest, I did not like Sawamura Chiyono."

"Why?"

"I recall a line from a French movie I saw a long time ago: 'Except for murder, she's a woman who's done everything.' That line came to mind when I first met Mrs. Sawamura. I had an impression that she was probably a person like that. And yet she put on an air of innocence, which was all an act, doing her utmost to play the virtuous person and pretending that she was living in a manner that transcended all things."

"Huh . . . Why did you get that impression?"

"The movements of her face and her eyes were at odds with each other; it gave me the creeps. I'm not sure how to describe it . . . You know what I mean, don't you? The feeling that someone is wearing several masks, and keeps changing them around. Even if that person's face changes, the eyes stay the same. That's really creepy, isn't it?"

"So, what was your 'acting'?"

"Even though I didn't like her, I pretended to. Through my choice of words and my attitude, I pretended to adore her."

"Hmm." Tetsuyuki was not surprised that Yōko had engaged in such acting; rather, he was surprised at the eye she had for seeing through Sawamura Chiyono. Just as his mother had said, "She's had a privileged upbringing, but I think that even tomorrow she'd be able to put off a bill collector." He was impressed with his mother's insight.

"Yesterday, when I opened the doors on the coffin, Mrs. Sawamura's masks had all been taken away."

Cocking her head slightly, Yōko pondered Tetsuyuki's words, but did not ask about them. As usual, the two of them parted at the ticket gate of the Hankyū Line.

Tetsuyuki returned to his apartment to find Isogai sitting on the stairs. Whether because of the cold or because of his heart condition, his face was pale and bloodless. They had often seen each other in passing at the hotel, but had been too busy to talk and had just said hello to one another.

"How long have you been sitting here?"

"Over three hours."

"What's up?"

"Is that lizard still alive?"

"Yeah. It's the season for hibernation, so it rarely eats anything, but it's alive."

Still sitting on the iron steps, Isogai said, "Let me stay here tonight."

"Okay. Is something wrong?"

Getting up as if with great effort, Isogai's eyes followed a group of children running through the alley as he murmured, "I want to die."

Tetsuyuki fixed his gaze on Isogai. In the distant sky, three kites were being flown. As he was searching for some words of encouragement, his feelings became indifferent and he locked the room without saying a word. He wished that Isogai would just go home. If he wanted to die, he could just die, couldn't he?

Isogai sat down on the floor, leaning against the wall and staring at Kin, whose tail was moving like the pendulum of a clock that was winding down. Tetsuyuki tried giving him some larvae, but he would not eat. He spread his futon and changed into his pajamas. "I'm tired, so I'm going to bed."

"That quilt smells of a woman." A slight smile came to Isogai's lips, but his eyes were on Kin. To be sure, yesterday afternoon Yōko had indeed come to this room, but after putting Tetsuyuki to bed she had spent the time straightening the kitchen and jotting down notes for her graduation thesis, and her scent could hardly have permeated the quilts. Tetsuyuki surmised that Isogai's hypersensitivity must be due to being overwrought.

"Anyone becomes nihilistic when they're exhausted. Get a good rest, and you'll feel better."

"Just to do an ordinary job, my heart is taxed as if it had been many hours at hard labor. And it's the same even if I'm just sitting still. I can neither work nor play. I wish it would just stop." Tetsuyuki had pulled the quilts over his head, and had his eyes closed. "I'm sick of everything. I'm really sick of it."

Those were the kinds of things I said to Kin when another man came into Yōko's life, Tetsuyuki thought to himself as he recalled that night several months ago. He poked his head out of the quilts and, taking the room key out of his trouser pocket, set it by Isogai's side. "I'm going to sleep, so lock up when you leave, okay? You can slip the key back inside underneath the door."

Fantasizing about making love with Yōko had become the most effective way for Tetsuyuki to fall asleep, and it worked.

The lights of dusk flickered between the curtains, which made him think of his mother. After a recurring unpleasant and incoherent dream, he awoke feeling not at all rested. Isogai had still not gone home.

"You slept well, snoring away. Light the heater."

Tetsuyuki put a sweater on over his pajamas and lit the kerosene heater, spreading his hands over it in anticipation of the growing flame. "While I was asleep, were you watching Kin the whole time?"

"Yeah."

"When April comes around, I'm going to pull that nail out of him."

"April?"

"I have this feeling that if I pulled it out now, he'd die. It'd be better to wait for spring."

"Let's start a revolution." Isogai spoke in a calm but strangely firm tone of voice.

"Revolution? What are you talking about?" Tetsuyuki turned toward Isogai with an amused snort.

"I'm the object of this revolution. I'm terrified, but I'm going to go through with it."

Tetsuyuki stood up and turned on the light. "Great! Let's go to the hospital tomorrow. I'll go with you." Tetsuyuki spoke as if he would be the one receiving the operation.

"In Chisato there's a large hospital that specializes in heart diseases. In my pocket I've been carrying around a letter of introduction to be admitted." Isogai pulled out a folded envelope and rested it on his palm, murmuring with a slight smile, "Every time I look at this, it feels as if I'm carrying around a pistol for my own suicide."

"Heart surgery in Japan is among the best in the world. Don't worry, it'll be a success."

"That's easy for you to say. After they use a saw to cut away ribs, they'll connect my arteries to an artificial heart . . . just thinking about it, everything goes dark before my eyes. I want to run away, but there's no place to escape." Isogai pointed at Kin. "I'm a living creature, and so is he. If he can stay alive after all he's been subjected to, I ought to be able to as well."

A little of the meat was left from yesterday's shopping, and there were potatoes and cabbage. Tetsuyuki switched on the rice cooker, and chopped things up. He melted some butter in the frying pan, sautéed the ingredients and, seasoning them with soy sauce and pepper, served everything up in dishes, which he set on the small dining table.

"Stay here the rest of the night."

"Okay. I never intended to go home."

"You never really intended to die, did you? You came here to build up the resolve to have surgery. You owe thanks to Kin for that." Tetsuyuki decided he would do whatever it took to show that he could pull the nail out without killing Kin. Tears came to his eyes. As the two ate, they thought of how to do it.

"Since the nail has become a part of the internal organs, it should be pulled out all at once. Then you'd have to make a wooden box to keep him in, and take care of him until the wound heals. Otherwise, the moment you let him go outside, a snake or carnivorous bird would make a meal of him." This was Isogai's suggestion. Tetsuyuki had thought of the same thing, but somewhere in his mind a very different idea flickered. Kin was now quite alive. If the nail were pulled out, he might die, but if the nail were left in, he would continue to live if given

267

food and water. Tetsuyuki did not want to inflict pain on him all over again; he wanted him to keep on living. Most of all, he did not want to part from him.

He sometimes thought that he should use a saw and chisel to free Kin from the pillar, but leave the nail in him. But then part of the pillar would be chipped out and his landlady would demand he pay for the repairs. If it were a matter of a torn sliding panel or a broken window, the amount would not be so great, but replacing part of a pillar would be a sizable cost. Tetsuyuki described this alternative plan to Isogai, who hemmed as he thought about it.

"You'd have to come up with a good excuse—an unavoidable accident."

"What kind of unavoidable accident would result in part of a pillar being chipped away?"

"I don't know. But I think you could come up with one."

"Think of something. It's already been determined that I'll be moving out in April to live with my mom. I can't leave Kin here like this. I'll either have to pull the nail out or cut the pillar out and take him with me."

The two of them came up with a few plans, but all were either impractical or were not "unavoidable."

"How about saying that rats chewed on the pillar?"

"That's a dumb idea. Who'd ever believe it?" Tetsuyuki glared at Isogai out of the corner of his eye. In the end, they got into bed without either of them being able to hit on a good idea. Since there was only one set of quilts, they had to share them, sleeping with their backs to each other. The woman who lived alone next door opened her window and called her cat.

"This place is so cheaply constructed, I can hear that lady talking to her cat. Sometimes she even makes sounds like a ghost cat, and argues with her pet." Hearing Tetsuyuki's muffled explanation, Isogai sat up suddenly.

"A cat!"

"A cat?"

"You could use a cat."

"How?"

"You could say you had some dried fish hanging on the pillar, and forgot to close the window. When you came back at night, the cat lunged at you in the dark. You were surprised, not knowing that it was the cat from next door, and started slashing with a butcher knife in order to defend yourself. The cat was surprised too, and kept lunging. The knife struck the pillar, making deep cuts in it and carving out a piece. How does that sound?"

"There's still a problem with it. If it were the landlady's cat, then she wouldn't be able to complain. But the cat belongs to the lady next door, who's no relation to the landlady. She'd make one or the other of us pay."

"Doesn't the landlady keep a cat?"

"No. She's the kind who'd never spend a cent she didn't have to. You think she'd ever feed a cat or a dog?"

Isogai sighed. "I'm tired. And my head's aching. There's nothing for it but to pull the nail out. Even if he dies, Kin-chan will be happier that way. It could hardly be crueler than to keep him alive this way." Isogai's words appeared to be speaking for his own state of mind.

"So, you won't have changed your mind when tomorrow rolls around, will you? You're afraid of surgery after all . . ."

"I am afraid of surgery. Why shouldn't I be? But I've already made up my mind. It took me five years to come to this resolution."

Tetsuyuki felt an urge to tell Isogai about Sawamura Chiyono: about the incident with Mr. and Mrs. Lang, and about the various pronouncements she made. And about her face in death. It took a long time for him to explain everything, since he was unable to avoid mentioning Yōko as well. From the beginning of his story, he got sidetracked talking about his and Yōko's romance and their future plans, and it took nearly forty minutes before he was able to address the main topic. At the end of Tetsuyuki's story, Isogai mumbled, "I guess that means that if you think with your head alone, it won't do you any good."

"What do you mean by that?" No answer was forthcoming from Isogai, so Tetsuyuki knocked against Isogai's buttocks with his own. "Are you asleep?"

Isogai finally responded. "I think that what she said was correct. Of course, without dying there's no way to know for sure, but I think that while you're alive if you really believe with every fiber of your being that you'll be born again, that you'll die again and be born again, then no matter what kind of painful experiences you have in the world, you'll remain impassive. However, if that's just something you use as self-defense against a fear of death, then it won't be of any use to you. No one truly believes in this ideology in their heart. Try listening to a sermon by a priest at a tourist temple in Kyoto or Nara and it sounds so idiotic that you want to throw a rock at them. Even authors who write difficult novels don't really believe in their heart of hearts the ideas and philosophies they write about. No matter what lofty things they write or say, they're not able to save even one unhappy person, much less solve the problems of those who are nearest and dearest to them, are they?"

"So, what do you have to do to believe with every fiber of your being?"

"You have to move something to the level of actual practice."

"What is 'something'? And what kind of practice amounts to 'actual practice'?"

"I don't know. If I did, I wouldn't have agonized for five years about whether to have surgery."

Tetsuyuki crawled out of bed and turned on the light. He moved his face close to Kin and grabbed the unyielding nail. For some reason, that nail that refused to budge brought to the back of his mind the image of Sawamura Chiyono's face in death, and he answered Isogai's intent stare: "I'm going to pull the nail out in April."

11

It was the day after Tetsuyuki completed his examinations for graduation when Isogai, the referral letter in hand, headed for the cardiovascular hospital in Senri. Tetsuyuki, whom Isogai had beseeched to accompany him, was made to wait nearly three hours in this hospital, which boasted all the latest equipment. When Isogai finally came back, he sat down next to Tetsuyuki. "They'll still be doing some tests on me this afternoon."

"Will they be able to operate?"

"It seems that's what the tests will determine. But they talked as if they'd have to operate in any case. From what they said, I could be admitted even today."

"But you're not prepared to be admitted, are you?"

His pale face cast down, Isogai thought for a while then took a notebook out of his jacket pocket and went to a public phone.

"Who're you going to call?"

"The place where my sister works. I'll have her bring pajamas, a change of underwear, and toiletries."

"You'll need slippers too."

"Yeah, you're right."

Not two hours had passed before Isogai's sister showed up in the waiting room, having apparently been informed of Tetsuyuki's features and the color of his sweater, for she approached him with no hesitation. "Are you Mr. Iryō?"

Tetsuyuki stood up and they exchanged greetings. The comment Isogai had once made that his sister was really cute was not off the mark. Dazed by her attractiveness, Tetsuyuki was unable to follow his greeting with appropriate words.

"Has my brother been assigned a room?"

Tetsuyuki took her to the nurses' station. A surly young nurse showed them to the room, pointing to a bed by the window and saying simply, "There." Then she returned to her station. It was a room for four occupants; a boy of middle school age, a middle-aged man with piercing eyes, and a corpulent elderly man were lying in their respective beds.

Isogai's sister set on the bed the new pajamas she had hurriedly purchased, but appeared confused about where to put the large paper bag containing changes of underwear and toiletries. Tetsuyuki pointed to a corner by the wall. "You could put them here for now, Miss Isogai . . ."

"Please call me Kaori."

"Don't you need to get back to work, Kaori?"

"No, they let me off early."

They returned to the waiting room and sat down together on a bench. "Please don't think I'm just saying this because I'm not related, but I hear that the success rate for operations for valve disorders is nearly one hundred percent . . ." Tetsuyuki commented, noticing the unusual shade of the whites of Kaori's eyes, which suggested an illness even more severe than her brother's. He sensed a shadow of unhappiness on her attractive face.

"There's plenty to be afraid of, but it's not as if he had to set out swimming to America across the Pacific Ocean or anything like that." Kaori raised her head and gave Tetsuyuki a dubious look. "But once you think, 'Oh hell, just do it!' and set out, then it's 'What? That one step was all there was to it?' I've begun to think that, as long as you're determined, everything in life is like that."

Kaori did not respond, but after some time had passed, said, "Thank you for accompanying my brother today." She stood up and bowed politely. Tetsuyuki had to leave.

Arriving at the Umeda Hankyū Line station, he took the escalator down to the subterranean mall, wondering how he might kill some time. He glanced through the window of a coffee shop to see Nakazawa Masami leaning against the glass wall panel as he drank his coffee alone. Tetsuyuki did not feel like wandering about aimlessly, and so he went on in. He tapped Nakazawa on the shoulder. "Are you by yourself?" He intended to move along if Nakazawa was waiting for someone.

"Oh, it's been a while, hasn't it?"

"Sure has. Since last summer, when I was refused a loan."

Nakazawa Masami moved only his eyes to look up at Tetsuyuki, but smiled slightly as he said in a casual tone, "Well, have a seat. But you've got to pay for your own coffee."

"I owe you for a lot. I don't know how many times I've had you feed me, or how many days you've put me up. When I'm able to, I want to make it up to you somehow."

"What noble sentiments! It sounds as if you want to break off all ties with me."

To be sure, that was Tetsuyuki's intention, but he made a point of laughing and feigning otherwise.

"There'd be no need to repay someone you intended to break all ties with, would there? Don't take it so cynically."

"Cynically? Why should I be cynical toward you? Don't say such foolish things."

Nakazawa smiled as he spoke, but a wrinkle resembling a dimple appeared at the corner of his mouth, expanding and contracting like the mouth of a goldfish, an unfailing indicator that his pride had been wounded.

Tetsuyuki inferred that their argument about *Lamenting the Deviations* had left more of a stubborn anger within Nakazawa than he had imagined. Perhaps anger at a total rejection of a system of thought in which one believes—especially if it is religion—is greater and deeper than even the one who is rejected is capable of understanding. But he had no desire to rehash the argument and instead was about to ask him whether he planned to inherit his father's business after graduating or seek employment in a different company. But before he could get the question out, Nakazawa spoke first.

"Do you still hold to your theory that Shinran didn't exist?"

After sipping some coffee, Tetsuyuki answered calmly, "Let's forget about that topic. I wasn't in my right frame of mind then. People are free to hold whatever religious beliefs they wish. It isn't as if I was rejecting you."

"That doesn't answer my question. I asked about your theory of Shinran's nonexistence."

"I don't care whether he existed or not. If you think he existed, then he probably did."

"It isn't a matter of what I think. Shinran actually existed. There's a ton of evidence. It's a historical fact."

"Okay, fine, let's say he did."

"That's not recognizing the fact. I want you to recognize it."

"And if you get me to recognize it, what does that matter?"

Nakazawa smiled gloatingly and leaned closer. "That day, you said this to me: '*Lamenting the Deviations* is a collection of words that rob people of their vitality. Reading it makes me sick of living.' Do you remember?"

"Yeah, I remember. And after that, I said, 'It's absurd for a rich man's kid who'll one day inherit this building to say "Hell will surely be my final abode."'"

"What's absurd is to place joining a religion on the same level as the question of whether one is rich or poor. Don't you think so?"

"Yeah, you're right. After all, there are children of privilege who benefit greatly from capitalism but end up as Communists."

Holding up two fingers, Nakazawa smiled. "With that, you've now recognized two errors in the impertinent comments you made then."

"Enough of this. I don't feel like arguing today. I came into this shop because I saw you for the first time in a while."

But Nakazawa would not give up, and continued talking triumphantly. "Do you realize how many illuminating insights *Lamenting the Deviations* has opened up for people? Do you realize how it has given people courage to live? Using logic, tell me why it's a hellish book."

His chin resting in his hand, Tetsuyuki stared into Nakazawa's eyes. A faint whiff of cologne wafted from Nakazawa's chest, which for some reason angered Tetsuyuki.

"Well then, in order for me to explain logically, answer this question." Nakazawa nodded and folded his arms. "What is death (*ōjō*)?"

"It's to go (*ō*) and then be reborn (*jō*) in paradise."

"Where does one 'go'?"

"To the Pure Land, I suppose."

"And where is that?"

"You'll find out when you die."

"It's something I can't know until I die? That is to say, asking for rebirth in paradise is asking for death? 'Illuminating insights' that can be obtained by asking for death, or 'the courage to live' . . . what exactly are they? And it's not at all the same thing as the saying 'Fortune favors the bold.' Where is paradise? Show it to me."

"Perhaps it doesn't exist. But by using the device of having the people dream of an imaginary Pure Land, Shinran helped them to overcome the sufferings of reality. The Pure Land is within each of us, but if he had taught that to the people of that time, what would it have amounted to? The real significance of *Lamenting the Deviations* is the depth of its ideas."

"But *Lamenting the Deviations* maintains that even if you want to abandon attachment to this world there's no way you can do it, and that's okay. Eventually, your ties to this world will be exhausted and you'll die whether you want to or not. Even as you tell everyone that it's okay, you just keep telling them to ask for rebirth in paradise, don't you? In the end, that's the same as telling them, 'Hurry up and die, hurry up and die,' isn't it? But even if they're told to, people don't just die. They want to live, after all. And Shinran himself no doubt felt the same way. So the idea of chanting such prayers creates people who're dead while still alive. The 'illuminating insights' and joy given by *Lamenting the Deviations* are like the morphine given to sick patients to relieve their pain. If the pain vanishes, then they are under the illusion that the illness is cured. But that morphine is a virulent poison that hastens the patient's demise. That's why I called *Lamenting the Deviations* a hellish book. Sometimes nihilism is a sweet liquor. But the liquor of nihilism brewed in the cask of such chanting will make anyone who deeply imbibes of it suddenly hang himself, jump off a tall building, or jump in front of a train. That's because it's a liquor that draws out a resignation colored by the lowest depths of the spirit."

"You've only given *Lamenting the Deviations* a superficial reading, so I suppose it's no wonder you think that way. But that's because you don't even know how deep or violent Shinran's inner conflicts were. It's useless to argue with sensibilities that can't even grasp that." Nakazawa glared with a sneering smile, his cigarette still in his mouth. Then the smile disappeared. "In this subterranean mall there are tens of thousands of guys like you wandering around."

"What kind of guys are 'guys like me'?"

"Antireligious idealists."

A spontaneous smile spread on Tetsuyuki's face. "Do you chant 'Hail Amitabha Buddha' every day?"

"I don't chant, but Buddha always exists in my heart."

"Religion is practice, isn't it? Aren't you the real idealist, you who don't chant anything but just keep it in your heart?" Nakazawa reddened. Tetsuyuki continued as he placed his money for the coffee on the table, "I'm neither an atheist nor antireligious. It's just that, whether gods or buddhas as expedient means, I can't believe in any religion that posits something outside of myself. I think I would lend an ear if it were a religion that affirmed what is absolutely and definitively within me. A certain lizard taught me that."

"A lizard?"

Tetsuyuki stood up and looked down at Nakazawa. "I'm far more reverent toward religion than you are. Things like 'Heaven' or 'Pure Land' were probably meant as metaphors, and through some dialectical process came to be thought of as actually existing places. Intellectuals call that 'back thinking' or something like that. So what is 'back thinking'? Ultimately, isn't it just taking a defiant attitude because you don't understand something? And that's why I called Shinran a loser. His agonizing over defiling himself with women is idiotic. Sex is just part of Mother Nature, isn't it? It's the intellectuals who are impressed that a priest hypocritically transformed his indulgence into enlightenment. No matter who manipulates the paradoxes through whatever theory or rhetoric, I'll go on calling Shinran a loser."

Wishing to respond, Nakazawa grabbed Tetsuyuki's wrist, but the latter said with a nonchalant smile, "Take care. As I said, somehow I'll pay back your kindness." Nakazawa released his grip.

Tetsuyuki thought as he walked through the crowd: it was definitely not out of friendship that Nakazawa Masami had lent him money and let him stay in his room those many times. For one thing he did it to combat boredom, and for another, to gain a feeling of satisfaction with himself for having done something for someone else. But thanks to Nakazawa, he had been helped out many times. Nakazawa would no doubt refuse it, but some day he would pay him back with sincere feelings. He wished that such a day would come soon.

He was not in an agitated state, but one phrase that was not the product of self-possessed thinking came to mind: "I'm far more reverent toward religion than you are." Was that really true? Tetsuyuki slowly ascended stairs littered with newspapers and advertising flyers. The February wind made his flesh contract. How are gods and buddhas different? The Bible is a single work, but why is the vast corpus of Buddhist scripture divided into various sutras? Looking at Kin he realized that there was an enormous power of life—a power of regeneration—in fleas, lice, and dandelions as well as in dogs or tigers or human beings. All have this power within them. *There's neither a windup spring nor batteries in my body, and yet my hands and legs move freely. My heart*

*beats, and my blood is constantly flowing. And this thing I call my mind
goes on moment by moment ceaselessly being born even as it changes,
quite apart from my ability to do anything about it. Such a reality is very
strange, isn't it? And yet all living things die. Why do they die?*

Various kinds of illumination moved in the dusk of the me-
tropolis. The time was approaching when he would pull the
nail out. Kin appeared everywhere in Tetsuyuki's field of vision, but what he saw was not a lizard; it seemed like a congeal-
ment of shining life in the guise of a lizard. Sensing something
of infinite power and purity, he came to a standstill. But that
scene of bliss lasted for one blink, then vanished. He looked up
at the sky in an attempt to recall the same ecstasy, but Kin had
become nothing more than a lizard.

That night there were many vacant rooms in the hotel, and
Tetsuyuki had time to call Yōko twice during his shift. During
the first call, she told him that through her father's connections
she had secured employment with a mid-level company. He
called a second time because he had forgotten to ask about her
starting salary, and excitedly ran to the public phone.

"That's three thousand yen more than I'll make. And
they say that it's hard for women who graduate with four-year
degrees to get jobs . . ."

"Yeah, but you'll get more in bonuses than I will. My base
salary is less."

"I can't say I like this. It seems no matter what, you always
have better luck than I do."

"After we're married, we'll both share the same fate,
won't we?"

Yōko was concerned about the results of Tetsuyuki's graduation examinations.

"The results were doubtful in only one subject, but they said they'd let me take a makeup exam."

Yōko lowered her voice. "It's not much longer."

"Yeah." After he hung up, Tetsuyuki wondered what Yōko was referring to when she said "It's not much longer," but he concluded happily that "not much longer" and everything would happen: he would graduate, move out of the apartment in Suminodō, pull the nail out of Kin's back, and live together with Yōko and his mother.

Buffeted by cold winds sweeping off Mount Ikoma, he arrived at his apartment and immediately spread his futon. Then he boiled some water and made hot whiskey. He was waiting for his foot warmer to heat and had begun to sip the hot whiskey, when a man's voice came from outside the door.

"I'd like to ask about your electric meter."

Tetsuyuki went near the door. "This late at night?"

"You were out during the day."

The moment Tetsuyuki opened the door a pair of brawny arms grabbed him by the collar and shoved him against the wall. "Don't make any noise," the man whispered and, motioning with his chin, dragged Tetsuyuki down the stairs. He felt a strange aching all over his body and his feet became tangled. He was shoved into a waiting car. The man did not release his grip on Tetsuyuki's collar even after the car set off.

He did not recognize the driver, but concluded that he must also be one of the henchmen of the collector Kobori. Tetsuyuki shuddered at the thought that he might be taken deep into the mountains of Ikoma and killed. But the car turned right on the highway and stopped by a river. There were no streetlights, only a large field with no houses around.

The man gripping his collar said, "You thought you could slight us, didn't you?" The driver appeared to be the lookout, maintaining silence as he watched in the darkness.

"Because of you, my buddy got five years in the slammer. So, you're prepared for what you've got coming, right?"

"What're you going to do with me?"

"Kill you."

"What would I have to do not to be killed?"

"It'd have to feel the same as five years in the clink. And what's more, we still haven't turned your old man's promissory notes into cash."

"I'll pay the money."

"With interest!"

"I'll pay the interest, too," Tetsuyuki pleaded.

"Fine. With interest that'll be one point five million yen."

"One point five million . . ."

"And when Kobori gets out of the cooler, you'll have to make a suitable apology. That's five years! Five years of stinking food, all because of you."

"One point five million yen . . . even if you stood me on my head, I don't have that much money."

"Well then, you'll die here."

The strength drained from Tetsuyuki's body. If they'd come after him no matter where he ran, he'd fight back. Did the man intend to kill him right there in the car? Or take him to a dark field with no one around to kill him? If he were dragged out of the car, he'd have a chance to run for it. He had no other choice. He murmured, "Please kill me." The driver looked at him for the first time and said, "You mean it?"

"No matter how much I work, everything is eaten up by my dad's debts. I'm tired of this. There's no point in going on living. Please kill me." This acting was a matter of life and death for Tetsuyuki. The two men looked at each other.

"Okay, I'll kill you. Three punches for each of the five years Kobori spends in the slammer. That's fifteen punches. And they won't be with an open hand. No one survives fifteen of my punches."

The driver got out of the car and opened the back seat door. Tetsuyuki was pulled out, remaining in the grip of the two large men and unable to escape.

With the first punch he felt as if his face had been crushed. His legs were numb and he was not even able to stand up, much less run away. He could hear nothing and felt nauseated. Grabbed by the collar, he was forced to stand. The second punch was more violent than the first, but the third seemed to be poorly aimed and only grazed his cheek. The fourth punch landed in the middle of his face, and he could hear his nose breaking. His entire face had become slimy, though he did not know where the blood was coming from. He desperately stood up and tried to run away. The man seemed to misunderstand his motive.

"Seems this punk really intends to get fifteen punches."

The man thought for a moment. "Hey, hurry up and kick the bucket!"

Only half conscious, Tetsuyuki thought he was running in the direction of escape, but instead ran right into the man. Unable even to sense that the fifth punch was lighter than the others, Tetsuyuki again stood up and clung to the man. Then he could understand nothing that was going on. Above his neck there were netlike cracks in all of his bones, and, hallucinating that blood was gushing out of those cracks, a fear of death welled up from within him.

A hollow sound like that of a crane became alternately louder and softer. After that, he could sometimes hear the sound of human voices. It was only after some time had passed that he realized it was the voices of the two men.

"This kid's gonna die. How long do you plan to stick around? We should beat it, and fast."

Like whispering in a large cathedral, the man's words momentarily brought Tetsuyuki to consciousness. He realized that he was not lying on the ground of an embankment, but on the futon in his apartment.

"Idiot! We're not dealing with a child messenger here. Unless we settle the matter once and for all, we can't just give up on the promissory notes." It was the voice of the man who had beaten him. The same man moved his face close to Tetsuyuki's. "Hey, don't you have anything of value? Anything would do. I'll return these promissory notes to you in exchange for it."

Tetsuyuki had nothing of value. Emitting a groan through the searing pain of his face, he barely managed to shake his head. He wanted to be taken to a hospital. If left in this condition, he would die. But he could produce no voice. He raised his arm in an attempt to grasp the man's thick shoulder, and on his wrist was fastened the Rolex watch he had received from Yōko. The man mistook Tetsuyuki's action as wanting to show him the watch, a thing of value. The man snatched the watch.

"It's old but hey, it's a Rolex."

Tetsuyuki had no strength to resist. At length the cranelike sound receded, and everything fell silent.

His right leg was numb. He pounded on the floor with his right hand. He wanted someone to come help, anyone. He thought perhaps someone living in the apartment building would think the pounding suspicious and come look. The pounding caused vibrations that were unbearable inside his brain, and yet actually it produced a sound no greater than that of a rolled-up newspaper. He no longer sensed light, sound, or temperature.

He was playing baseball in the middle of a shopping arcade whose lights were all out. This "baseball" game used a bamboo broom handle for a bat and wadded newspaper secured with cellophane tape for a ball. Minoru pitched the ball, and Tetsuyuki struck at it. Having no bounce in it, the ball rolled, entering the grilled pancake shop Full Moon, whose door was slightly ajar. Tetsuyuki cautiously peered inside. Three old men were playing "flower" cards with the proprietress of the shop. Every night those three old men would show up at Full Moon to play cards, and she always trounced them.

"Don't break the glass." The proprietress—who looked about thirty but at the same time also past sixty—scolded him. One of the old men picked up the newspaper ball.

"You think this ball could break glass? Huh, Tetchin?" People who had known Tetsuyuki since he was little called him Tetchin. One of the pancakes sizzling on the grill was almost done, and the bonito flakes sprinkled on it were writhing.

"If you don't eat it right away, it'll burn," Tetsuyuki reminded them in a loud voice, though he knew that the three old men had only ordered it but wouldn't eat it. They had no time for that. Each held his fan-shaped hand of cards at eye level, and while scattering the ashes from their cigarettes would say such things as "Who's got the Priest? It's probably that vixen," or "Someone toss in the Pine, or else I'll be done in by the Red Poetry Ribbon."

Tetsuyuki asked the old man: "Then, is it okay if Minoru and I eat it?"

"You just ate, didn't you?" Another man added, "Well, at fifteen or sixteen they're bottomless pits. They can eat any amount."

"So then, it's okay if we eat it?"

Tetsuyuki called Minoru and, by their own leave taking two stainless-steel spatulas in hand, sat down, turned off the gas burner, and cut the pancake in two. Staring at the old men, the proprietress bared her lipstick-stained teeth and laughed. "You guys are all going to be dead in another hour."

The three old men all set their cards on the table in unison. Tetsuyuki's maneuvering of the spatula came to a standstill as he looked at the faces of the old men, which had taken on an ashen cast. The door of the shop opened and in came a lizard, and then another one. Before he knew it, so many lizards had come rushing into Full Moon that there was no room to move. Even the walls and ceiling were thickly covered with them, and at length, the ankles of the three old men were buried in their glossiness. Like the surface of the sea at high tide, the number of lizards swelled up from the floor of the shop. Tetsuyuki held several of them on the palm of his hand after they had eaten up his pancake. One of the old men was crying. "There are lots of things I've left undone. Please don't tell me I have only one hour left."

The lizards kept pouring into the shop, piling on top of one another until the old men were waist-deep in them. There was also a steady stream of them falling from the ceiling.

"What're the things you've left undone?" another old man asked, with an expression on his face as if he were the only one resigned to what was about to happen.

"Yōko, and the child she and I created together. I want to see them and apologize to them."

"Where are they now?"

"They're nearby. I know they're living somewhere close, but I can't seem to find them."

"Why did you become separated? Wasn't it because you reduced them to poverty? And what's more, you hit her just because she talked to another man."

"Yes, and I want to apologize for that, too."

At that, the old man who had been silent mumbled, "If

288

our lives are two feet long, then the part taken up by dealings between men and women is just half an inch. And yet, if it weren't for that half inch, it would never turn into two feet." Then he laughed loudly and sank into an ocean of lizards. Tetsuyuki stood up and looked for Minoru, who was nowhere to be found.

"I'll take you to that woman named Yōko and her kid."

"Tetchin, you know where they are?"

"I do."

"Where? Where are they?" Those were his last words before the two remaining old men were overcome by a wave of lizards and never resurfaced.

Fighting his way through the lizards, Tetsuyuki exited Full Moon, running through the shopping arcade and down a gray path. He dashed into a phone booth and dialed Yōko's house, but his fingers and his will were at odds with each other: when he tried to dial 2 he dialed 6 instead and, becoming flustered, started over. No matter how many times he tried, he was unable to dial the number he wanted.

He had not noticed that lizards had entered the phone booth as well, their writhing bodies progressively burying his legs, abdomen, and chest. He stood on his tiptoes. The lizards finally reached his nostrils and stopped there. The phone rang. It must be Yōko. But if he moved even slightly he would sink into the mass of lizards, and would be unable to take Yōko's call.

He wondered if Kin was not somewhere among them, and called out, "Kin-chan, Kin-chan."

In Tetsuyuki's field of vision there appeared the morning sun of winter and the form of Kin nailed to the pillar. His body was chilled to the bone and he was shivering in short bursts. His right leg had recovered from its numbness, but during his dream the pain in his nose had increased in severity and his face kept cramping. He tried reaching his hand to his face. Something like a hardened membrane was stuck to it from beneath his nose over his chin and extending to the apertures of his ears. Apparently he had gotten a crick in his neck from his beating, and was unable to move it. Using his fingernail, he scratched what was stuck to his face: it was dried blood.

His nose was swollen, and even without a doctor's diagnosis he knew that it was broken; he could tell that a piece of bone moved when he endured the pain of pressing it. He could hardly open his left eye, and both cheekbones ached. It occurred to him that they might also be fractured. But his headache had vanished. Rolling his body over toward the closet, he was barely able to pull out his quilt.

He was unable to recall any blows except to his head, and yet he felt pain in his right ribs. When he was beaten and fell down in the frozen field he had probably injured them on a rock or something. He felt a burning sensation in his face and wanted to cool it with a wet towel, but was unable to get up.

He could hear the footsteps of the woman who lived alone in the apartment next door, and pounded repeatedly on the wall with his fist. There was no one aside from that sickly woman to whom he could appeal for help. At one point he gave up, but renewing his resolve, he began banging against the wall with his foot. He kept kicking against the wall with all his might. He heard her opening the door.

"Mr. Iryō," she called with her thin voice. He opened his mouth and was about to answer, but then realized he needed to hide Kin. Pulling a handkerchief out of the back pocket of his trousers, he grasped the pillar and raised his body, struggling against dizziness and nausea. The moment he placed the handkerchief over the nail piercing Kin's back, he fell over, making a great noise.

"What's wrong, Mr. Iryō?"

The door was not locked. Tetsuyuki turned his face toward the door, and the moment his neighbor saw him she stooped down and let out a long, hoarse scream. An office worker in the neighborhood who had just left for work came into Tetsuyuki's apartment in his overcoat, and another man in his thirties who lived on the corner of the alley but whom Tetsuyuki had never met also entered. The three of them showered him with questions.

"What happened? Were you robbed?"

"Hey, we need to call an ambulance."

"Did you get in a fight or something?"

"Can you see?" Tetsuyuki nodded.

"Are you conscious?" He nodded again.

What made them turn pale and become alarmed was the fact that blood from his nose had formed a large, dark red circle on the front of his sweater and on the quilt, leading them to believe that he had been stabbed in the chest or stomach.

Tetsuyuki was taken by ambulance to a hospital on the

Hanna Freeway, where the doctors immediately took an X-ray of his head. His nose was indeed broken.

"If the break had been even just one centimeter deeper, it would have killed you."

"Is it only my nose that is broken?"

The doctor answered in the affirmative, and then explained that after the initial treatment he would do an electroencephalogram.

"Do you live alone?"

"Yes."

"Your parents or siblings?"

Tetsuyuki did not want his mother to know about it. It was over now. The villains had left his father's promissory notes, and would never come again. He wanted to keep this a secret from his mother. He gave the doctor Yōko's home telephone number.

After the blood had been wiped away and he had been moved to a private room, a nurse came and put an ice bag on his face. As she exited, a young police detective came in and sat down beside the bed.

"You were threatened and beaten by a collector once before, weren't you?"

"Yes."

"This was their henchmen, wasn't it?"

"Yes."

"You have no legal responsibility to pay back your father's promissory notes. That was a despicable thing they did to you."

Tetsuyuki expected to be asked about various other things, but the detective got up to leave the room.

"Please don't arrest them. If you do, their partners will just come and get back at me. It's all over now. They took my watch in exchange for the promissory notes." The detective made no reply. "Even if you arrest them, they'll get out of prison after five or six years, won't they? And then I'll have to live in fear again. I won't press charges . . ."

The wooden expression of the detective then broke into a smile. "Uh, I was surprised at that lizard on the pillar. Is that some kind of charm?"

Tetsuyuki closed his eyes. The door shut, and the sound of the detective's bold gait receded. Since the detective entered his room, the landlady must have accompanied him. And she no doubt also saw Kin. At that thought, it occurred to him that he might be evicted before April.

That miserly landlady would be certain to demand payment for the pillar, but even if she got the money she would simply install a new tenant without repairing it. Tetsuyuki resolved that he would not pay. It was because the landlady had not switched on the electricity that the lizard ended up getting nailed to the pillar, and he as tenant ended up in the situation of having to share the space with the reptile. What, after all, did she intend to do about his psychological stress? He would let all that loose on her in no uncertain terms, and that would take the edge off her hostility.

Tetsuyuki started to feel a bit better. He recalled fragments of his dream. He understood vaguely what the ocean of lizards was that had engulfed the three old men. No matter how severe the laws that human beings create, they never truly punish a guilty person. But you can never completely evade the law that creates human beings, no matter what you do. And there is such a law. There is a law that created the myriad living things, including flowers and trees. There are invisible, imperative laws. They make the seasons go through their cycles, and the tides advance and recede. They make human beings happy or unhappy, animating them and destroying them. If that were not so, then what was the reason that Kin—one worthless lizard—should go on living?

There must be a deep meaning in the dream he saw last night—during a time when he could easily have died—about the old man lamenting the things left undone as he was sinking in a sea of lizards. There are no doubt many people who die that way, and it is because they have violated a law. Though not applicable to rules created by human beings, the ocean that swallows those who are guilty of great sins leads them into a fathomless darkness that symbolizes everything horrifying, like lizards and snakes. Sawamura Chiyono was probably one of those human beings. Half asleep, Tetsuyuki's thoughts branched out from one thing to another.

Tetsuyuki pricked his ears up with a start. He could definitely hear busy footsteps: Yōko's. They brought tears to his eyes. He could not tell whether he was still dreaming or was out of his mind.

Yōko opened the door without knocking. The moment their eyes met Tetsuyuki raised one arm as if taking an oath. "As long as I'm alive, I'll never hit you. And even if you dance with another man, I won't get jealous."

She timidly approached and peered into his face, which was mostly hidden by the ice bag. She sighed deeply and then began to cry.

"Yōko, my luck has really been rotten. I wasn't able to die even after being thrashed by a guy who was like a pro wrestler."

"Idiot . . ."

"They returned my dad's promissory notes. Even though they said they'd kill me, after I lost consciousness they brought me back to my apartment. That was kind of them."

"Such people ought to die."

"If you say that, you'll be the one who dies. While I've been half awake just now, I've been thinking about a lot of different things. I've turned into a philosopher. I've arrived at a great enlightenment, nothing like empty academic theorizing."

Yōko gently lifted the ice bag. "Do you realize what your face is like?"

"I have a pretty good idea. From my nose on up I'm a monster with no eyes, and from my nose down . . ."

"It's worse than you imagine. Someone who has no idea what his face is like could hardly have arrived at a great enlightenment, could he?" Yōko laughed and cried at the same time. Then she softly brushed her lips against his face.

"Keep this a secret from my mom." Without responding, Yōko put the ice bag back into place. "In place of money, they took your watch. The Rolex. Sorry about that."

The examination that afternoon showed no irregularities in brain waves, but revealed cracks in two of his ribs. He was told he would need three weeks for a full recovery. That evening, Yōko's parents visited. From their expressions, Tetsuyuki guessed that they planned to use this incident as an occasion to settle his relationship with their daughter.

"Things in life never go according to plan, do they?" Yōko's father said, looking directly at his daughter. The expression on her face was fuller than usual, but she again broke out in tears. Tetsuyuki then realized that his assumption had been incorrect.

Removing the ice bag himself, he said as a preliminary, "I'm sorry to have to meet you with a face like this." Then he prepared himself to say what would sooner or later have to be said. Apparently amused by his manner of speaking, her parents smiled and straightened themselves.

Tetsuyuki announced that he wished to marry Yōko, that the matter of his father's debts had been settled by last night's incident, that he had secured employment, and that he was about to graduate. Yōko's father had already made up his mind.

"Since you are an only child and so is she, I'd like to express some of my hopes."

"Certainly."

"There's the expression 'close enough that the soup doesn't grow cold,' and we'd like you to live in such a location."

"We intend to. Thank you."

"But, that's really an awful face, isn't it? It's been a long time since I've seen you, but as soon as I walked into this room, I thought, 'What an ugly man my daughter has fallen in love with!'"

"Until last night, I was quite handsome."

After Yōko's parents left, the two were alone again.

"Can you stay here today?"

"My mom told me to take care of you."

They were about to embrace, but Yōko hurriedly returned to her chair when there was a knock at the door. Tetsuyuki supported the ice bag with both hands.

It was his landlady who came into the room. After her formal well-wishing, the heavily made-up, stout woman whose full-time occupation was that of beautician pressed him for an explanation of the lizard.

"The police detective was surprised, but I was frightened out of my wits. That's rented property, you know, not your own house. And it was clearly spelled out in the contract. As soon as you have recovered, I want you to move out. And I'll ask you to repair the pillar as well."

Tetsuyuki agreed to move out on the first Sunday of April, but responded that he would not pay to have the pillar repaired.

"It's your responsibility that a lizard got into the apartment. You knew three days before I rented the apartment the day and the time I would arrive with my luggage, but the electricity had not yet been turned on. It is of course the obligation of the property owner to see that such things are accomplished. I had no choice but to find a nail and pound it in the dark. I never imagined that a lizard would be there. Do you realize how unpleasant it has been for me every day because of that lizard? I'm going to leave it there, and you can take care of it later."

"But, but . . . how did that lizard stay alive for a whole year?"

"That's what I'd like to know. Anyway, since there are lots

tion.tion.tion.tion.tion.tion.tion.tion.tion.tion.tion.tion.tion.tion.tion.tion.tion.tion.tion.tion.tion.tion.tion.tion.tion.tion.tion.tion.tion.tion.tion.tion.tion.tion.

of cracks and crevices in this room, that lizard's spouse must have brought food for it when I was out."

"That's ridiculous, to say that lizards have husbands or wives . . ."

"I can't think of any other explanation."

After the landlady had left in high dudgeon, Yōko whispered and squeezed Tetsuyuki's hand. "That's right. It was the lizard's wife, his really cute wife, who faithfully brought him food."

12

Tetsuyuki decided to tell his mother that he had been assaulted and beaten by two or three unfamiliar drunk men, and asked Yōko to inform her, using this fiction. The following afternoon, his mother took three days off and came to see him.

"You really got roughed up badly. Anyone who would do that isn't human." After hearing his invented account, his mother spoke impassively, though she was usually one to cry on such occasions. "No matter what, time will play a major role . . ." she mumbled as she cast her gaze in the distance out the window, and then continued peeling the oranges Yōko had bought. This one hour alone with his mother was a rare occurrence. Aware of that, Yōko had limited herself to two phone calls a day, and did not stop by at all. Tetsuyuki was eager to find out the results of Isogai's examination. He asked Yōko to go to the hospital and inquire.

"They said that there are still no results, and that they have yet to do various tests. Even if they decide to go ahead with surgery, it will be another month or so."

When he returned to his room from the telephone at the nurses' station, his mother asked for the key to his apartment. "I need to wash the blood off your quilts, and you'll need more changes of clothing. And besides, I'd like to see where you've been living this past year."

The landlady had taken the key, but Tetsuyuki acted as if it had slipped his mind. "I handed it to Yōko, and she still has it. She's probably forgotten that it's in her purse."

"The landlady has a master key, doesn't she?"

"No, there's no master key. The person who lived there before lost his key, and it wasn't replaced. So the landlady told me that I absolutely must not lose it." He lied because he did not want his mother to see Kin. "And besides, I don't have anything that would amount to a change of clothes. Everything's dirty."

"Well, that's not hard to imagine." She had begun to get up, but again settled into her seat next to the bed. While stuffing orange segments into Tetsuyuki's mouth, she spoke in fits and starts about how she had spent the past year.

"I wonder why so many of the women who run places like diners, snack bars, or clubs are so temperamental. If one day you find them kind and thoughtful, the next day they're brusque and impossible to please, always haranguing and complaining. I always thought such a business just made women that way, but that's not the case."

"What do you mean?"

"Women like that don't get married, and before you know it, they'll be into something, whether the nightlife trade or some other line of work. I've come to understand that very well."

"In that case, we mustn't make a woman a president or prime minister."

"No, we mustn't. It'd be horrible."

His mother proclaimed after drawing a long breath that nothing was easy about her work. Tetsuyuki felt somewhat annoyed, expecting a sermon to begin. But on the contrary, his mother kept all distressful happenings to herself, punctuating her report with smiles and only talking about episodes with interesting customers or about the amusing tactics of the power struggles that are a solid reality even in a small restaurant employing only three people. Only at the very end did she say, "But you know, I'd really like to be able to think as I crawl between the covers at night, 'Ah, I'm happy.'"

After three o'clock that afternoon, Section Chief Shimazaki and Tsuruta came to visit. Seeing Tetsuyuki's face covered in gauze and adhesive plaster, they cried out in surprise. His mother expressed her thanks effusively, then left to do some shopping. Shimazaki had apparently heard from the doctor about the condition of the injuries. Frowning, he lowered his voice. "They say that if the break in the bone had been even one centimeter higher, it would have been fatal."

Fingering the adhesive plaster where the bone was broken, Tetsuyuki forced a smile. "It's totally ruined my good looks."

"If you don't look ahead while you walk, this world's a dangerous place." With that, Tsuruta gave a suggestive laugh. Shimazaki glared at him as if to imply that such a remark was uncalled for. But Tsuruta did not notice, and kept on in his playful tone.

"There was a sudden change in personnel. Mr. Shimazaki was promoted to manager. Mr. Miyake was exiled to Hakata as regional manager."

The hotel in Osaka was the company headquarters, but there were branches bearing the local place-names in Kyoto, Nara, Okayama, and Hakata, as well as two resorts. Of those, Hakata was the smallest, and the decision whether to remodel it completely or just close it had become urgent. Rumor had it that the management was leaning toward closure, and now Operations Chief Miyake was to be transferred there as regional manager. Tetsuyuki had no idea what methods he employed, but Tsuruta had indiscriminately broadcast within the company the relationship between the grill cook Yuriko and Miyake, who had a wife and children. Tetsuyuki fixed his gaze on the oily face of Tsuruta, who was a vulgar but quick-witted strategist of unimaginable abilities.

There were things Tetsuyuki wanted to ask Tsuruta, who also wanted to provide answers. Shimazaki, whose presence was a hindrance to such an exchange, took out a cigarette.

"If you light up in a patient's room, an ogre of a nurse will come scream at you." Then Tetsuyuki told him where the smoking room was located.

No sooner had Shimazaki said "I'm going to go have a smoke" and left than Tsuruta spoke with a smile. "You're really a bad one, aren't you? All that stuff about getting mixed up with some drunks is a lie, isn't it? You've done plenty of things to earn grudges against you, haven't you?"

"Why am I the bad one? That description fits you. There's

no way Miyake could even imagine that a bellboy like you could be the ringleader in getting him demoted to Hakata."

"It serves him right! After he made a plaything of Yuriko like that . . ."

"What's happened to Yuriko?"

"There are plenty of other jobs in Osaka. It's no concern of mine. You put me up to this. 'You'll be a bellboy until you retire.' That one phrase included a threat. It came as a shock, and I couldn't just stay still."

Shimazaki returned. He told Tetsuyuki to take care of himself and reminded him that the company entrance ceremony was set for April 2. Then he left, urging Tsuruta to go with him.

So, it was a total victory for the beanpole faction . . . Tetsuyuki thought of Yuriko, who was perhaps already sleeping with another man somewhere in Osaka.

"Mr. Iryō, I told you, didn't I, to leave the ice bag on all day today?" At the shrill voice of the head nurse, Tetsuyuki quickly placed the bag on his face.

The doctor had said that they would perform cosmetic surgery on the twisted nose bone as soon as the swelling had completely abated, but after his release and return to his apartment Tetsuyuki never once went back to the hospital. He would be able to take care of something like that anytime, and had many other things he needed to do.

He felt impatient: though it was already the middle of March, the weather had not warmed at all. Every time he saw a cherry tree he would check to see if the buds were swelling.

The day he had agreed upon with the landlady was getting close. He suddenly recalled having heard the word "keichitsu," and looked it up in the dictionary:

> . . . also *keichū*, or the emergence of insects that have spent the winter hibernating. One of twenty-four points in the ellipsis of the sun. When the sun is at 345 degrees longitude, during the second month of the lunar calendar. Around the sixth of March in the solar calendar.

Tetsuyuki tried setting the heater closer to the pillar in an attempt to hasten Kin's awakening, but decided against that out of fear that going against nature might actually weaken the lizard. So he endured the cold and spent a day without lighting the stove.

The day for keichitsu was already a week ago. He could see no signs of spring, but perhaps they were invisible only to humans; the rhythms had no doubt already begun in insects and other animals, and in humans as well. He began to get up, but again sat down with his face between his knees, averting his gaze from Kin.

An air mail letter arrived from Mr. and Mrs. Lang. Wondering how they had obtained his address, he tore it open. Two sheets were inside: one typed in German by Mr. Lang, and the other a handwritten translation into Japanese, its small characters lined up neatly.

Dear Tetsuyuki Iryō,

We are both keeping well in our Munich apartment, which is too spacious for an elderly old couple. My wife has discovered joy in planting vegetable seeds in our small garden plot, and I have found a modest purpose in life jotting down simple verses that suddenly pop into my mind. This feeling that I have become another Homer makes me realize that the many dreamlike happenings in my life were decidedly not dreams at all. I have written this letter wishing to share with you and your beautiful, charming girlfriend one of my poor poems. Please don't laugh at it. I worked as a printer, but my vocabulary is limited.

All things that fly in the sky
have two wings, and also one mirror.
And yet those that suppose
they have one wing and two mirrors
will at length fall to the depths of the earth.
The two wings work in unison,
and a mirror has a front and back.
How could anyone aware of that

undertake to lead another

into unhappiness?

I may make pretensions to be Homer, but
I racked my brains for ten days to write this
verse. I had a Japanese student in our neighborhood translate this letter for me. Kisses for
you and your girlfriend.

March 4, 19XX

Friedrich Lang

At first, Tetsuyuki was moved more by the phrase "the
many dreamlike happenings in my life were decidedly not
dreams at all" than by Mr. Lang's poem. But as he reread the
letter several times, he became more immersed in the verse,
whose literary quality he was unable to judge. That evening, he
shaved, shoved the envelope in his pocket, and set out. On the
way, he called both his mother and Isogai's hospital.

"I was in the hospital with a broken nose." Tetsuyuki can-
didly explained the circumstances.

After listening to the end, Isogai said, "I wonder why those
gangsters quit before they finished you off."

"I don't know. I suppose fate was more on my side than on
theirs."

"My surgery has been set for April twenty-fifth." Isogai said
nothing about the results of the examinations.

"My landlady found out about Kin, and she was hopping
mad. She told me to be out of the apartment by the first Sunday

of April. Of course, I'll take Kin with me. You'll be put under anesthesia and a skilled surgeon will stitch you up, but Kin won't be so lucky."

Tetsuyuki worried that what he said might make Isogai feel bad, but the latter just laughed. "You should try being a patient about to undergo heart surgery. I get so scared I can't sleep at night."

The moment he hung up, Tetsuyuki decided that even if pulling out the nail should kill Kin, he would lie about it to Isogai.

It was before eight o'clock that he arrived at Mukonosō Station. He wanted to try visiting Yōko's house without prior notice. But as he approached the house, he reconsidered, thinking that he should not presume upon them just because they had given permission for the marriage. He dashed to a public telephone. Yōko's mother answered, and asked, "Where are you now?" He ended up answering, "In Umeda," and so although he could see their house, he would have to kill some time before stopping by. Yōko angrily took the receiver from her mother.

"What have you been doing all day? I've been waiting for you to call, and I can't do anything but wait. You have to decide on a date to move, don't you?"

"Actually, I'm in your neighborhood, but without thinking I told your mom that I'm in Umeda. What should I do?"

"Why did you do that?"

"I guess I still feel awkward about visiting."

Saying that she would invent some excuse, Yōko hung up and within two minutes had exited the house.

"It isn't as if they've gladly given me their daughter, and it would be a bit impertinent of some guy she's been meeting in secret until recently to say, 'Well, I was just in the area,' wouldn't it?"

Sitting on a swing in the park, Tetsuyuki looked up at Yōko, who had just gotten out of the bath and smelled of soap. She reached out and lightly stroked his left cheek. "It's still a bit swollen here."

Without saying a word, Tetsuyuki handed her the letter from Mr. Lang.

"When did it arrive?"

"Today."

Not wanting her to feel chilled after her bath, he suggested that they go to a coffee shop somewhere, but she replied that her fur-lined coat was quite warm. She sat down on the swing next to him and read the letter by the light of the mercury lamp.

"Sawamura Chiyono's intuition turned out to be wrong. In the tea hut she had said: 'These two were not able to die here, but they will no doubt carry out their plan someplace else. This was a farewell tea ceremony . . .'"

Yōko made no response to his comment, but said in a thin voice, "I'm glad I didn't wash my hair. Somehow I had a feeling that you'd show up." Then she mumbled, "'Dreamlike . . .'"

He took the letter from Yōko. "Mr. Lang wrote that it made him realize it wasn't a dream." Tetsuyuki spoke even as he became aware of a strangely wonderful feeling welling up within him. It was decidedly not a dream, but it was like a dream . . . It was even hard for him to believe that his own nest—if only for a

short time—was a stifling boxlike place atop some metal stairs,
separated by a number of train connections and a thirty-minute
walk along a deserted country lane. Everything—whether the
incidents that had come up between himself and Yōko, the easily imagined life his mother was living, the days when he was
threatened by collectors, the power struggle between the fatso
and beanpole factions that was likely to continue, the major surgery Isogai would soon face—everything was contained within
the body of one lizard named Kin. Entertaining these thoughts,
he touched his bent nose with his index finger.

"Kin will probably die if I pull out the nail, won't he?"

"I've made a house for him." Yōko explained that for the
time being they would leave the nail in Kin after pulling it out
of the pillar. Then they would wait for the right time to pull the
nail out of his flesh, and keep him in a small wooden box until
the wound healed. When he was in good condition, they would
let him go. "I think that would be best. I made the box myself,
and put some round stones in it."

"When did you make it?" Tetsuyuki was surprised.

"Today. I sawed some wood, and pounded nails . . . I don't
know how many times I hit my fingers with the hammer. See,
I have blood blisters, don't I? I found pieces of board in the
storage shed, and my face and neck got all dusty. That's why I
took a bath."

"Why? Why did you do that?"

"Because I decided that you'll be moving the day after
tomorrow."

"The day after tomorrow?"

"You know that my cousin is an electrical contractor, don't you? He's working on some major construction projects, and the day after tomorrow is the only day he'll be able to lend us his truck. And that's why I hurried and made a house for Kin."

Tetsuyuki stood up, grasped Yōko's hand, and took off running. After paying quick but appropriate respects to her parents, he took the wooden box and went back to Mukonosō Station. The deformed box, measuring eight inches on each side, told of the great pains Yōko had expended in making it. At the ticket gate, she pulled a face at him.

"Idiot."

"I think I'm about to break down in tears."

"The truck will arrive the day after tomorrow at ten. If you're still asleep then, I'll kick you in the face."

Tetsuyuki wanted to say something wonderfully endearing but was in too exultant a state of mind and was not even able to reply coherently.

By the time he arrived at Suminodō Station, his feelings of exultation had subsided into a solemn tranquility. Walking against headwinds, he carried the box containing the round stones, pushing forward with his head down along the dark path. Locking the door, he caressed Kin's nose. Kin's tail shivered slightly. It occurred to Tetsuyuki that there were many things he must talk to Kin about before going through with it, but the moment he said "Kin-chan," he winced at the thought that he should pull the nail out of Kin's body at once rather than traumatizing him twice. Holding the pliers in his right hand, he gently held down Kin's body.

"You won't die. You won't die."

Kin's legs moved wildly, his tail writhing. Following an instantaneous creaking sound, the dislodged nail along with the pliers went flying up toward the ceiling. A piece of Kin's internal organs appeared on the finger Tetsuyuki had used to hold down the lizard, forming a red-and-yellow-green speck. He opened the box and released his fingers, but Kin's body remained stuck to the pillar, twisting like a mosquito larva. But he did not fall into the box. When he had been pierced by the nail, some flesh from his abdomen had hardened along with body fluids, causing him to adhere to the pillar. Tetsuyuki found the nail in a corner of the room. Using the point of the nail, he tried to scrape away the congealed matter. Kin was thrashing about violently. If Tetsuyuki were not careful, the wound would only grow wider. The nail that had for so long pierced him only created a fresh wound in his abdomen after it was pulled out.

At length, Kin fell to the floor. Getting down on all fours, Tetsuyuki cautiously placed the lizard on his palm, and then set him in the wooden box. With spasms in his neck and back, Kin hid between the stones, his mouth open.

Toward dawn, it began to rain. It was past noon when it stopped, and bright sunlight fell on the tatami floor and on Kin's box. Lying on his stomach, Tetsuyuki put his ear to the box.

"You won't die. You won't die . . . I had a dream, it was a long time ago. I turned into a lizard, and went through lots of lives and deaths."

There was no sound from inside the box. He barely

managed to suppress the urge to take out the stones to determine whether Kin was alive or dead.

"This is definitely spring sunlight. Kin-chan, when I pulled the nail out, spring arrived."

He spent that entire day telling Kin whatever came to mind. Years from now, if he recalled this period of living apart from his mother, all images would appear through the lens of this mysterious messenger named Kin. Tetsuyuki realized nothing had yet begun. He drank some saké, talked on, and occasionally peered between the stones as he waited for the next day. Tomorrow . . . tomorrow Yōko would come in the truck with her cousin. Thought of tomorrow brought panic and at the same time excitement. This must be what true bliss was like.

He awoke at eight o'clock on that awaited day. The unmistakable light of spring brought beads of perspiration around his neck and under his arms. Carrying the wooden box, he made several trips to the corner of the path. He wanted to wave his arms to greet Yōko by the side of the road rather than in his apartment. As he was waiting, he could no longer contain himself and removed the stones from the box one by one. Some were the size of hen's eggs; there were also pieces of brick.

"Kin-chan, stay alive," Tetsuyuki mumbled, his heart pounding. After removing all the stones, he stared for a long time into the box, occasionally raising his head like a marionette and looking off into the vast sky filled with spring light. Kin was not there.

TERU MIYAMOTO, born in Kobe in 1947, is among Japan's most widely read living authors. He has received Japan's most prestigious literary distinctions, including the Dazai Osamu Prize and the Akutagawa Prize. Several of his works have been made into award-winning movies, including *Maborosi*, directed by Hirokazu Kore-eda, the Oscar-nominated director of *Shoplifters*.

© Shintaro Shiratori

ROGER K. THOMAS is a professor of East Asian languages and cultures at Illinois State University, where he also directs the program in East Asian Studies. He has translated two of Teru Miyamoto's books, along with other works of modern Japanese fiction, including Enchi Fumiko's *A Tale of False Fortunes*, winner of the Japan-U.S. Friendship Commission Prize for the Translation of Japanese Literature.

© Michiko Thomas